Hide Away

Also by Dermot Bolger

POETRY
The Habit of Flesh
Finglas Lilies
No Waiting America
Internal Exiles
Leinster Street Ghosts
Taking My Letters Back
The Chosen Moment
External Affairs
The Venice Suite
That Which is Suddenly Precious
Other People's Lives

NOVELS
Night Shift
The Woman's Daughter
The Journey Home
Emily's Shoes
A Second Life
Father's Music
Temptation
The Valparaiso Voyage
The Family on Paradise Pier
The Fall of Ireland
Tanglewood
The Lonely Sea and Sky
An Ark of Light

YOUNG ADULT NOVEL
New Town Soul

SHORT STORIES
Secrets Never Told

COLLABORATIVE NOVELS
Finbar's Hotel
Ladies' Night at Finbar's Hotel

PLAYS
The Lament for Arthur Cleary
Blinded by the Light
In High Germany
The Holy Ground
One Last White Horse
April Bright
The Passion of Jerome
Consenting Adults
The Ballymun Trilogy
1: From These Green Heights
2: The Townlands of Brazil
3: The Consequences of Lightning
Walking the Road
The Parting Glass
Tea Chests and Dreams
Ulysses (a stage adaptation of the novel by James Joyce)
Bang Bang
Last Orders at the Dockside
The Messenger
Home, Boys, Home

Hide Away
A novel

Dermot Bolger

NEW ISLAND

HIDE AWAY
First published in 2024 by
New Island Books
Glenshesk House, 10 Richview Office Park
Clonskeagh, Dublin D14 V8C4
Republic of Ireland
www.newisland.ie

Copyright © Dermot Bolger, 2024

The right of Dermot Bolger to be identified as the author of this work has been asserted in accordance with the provisions of the Copyright and Related Rights Act, 2000.

Print ISBN: 978-1-84840-938-5
eBook ISBN: 978-1-84840-937-8

All rights reserved. The material in this publication is protected by copyright law. Except as may be permitted by law, no part of the material may be reproduced (including by storage in a retrieval system) or transmitted in any form or by any means; adapted; rented or lent without the written permission of the copyright owners.

This book is a work of fiction. While its plot has some roots in events that happened during the War of Independence and the Irish Civil War, and while it uses the real names of certain historical figures associated with those particular events, all the other events described here and all characters who possess fictitious names are entirely the product of the author's imagination. Any resemblance to any actual living person is entirely coincidental.

Sincere thanks to the artist Alan Counihan for permission to use, on the cover of this novel, a detail from a photograph taken from his 2014 installation, 'Personal Effects: A History of Possessions', which focused on belongings left behind by dead or discharged patients from St. Brendan's Psychiatric Hospital, Grangegorman.

British Library Cataloguing in Publication Data. A CIP catalogue record for this book is available from the British Library.

Set in Goudy Old Style in 12 pt on 15.3 pt
Typeset by JVR Creative India
Edited by Djinn von Noorden
Cover image detail by Alan Counihan
Printed by L&C, Poland, lcprinting.eu

The paper used in this book comes from the wood pulp of sustainably managed forests.

New Island received financial assistance from The Arts Council (An Chomhairle Ealaíon), Dublin, Ireland.

New Island Books is a member of Publishing Ireland.

10 9 8 7 6 5 4 3 2 1

For Diarmuid and Katie, setting forth

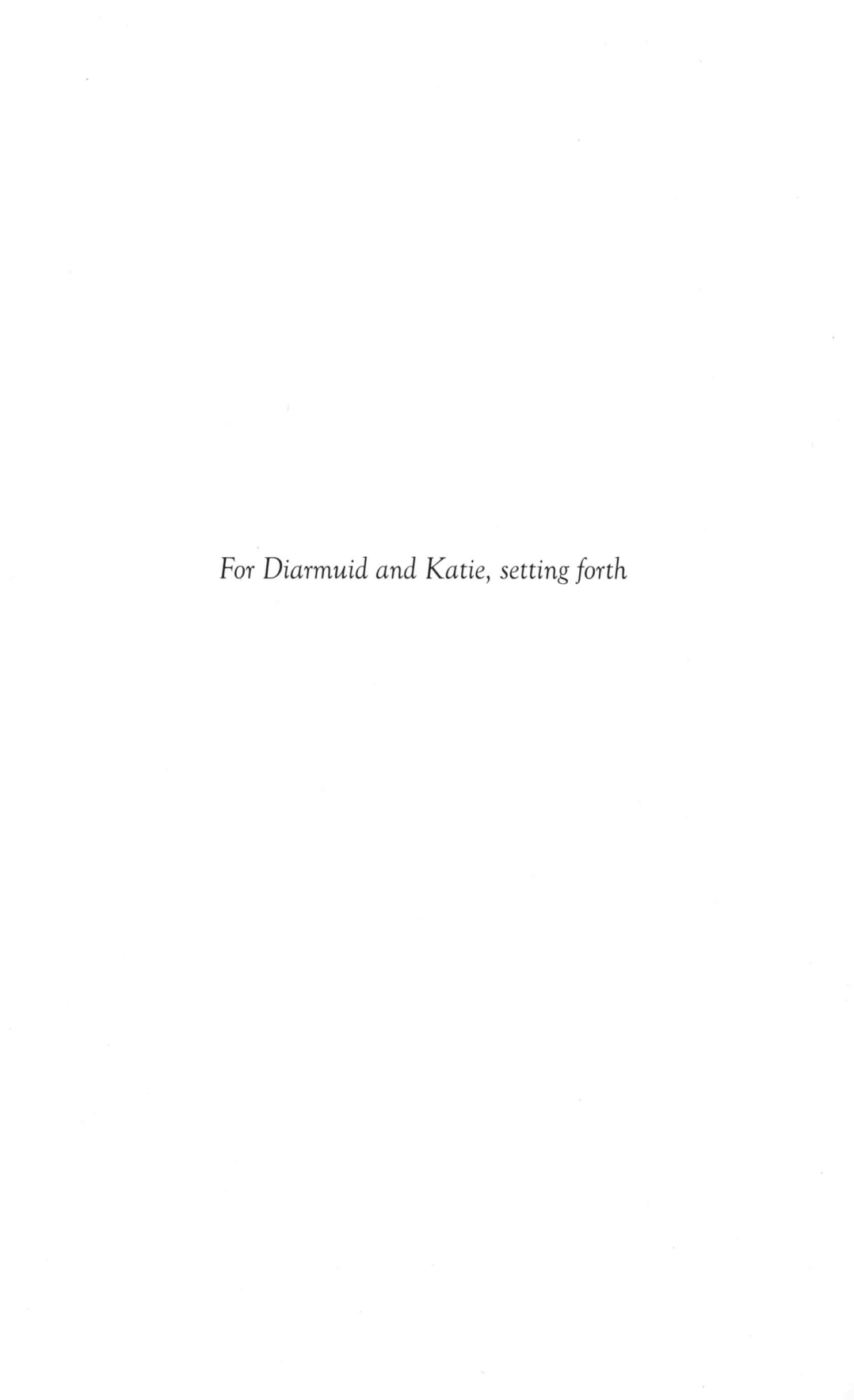

Prologue

Fairfax

25 March 1941: Night Crossing

They met on a voyage from darkness into light. Or so it seemed to Fairfax as he stood on the open deck of the mailboat navigating the night crossing to Dublin. After two years of enforced blackouts in England, Dublin's lights glittering in the distance looked so unnatural that this might be a journey into a different world. Or a journey back in time – where he often asked his patients to mentally travel – into a lost childhood, when lights could shine bright without a fear of attracting bombers, where the only things that might wake you were a cock crowing or a dog's bark – not the heart-stopping wail of air-raid sirens or the unearthly whoosh of a falling bomb foretelling the ferocious explosion to come.

He did not know the circumstances of how this woman standing on deck had left London twelve hours earlier. His own journey started in the blacked-out darkness he had grown accustomed to navigating. The headlights of the Wolseley Super Six driven by his friend Christopher, who collected Fairfax from his flat, were cloaked in cardboard with two pinpricks cut into them. This allowed not so much a beam of light as the ghost of a beam, to precariously guide them through unlit streets where even one loose curtain over a window could become a source of consternation and danger.

He didn't ask where Christopher had acquired the petrol to drive him to the station, and was too distraught to want to know what favours Christopher must have called in to circumnavigate regulations and procure the necessary documents to allow Fairfax to leave Britain.

Some work and travel permits had undoubtedly been procured during hushed conversations in the corridors of White's Club in St James's Street, a club steeped in arcane etiquette where gentleman could enjoy the company of fellow gentlemen in the billiards room, as if this Blitzkrieg were just another outside interference to be kept at bay until obsequious servants requested members to adjourn to the relative safety of the wine cellars. Other permits had possibly been acquired from contacts in more secretive clubs like Le Boeuf sur le Toit in Orange Street in Soho, where a different type of gentlemen could risk enjoying the company of other men in a more surreptitious manner.

Fairfax rarely frequented White's, which he found too stifling, or Le Boeuf sur le Toit, because its decor was too lascivious and its trade a bit too rough for a settled man like himself. But he was known on the fringes of these closeted circles and in other circles too. He frequented meetings of the British Psychoanalytical Society, which, following an influx of members fleeing Vienna, was now beset by schisms between Kleinian and Freudian factions. Since boyhood he had been a member of the local cricket club, where he enjoyed the relative anonymity of being known only for being not as good a medium-pace bowler as his older brother once was and for being considered a disappointment to his ambitious father.

For the past decade Fairfax had been able to partition his life between these different worlds because at heart all he cared about was the unshakable sanctuary that had been at the centre of his existence; the small haven he had created where he could be himself with the man whom he loved; that sanctum in Putney, which he had shared with his lover Charles and which he had thought could only ever be blown apart if a Heinkel had circled overhead and indiscriminately dropped an incendiary bomb on the flat. He could never have expected his world to be shattered by a blast on a shabby side street off the Old Kent Road in Southwark a fortnight ago, which caused two bodies to be found entwined amid the rubble.

When one secret was shattered in the circles in which Fairfax moved, there was always a fear of contamination, of other secrets being exposed among the shards. Therefore, some favours solicited by Christopher on his behalf had been given not only from sympathy for his loss but from self-interest. With his private sanctum destroyed, he might become dangerous to know. Nobody could gauge what secrets a man might inadvertently let slip when trying to make sense not only of a terrible loss but a heartrending sense of betrayal as well.

At the train station, Christopher had paused before getting out to seek a porter for his cases. 'You do know that Charles loved you?' he said.

Fairfax shook his head. 'I'm certain of nothing anymore.'

Christopher turned towards him, but even in the privacy of the Wolseley on a blacked-out street he was too nervous to risk putting a comforting hand on his knee.

'Charles was always just Charles. He was older than us. You saw in his eyes that he had seen ugly things we never had to see. Maybe he needed to do ugly things too, in Egypt or in Ireland during their damned unrest. I don't know because a gentleman doesn't tell. I just know that war was damnable back then and is damnable now. We're each made up of our contradictions. You know this better than most. You delve into contradictions every day with patients. Few people are just good or evil. Sometimes we yield to temptations that are simply opportunistic; acted out in one moment and forgotten in the next, with no intent to hurt anyone. Charles could show a streak of cruelty, but never towards you. I don't know how Charles ended up in that flat in Southwark, but from how Charles sometimes gazed at you, I never saw any man so much in love with another. Hold onto that thought and do nothing stupid. Boats have a hypnotic quality. Waves look inviting if you stare long enough. But any poor sod who ever jumped was already regretting the decision before his body entered the freezing waters.'

Fairfax had pondered those words since the train began its cautious journey from London, crawling through dark cities with the blacked-out carriage windows increasing his claustrophobia. There was the brief respite of being let out into the air to queue to board this packed mailboat. The crossing took eight hours longer than before the war, but even at sea some passengers felt apprehensive. Early in the war U-boats had laid mines that caused the MV *Munster* passenger ship to sink within sight of Liverpool. The Irish Sea was safer since the Royal Navy laid a nest of mines across the St George's Channel. But magnetic mines could break loose during storms and drift harmlessly until they found a metal hull to latch onto. No stage of this crossing was safe until they caught sight of the neutral, lit-up Irish coastline.

These lights were causing excitement on deck now, beckoning in the dark like the gateway to a luminous funfair. Three well-heeled English passengers paused beside him. Their stance betrayed how – although banned from wearing uniforms in Ireland – they were British army officers, availing of leave to indulge in the pleasures Dublin could offer. Restaurants where they could eat without fretting over ration cards; ballrooms to dance in without fear of air-raid sirens; shops awash with gifts of cosmetics for wives and girlfriends, if guilt required them to atone for any indiscretions during this spree, when pink gin and whiskey were flowing. He heard them make plans: dinner in Jammet's, then a wager on who could get furthest with any local Judy lining the walls of the Olympia Ballroom. They spoke of Dublin with childlike glee but also with spite, convinced that if they visited local harbours they would spy U-boats surfacing at night to be refuelled, and Kriegsmarine sailors nodding to sly fishermen in pubs, before those German crews disappeared to bring death to honest sailors on the Western Approaches.

'We'll gatecrash a dance at the Gresham,' one man said. 'It's easy to sweet-talk your way in and find a better class of Able Grable to ply with gin. If I lure one outside, I won't take no for an answer. If they're so free with favours for the Nazis, they can be free with them for us too.'

The others laughed and strode away, leaving him alone in the shadows. Fairfax had frequently travelled by yacht in rough seas, yet a fear of seasickness prevented him from venturing into the bar. Or maybe a fear of getting drawn into conversation with a fellow passenger from his own social class. He lacked the strength to go through the charade of spurious chitchat. Fairfax needed to be alone. Or as alone as one could be with so many passengers traversing this narrow deck, hurrying to join the singsong in the bar or pausing to marvel at the approaching city lights.

In truth, he was in hiding in this semi-darkness, hoping nobody would recognise him. In his early twenties it was the sort of shadowy darkness he had furtively sought out, torn between fear and excitement, between physical needs he tried to suppress and a fear of assault and blackmail, arrest and the disgrace of a court case. Before the war, such clandestine pockets of darkness were hard to find. But, as Charles had recently remarked, the blackout transformed all of London into a vast version of Hampstead Heath, brimming with sexual possibilities. Charles had given him a long glance after saying this, before adding with a laugh, 'That is, if we still needed to seek such encounters, dear heart, which thankfully we don't, as we have each other. All I'm seeking these days is a pot of tea stewed with leaves only previously used twice.'

Back then Fairfax hadn't thought much about Charles's observation. But now what he recalled most was his long glance. Had Charles been trying to tell him something? Or hoping to lure him into a reply that bestowed permission to go 'bunburying', to use his favourite Wilde euphemism?

Maybe Charles meant nothing by it. The Blitz had taught him not to read portents into people's final remarks. Death came too randomly. No Londoner knew when an incendiary bomb would devastate their home or if they would reach a bomb shelter in time or if their Morrison shelter, doubling as a kitchen table, would bear the weight of rubble until they were dug out. Death could strike as mundanely on Westminster Bridge as on the Clapham omnibus. But surely a cosmopolitan ex-army officer like Charles could never have expected it to seek him out in a bed in that cheap lodging house in Southwark.

Not that Fairfax knew how threadbare the room had been. Little had remained standing by the time the air-raid warden on the scene recognised that Charles – even when naked – did not belong there. Too well fed and groomed in contrast to the equally naked Irish labourer whose body was entwined with his. The warden had searched Charles's jacket, still attached on the collapsed bedstead, and, seeing Charles's former rank, deserted his post to telephone the number on his business card. Fairfax recalled the warden's deferential phone manner as he asked firstly if Fairfax was acquainted with a Mr Charles Willoughby and then, after a pause, if he knew of an Irishman with travel papers that gave his name as James Bourke. The warden had been very hesitant with his questions, sensing from the details on Charles's business card that he might be dealing with the sort of people who knew important people who would want any scandal to be hushed up.

Fairfax now wondered whether he had spent ten years intimately getting to know Charles, only to discover that he didn't truly know him at all. Their age difference meant that Charles had witnessed butchery and horrors in the Dardanelles and Egypt that Fairfax's youth shielded him from until his first posting to France during the final months of the Great War. But if he never witnessed whatever horrors Charles endured, Fairfax had witnessed the nightmares that arose from the trauma of those unmentioned events. On some nights Charles would shudder and shout out in his sleep, waking in such dazed confusion that he could only regain his equilibrium by spooning into Fairfax's body, nuzzling his naked back and then, as his breathing slowly returned to normal, planting a kiss on Fairfax's ear before murmuring, 'Ambushed again, dear heart. Hope I didn't frighten you.'

But on other nights, Charles's hardened state of arousal upon wakening had allowed for no such endearments, with Fairfax knowing that the silent fucking he was about to receive would be long and merciless. This rough sex felt both intimate and anonymous, with Fairfax occluded from whatever memories made his lover's cock so rigid. Only once had he deciphered a whisper – 'beg for it to the hilt ... tight Irish arse ...' – words so barely audible that he was unsure if Charles was awake or asleep, fantasising or reliving a memory. These uncharacteristic outbursts of sexual dominance – over which Charles, in his agitation, appeared to have little control – left Fairfax feeling bruised, inside and out, and yet oddly loved and needed. In those moments he became the poultice for Charles's pain, even if Charles was so exhausted by his climax that he generally fell back asleep within moments, barely aware of Fairfax being left to spill his own seed across his lover's naked chest, adorned with the scar of a bullet hole, the souvenir of an ambush in Tipperary in 1920.

But generally, their sex was not like that. It was companionable and relatively gentle, if lacking the intensity of the early years when every coupling felt like a treasure snatched from a judgemental world. Charles's unexpected violence during those rare nocturnal couplings was never mentioned, though, sometimes next morning, he would kiss Fairfax's neck lightly and murmur, 'Hope I wasn't over boisterous last night, dear heart. I was barely awake. I don't know what came over me. I'd never intentionally hurt you. I love you too much. You know that, don't you?'

Standing on the deck of this ship now, he was certain of nothing. The first rule for any psychoanalyst was to never psychoanalyse one's partner. Charles and he lived together for so long that it felt akin to a marriage. Charles professed little patience for his field of 'quack medicine', as he sometimes disparaged it. But even if Fairfax had persuaded him to lie on a couch, Charles could never have been lured into reliving what turned him into a predator on nights when his unloosened brutality scared and excited them both. Fairfax wasn't sure if this sadism stemmed from experiences in Egypt or serving in Ireland after the Great War or if this quirk of sadism was always latent inside Charles and might have emerged anyway, even if war had not interrupted his career as a stockbroker and a name in Lloyds.

Mostly they had kept their very different public lives separate, despite very occasionally pretending to be brothers. Charles had enjoyed immersing himself in risks and profits from stocks and shares, deals involving tangible commodities. It had been a mistake to lure him some months ago to a fractious meeting of the British Psychoanalytical Society, where the conceptual theories being passionately espoused merely exasperated him.

This had led to a rare row, after Charles opened the whiskey decanter back in their flat. But also to a rarer glimpse into Charles's time in Ireland, as he mocked the debate he had been forced to sit through. It was also the first occasion that Fairfax heard the name of the asylum to which he was now travelling to take up his new post.

'All your theorists can do is just drone on about vague abstractions,' Charles had snorted after several whiskies. 'God help any poor bastard seeking help from them. Don't tell me you honestly believe that lying on a couch and bleating out your inner thoughts does anyone any good? People who go mad need to be shaken out of madness. I know. I saw the inside of an asylum while you were still in boarding school. Grangegorman in Dublin – a hellhole in which, to be honest, you'd be too soft to ever work. Don't worry; I wasn't in Grangegorman to be dosed with strychnine syrup or plunged into hot and cold baths to revive my spirits and scrunch up my scrotum. I rarely set foot in the main asylum there, thank God, because it was rife with tuberculosis and dysentery. The army kept our shell-shocked soldiers in a separate military wing and blotted their names out of the asylum's records, so our lads could walk away with no stain of ever being certified as insane. They were honest, decent chaps, sunk into themselves after enduring such horrors that they heard voices and explosions in their sleep or even when awake. The doctors did their best, but with proper drugs, not abstract nonsense. There's no point in asking a man suffering from neurasthenia if he wet the bed as a child, when he's so disturbed after seeing his pals blown to shreds that he's shitting himself in his sleep.'

'What were you doing visiting that asylum?' Fairfax had asked, humiliated at how the evening had gone. 'Shouting at patients to buck up?'

'I was helping those lads who could do so to buck up,' Charles replied. 'With those who couldn't, I just sat with them, sharing cigarettes or helping to write letters. It was the first time many had ever properly spoken to an officer, though some were so feeble-minded they could barely form a sentence. But when I saw a spark returning to other chaps, I did as much good as any doctor. The Irish Automobile Association put a motor at my disposal. I'd take them out of that rancid asylum and out of themselves. Fresh air in the Wicklow hills, the freedom to swim naked in a lake and then just lie there, feeling the sun on their pelt. Sometimes doctors were angry with me bringing them back so late, but during their day with me they felt like men again, not just patients to be pitied.'

'And what kept you and them so late up the Wicklow hills?' Fairfax remembered feeling an irrational stab of jealousy.

Charles had fixed him with a stare. 'Few stayed up there late with me but any who lingered did so willingly. Our kind can always find tell-tale signs to recognise each other, even in those who never faced up to admitting their nature to themselves. Stretching out naked after a swim is the easy way to sort the wheat from the chaff. I'd just lie there, smoking, gazing up and, if it was in their nature, then I'd pretty soon sense their furtive glances at my body. Some lads were so innocent I was often their first time. "What if I can't keep a stiff upper lip, Sir," one Dublin lad asked me. "Don't worry," I said, "it isn't your lip that I'll teach you how to keep stiff."'

Charles had laughed, expecting him to join in, but whiskey had soured the mood between them.

'Is that where you learnt to be rough?' Fairfax had felt a need to hurt him.

Charles's smile disappeared. 'I was rough to no man in Ireland. Not back then, just after the Armistice when it was still safe for an officer to drive about. Ireland changed soon after. You never knew what baby-faced cornerboy was lying in wait to put a cowardly bullet in your back. After the murders started, everything was off the table or, if the ghastlier of my fellow officers were drunk enough, I'd find men bent across it.'

Their quarrel had lasted for days, neither of them knowing how to resolve it, angrier with themselves than with each other. Finally, Charles had found the consolatory words. 'I spoke out of turn the other night, dear heart. The whiskey talking. I've no doubt that you do good in your work. Don't think of me badly. Any encounters I had before I met you needed to be furtive and quick, with often no words spoken. But it kills me that you might think I ever took advantage of any man.'

'It kills me that you think me too soft to work in an asylum like Grangegorman.'

Charles had reached his hand across the table. 'I don't think you're soft, dear heart. It took moral courage for you to resign from your last job over the ragging of that conscientious objector which went too far. I don't think of Ireland often. I've forgotten most of my good memories and can't forget my bad ones about that blasted country. Promise me you'll never think of working there. The asylums would break your health and then break your heart.'

He was on this boat now partly to prove Charles wrong in thinking that he lacked the strength to cope in somewhere like Grangegorman. Even if working in such a place gradually decimated his soul, having to focus on the labour involved might just save him from thoughts of killing himself. Remembering any conversation with Charles now anguished Fairfax. He was overwhelmed by grief, yet even this grief was soured by a paralysing anger at having been betrayed in a cheap lodging house.

His thoughts kept returning to the night when he was summoned to that collapsed building in Southwick, but he was so lost in self-absorption that it took him a while to realise why.

Then gradually Fairfax became aware his gaze had honed in on a solitary figure at the rail. It was windy on deck in this hour before dawn, yet she seemed oblivious to the cold. She gazed at Dublin's distant lights but seemed barely aware of them. He had never seen anyone look so alone and lost. The lighting on deck was so dim that it defied logic to feel convinced that he recognised her, having only glimpsed her twice before. Their first encounter had possessed a nightmarish quality when she arrived at the rubble of her former home in Southwark to find neighbours digging with their bare hands and pointedly ignoring Fairfax, who was sobbing and openly stroking Charles's forehead. He had been saying God knows what, with all normal discretion gone, while Charles's body lay beneath the same blanket that concealed the naked corpse of the husband who had betrayed this woman.

The second was a glimpse of her being consoled by other Irish emigrants two days later at James Bourke's funeral in an RC church, where Fairfax had tried to sit unobtrusively in the back pew, knowing that he was intruding on someone else's grief but unable to stay away from what had felt like a final link to Charles. He had known, from her venomous glare when glimpsing him there, that she resented his presence.

If he approached now on deck, she might suspect him of stalking her. Her presence on board made sense. She was presumably returning home to be consoled by her kin. But his presence here would be inexplicable to her, voyaging to a city where he knew nobody and hoped that nobody knew him. Fairfax had never even previously visited Ireland, put off by Charles's reticence about discussing his army years there, which he had dismissed as 'a shambles of brutality and brandy, best forgotten'.

It was the cruellest irony that, during this crossing, Fairfax had chanced upon the only person who might understand the paradoxical emotions destroying him. He had no right to further intrude on this widow's grief and might have remained watching from the shadows if something about the way that she kept leaning over the rail had not alarmed him. Those waters were icy. Nobody was paying her attention, yet surely someone would hear the splash. He had no idea how long it would take this creaking ship to turn and try to search the waves into which she might disappear.

Her death should be her own business. She had endured enough. Fairfax had no right to interfere. But the Hippocratic Oath he once swore – the *primum non nocere* clause – made him step forth and grip her elbow when her body lurched forward as the ship struck a wave. She recoiled from his touch, even before recognising him. When she did, she was so startled that it took her a moment to speak.

'What the hell do you want? Haven't your sort already done enough to me! Get away or I'll scream to let folk know what class of deviant you are!'

'Please,' he said, 'I don't mean to alarm you. I was just worried.'

'About what?' She glanced at the waves. 'That I'd jump? Why would that worry you? It would be one less person alive who knows your dirty secret.' She paused and stared at him angrily. 'What are you even doing here?'

'Not spying on you, I swear. But it's slippery out here. So just promise you'll move back from the rail.'

'What would you do if I jumped? Dive in to rescue me like a gallant gent?'

'I might dive in,' Fairfax replied after a pause. 'Not to rescue but follow you. There has been no day in the past fortnight when I haven't thought about escaping this pain by ending it all.'

His words lessened her aggressive tone. 'I've not thought about you,' she said. 'Beyond thinking that I'd like to put a knife in you. But what good would that do? The night I came home to find you sobbing over those two bodies, I realised you were as duped as I was. Equally clueless. Even when you think you know men, you can't trust them. But my Jem wasn't like your perverted friend. Jem was from Dominick Street in Dublin. He had trials playing soccer for Bohemians. You don't get queers in Dominick Street.'

'Are you sure?'

She shook her head. 'A fortnight ago I thought I understood my world. But not anymore.' Her tone sharpened. 'You had no right to attend Jem's funeral. People were asking who you were.'

'What did you say?'

'I lied and said you were the warden who found his body, piled among other bodies in the hallway, all of them trying to reach the air-raid shelter.' She paused. 'The sirens were going. The tube station only a hundred yards away was packed with people. I keep asking, why hadn't they enough sense to get to safety with everyone else?'

She glanced away. 'But that's the old naive me thinking. They didn't want to be with other people. The sirens must have sounded like music. It meant that every other flat in the house was empty and they could do as they pleased, as loudly as they pleased. But it makes no sense because my Jem wasn't like that.' Her voice lost conviction. 'Or was he? Was money involved? We found it hard to make ends meet, but Jem wouldn't ... not that way ... even if we had debts I didn't know of. Jem liked to gamble ... he liked risk ... but he'd never do such a thing.' She turned to Fairfax. 'At least have the decency to explain all this to me.'

'If I could, I would. I didn't know your Jem, or James as he was called on his work permit. But maybe I didn't know my friend Charles either, despite ten years under one roof.'

'Ten years.' She took this in. 'Jem and me only had eighteen months. But they were eighteen natural months. We were a married couple.'

'I know,' he replied softly. 'But grief isn't a competition.'

She nodded. Both lapsed into silence. There was just the splash of waves against the hull, a whistling sea breeze and murmurs of conversations around them. No other passengers lingered to eavesdrop or pay them any heed. They could think of little to say, having nothing in common. Nothing and everything. Sharing the accidental and unwelcome bond of being the keepers of each other's secret. Perhaps it was good to know so little about each other. No words exchanged here would get back to anyone who knew either of them. A secret unshared can drive a person into the depths of insanity. Talk was as essential a cure for the mind as penicillin was for the body. To keep the truth hidden away was an invisible form of cancer. Fairfax knew this, as a psychoanalyst. But he felt as lost as any patient who ever lay on his couch.

He thought of Luke 4:23 in the King James Bible. 'Physician, heal thyself.' Fairfax didn't share this quotation with her. Roman Catholics – as far as he knew – were not encouraged to read the Bible and certainly not the version reshaped by forty-five Protestant biblical scholars to elevate their king. Glancing at her face, as she stared towards Dublin's lights, he knew that when this boat docked she would disappear from his life. The only thing they would take away were the hidden aspects of each other's lives. She could never talk about this without it bringing judgement on her late husband. She felt his gaze and looked up.

'What sort of welcome will you get from your family?' Fairfax asked.

'It will beat the welcome I got in England when I made this crossing two years ago. Men spraying delousing powder over my hair and a stuck-up Foxrock Dublin Protestant doctor looking down her nose as she made me strip to my shift to check for lice and ask how often I washed. I'll take that guff from your sort but not from the likes of her.'

'Is a Foxrock Dublin Protestant not one of your own?'

'They're neither flesh nor fowl,' she replied bitterly. 'I had to pretend to be twenty-two to get a permit to go to England. The Garda stamping my travel pass knew I was too young, but also knew there were enough of us sharing one bed and my parents needed me to be sending home a few bob. But I only had to bluff my way in. Jem had to tell outright lies because he had been an agricultural labourer and Dev is forcing them buckos to remain in Ireland and work for a pittance.' She looked at him. 'Before Jem left the Dominick Street flats to get a job on a farm in Meath, he said that he had never once eaten a piece of fruit or a fresh vegetable. But he just wanted to get away from Dublin and spun lies to persuade a farmer to take him on. I used to laugh with him about the other lies he spun to get his travel pass to London because Jem was great at spinning yarns. I just didn't know he was spinning them to me.'

'I'm sorry,' he said softly. 'I know how you feel.'

Her face hardened. 'It has nothing to do with you, and you have nothing to do with me. When you saw me at this rail, why couldn't you have just walked on?'

'You looked so alone,' he said.

'I am alone.'

'You have family waiting. I don't know a soul in Dublin.'

'Then why come here?'

'Sometimes you need to go where nobody knows you.'

'I'm being bitchy,' she said quietly. 'I can't help it. I'm so angry. I should be angry with Hitler but I'm too busy being angry with Jem. I want to take him in my arms, yet I want to scratch out his eyes. What unearthly class of man was he?'

'Why ask me?' Fairfax said. 'You were married to him.'

'The best eighteen months of my life. He had his oddities, but I thought nothing of them because I knew nothing about life.'

'Did you love him?'

'He swept me off my feet. Six weeks between the night we met and our wedding. I couldn't believe he picked me instead of every other girl dying for him to put a ring on them. For the first time I felt special. Now I feel that something must be wrong with me.'

'There's nothing wrong with you.'

'There sure as hell was something wrong with him. And you too. No disrespect.'

He produced a leather notebook, wrote some words on a page and tore it out. 'This is my address in Dublin if there is anything I can ever do for you.'

She glanced at the slip of paper and nodded.

'It's good you're going in for treatment,' she said. 'I didn't know they treated your abnormality in there, but, God knows, they treat every other affliction.'

'I'm not there as a patient,' he said. 'I'm going to work as a doctor.'

'Of your own free will?'

His nod was rewarded with a look of incredulity.

'Surely a man of your education can find a better job?'

'If I wanted to, yes, but I don't. I need to get away from London. I also want to do some good.'

'You want to hide away, you mean? Well, your secret will be safe in Grangegorman. Those walls hold thousands of them.'

'Have you been inside that asylum?'

A defensiveness entered her voice. 'Are you accusing me of being astray in the head? No amadáns in my family ever needed to be carted off to that puzzle factory.' She paused. My professional instincts cautioned me against speaking before she spoke again. 'Though just because no one ever needed to be, doesn't mean that nobody ever was. I've a class of aunt locked up in Grangegorman.'

'What class of aunt?'

'The class no one mentions. She lived under her mother's roof for fifty years, though I'm not sure of her exact age and by now she probably doesn't know herself.'

'Do you mean that she is delusional?'

'I mean that she was in her brother's way after he inherited the farm when their mother – a vindictive hag – had the decency to finally oblige him by dying. I suppose nobody can blame him for wanting to make a spinster sister disappear. But in my book he's a hard-hearted bastard. In London I earned fifty-six bob a week as a carney girl in a munitions factory. Dirty work, my hair yellow from ladling sulphur, but it was more than my uncle earned from his tight-fisted mother in a month. Thirty years at her beck and call, running the farm for pocket money. I saw him collect old washers, to have something to jangle in his pocket that sounded like coins when he went out. He slaved from dawn to dusk because of the prize his mother dangled before him; that he could move in a young wife under her roof once she was dead. Until then, she would buck no rival and have no painted hussy, as she called them, preening as the woman of the house. Not that you'd find many painted hussies in Castleblaney, unless they can make mascara from cowshite. But you'll find women desperate enough to flutter their eye at an ageing bachelor with fifty-two acres and lumbago. My uncle was no great catch but the sea doesn't come in as far as Castleblaney so there's not many fish to choose from. Women will settle for a man who's already old, and will make them old by having babies as he tries to catch up for lost time while he has some *faloorum, fadidle eye-oorum* left in him. But they'll not move into a house with a spinster sister-in-law moping in the kitchen.'

'You are referring to your aunt?'

'Nobody refers to her. She'd have been better in a coffin than in Grangegorman. If she was under the ground, no nightly rosary would be said without her name being included among the prayers for the departed. When you're dead, queer habits are recalled as amusing quirks, not used as nails to crucify you.'

'Had she quirks?'

The woman turned to him. 'You have some cheek asking. It's more than quirks that you and your blaggard friend had.'

'My relationship with Charles had to be undefined. A case of *acta non verba*.'

'I mightn't know Latin, but I know that sin is sin in any language. And I now know something of your filthy codology. Everything arseways and back to front. But I was so innocent leaving Castleblaney that I didn't know that men like you existed. I was so innocent that it wasn't until the older women I work with rushed to an air-raid shelter and our tongues loosened, that I got some clue because they started laughing when I described how Jem and I went at it. Before that I presumed a girl was always meant to kneel up, like Jem instructed me to, because I had no one to tell me any different.'

She stared again towards Dublin's lights creeping closer. A passenger walking behind them pointed out the flash from the Bailey lighthouse to his travelling companion. Fairfax knew that she felt exposed for having said too much. It was presumptuous to think that he could fathom the cocktail of emotions she must be enduring. But something of her conflicted feelings surely echoed his own unbearable grief that was relieved only by surges of fury at having been betrayed. She and Fairfax seemed separated from every passenger on deck and yet, despite their similar grief, equally separated from each other.

'You needn't tell me such details,' he whispered. 'These are not matters to discuss with a stranger.'

She turned to him, her eyes betraying how long since she last slept. 'Who the hell else can I ever discuss all this with? Not even with a priest in confession, although it's a mortal sin to hold anything back. But if the punishment for a false confession is hell, I'll take it because this feels like hell. I'm only talking to you because, after this boat docks, I'll never see you again and you'll encounter no member of my family.'

'Except maybe your aunt in Grangegorman.'

'I've not told you her name.'

'Trust me. I would never betray your confidence.'

She looked away, wounded. 'I'd have trusted Jem with my life. I'm so broken I'll never trust anyone ever again.'

'I know.'

'How could you know?' she said angrily. 'You haven't lost a husband.' She stared at him closely. 'Don't say you thought of your friend like that. Your loss is nothing compared to mine.'

'I don't presume to fathom the depth of your loss,' he replied. 'Please don't presume to fathom mine.'

'They're not alike.'

'No. When you disembark, you can discuss yours. Widowhood gives you status. People will sympathise, make allowances, understand you are grieving. I'll never be able to speak of this again. For years I needed to hide my love. Now I must hide my grief.'

'You won't be able to hide if I write to tell the Superintendent in Grangegorman that you were in an unnatural relationship.'

He nodded. 'If that's your wish then I can't stop you.'

She looked away, her anger dissipating. 'I'd never do that, because I'd also have to say how my husband was in an unnatural relationship with the same man.'

'Had you no idea?' Fairfax asked.

'Had you?'

He shook his head. 'The life I am forced to lead has made me used to deception, threats of blackmail and disgrace. When you met Jem, I imagine that your friends were thrilled to see you settle down. With men like me, the pressures are reversed. Shared domesticity is dangerous and frowned on. Short liaisons are safer. But Charles and I never cared what our friends thought. In our early days we had adventures, sampling the delights that Morocco can offer. But we saw men there grow old and foolish and none of those temptations matched the joy of being able to turn a key in a front door and call someone's name; the pleasure of sharing a bowl of soup in companionable silence. We no longer needed to seek release in dark alleyways. What we possessed was too precious. We both understood that, or I thought we did, until that air-raid warden scrambling through the wreckage recognised that Charles was a toff. When he phoned, he asked no questions, but people who hear my accent rarely do. He covered their bodies with a sheet until I arrived and went back to helping to dig in the rubble.'

'What would the warden have done if he'd discovered Jem with another navvy?'

He shook his head. 'I don't know.'

'It's your country, you should know.'

'It has never felt like mine. I don't feel that I possess a country but I possess a vocation. I am a doctor. I try to help people trapped in pain to at least understand their pain. I don't mend broken bones. I deal with invisible wounds, maybe because my private life had to be invisible until Hitler blew both of our worlds apart.'

'Hitler robbed me of my husband, but your friend robbed me of my right to grieve.' She looked up at me. 'How can I grieve someone I loved but then discovered that I never truly knew?'

'Were no hints dropped?'

She gave a wistful laugh. 'You don't know Irishmen. They're like closed fists. You'd decode Greek quicker. Even talkative Irishmen don't say anything beyond bluster. Discussing the weather or Gaelic football or Queen Victoria being a bitch. They've never forgotten her heartlessness during the Famine, but don't ask if any of their own families starved to death, because the shutters come down on things they want to forget.' She paused. 'Mother of Jesus, why couldn't Jem have been found shacked up with a cheap floozy? I'd hate him but at least I'd understand him.' She looked away. 'When I said he asked me to kneel up, I don't mean we did anything unnatural. I knelt because he liked it. But I didn't like it. I kept thinking I must be so ugly that he can't bear to look into my face.'

'You mustn't think like that,' he assured her.

'How should I think?'

'That he loved you because I'm sure he did. If he'd been with another woman then I'd suspect that he didn't love you because what could she give him that you couldn't? But maybe deep inside – and I doubt he understood it himself – he needed something no woman could give. It's a curious consolation, but all I can think to give you.'

She stared at him. 'If that's my only consolation, it leaves you with no consolation at all. I don't know what pleasures my Jem gave your friend, but they were nothing you couldn't have given just as easily.'

'I know.'

'So where does that leave you?'

'On my way to a job in Dublin. That was plan A anyway.'

'What was plan B?'

The boat had steered its way between two long stone piers stretching into Dublin Bay. More people came on deck, attracted by the lights and sense of arrival.

'What a friend in London cautioned me against. A dark crossing on a crowded boat. Nobody would miss a passenger who slipped overboard.'

'What stopped you?'

'I think you did.'

'Get away out of that.' She blushed. 'You don't even know me.'

'From how you were stood alone, gripping this rail, I feared for you and I wanted to see you safely to shore.'

'I never asked you to play at being my saviour.'

'Maybe it was you saving me.'

'Or maybe the thought of how long it might take to drown, floundering among those waves.'

He nodded. 'Maybe you're right and I'm a coward.'

She shook her head. 'I was thinking of myself floundering in those waves before you appeared. Maybe we saved each other or for me maybe it was the thought of suicide being a mortal sin. I'd go straight to hell. Jem – for all he did – was still a decent man who would only be condemned to purgatory. So it wasn't the fear of not seeing God's face that stopped me. It was the fear that I'd never see Jem again to ask if our love was real. The fires of hell are nothing compared to the need for answers.'

'I know,' he said softly.

For the slightest half second she placed her cold hand over his on the rail.

'I know you know,' she said. 'Jem was gentle. Never laid a finger on me. But I'd sooner he'd have beaten me black and blue than leave me like this, burdened by his secrets.'

Fairfax was silent while the three off-duty army officers he had overheard earlier came out on deck, keen to be the first passengers off. Even after they moved away, he hesitated. 'Charles was a gentleman,' he said finally. 'But he wasn't always gentle. With men like us, sometimes the older man is dominant. The younger man accepts this because it makes him still feel young in his lover's eyes.'

Anxiety entered her voice. 'You don't think Charles ever hurt my Jem?'

He shook his head. 'When I saw how your husband's body was strong and toughened from manual work, I knew Charles was after something I couldn't give. Maybe I'd become too compliant for his tastes. Do you know anything about radium?'

'No.'

'It's powerful but has a poisonous toxicity. Maybe all power is toxic. Charles liked me to kneel up too. He chain-smoked. One night recently, when we were doing what men do, he shocked me by stubbing out a cigarette butt on my skin.'

The woman blessed herself. 'That would shock anyone.'

'I wasn't shocked by him,' Fairfax said. 'I was shocked by myself. Shocked to discover that I found myself excited by that pain.'

'Mother of Jesus. What class of man are you?'

'One, it seems, who didn't know my own nature. Charles leaned over me that night and whispered, "In Ireland that's what we used to call doing an Igoe." But if Charles had tried to do that with your husband, then Jem would have broken his jaw. I didn't and maybe that was when I lost his respect by not lashing out. Grangegorman sounds like hell but if I can find one patient who needs my help then just maybe I can cure him in lieu of curing myself. It's not much but just now it's the only thought that gives my life any purpose.'

The ship was docking at its berth on the North Wall, ropes being tied up, a rudimentary gangway waiting to be put in place.

'You won't be able to do much for my aunt,' she said. 'You can't cure someone who wasn't mad in the first place.'

'Then how did your family get her admitted?'

'A note from the local priest. Priests know what side their bread is buttered on. When a postal order arrives from England, a shilling falls into a priest's palm every time the money changes hands. There's cash in weddings and christenings, and no married farmer wants to be shamed when the priest reads out the exact sum that each parishioner contributes to the Easter dues. A spinster is useful for arranging altar flowers but the only money a priest will earn from her is from her funeral. Everyone saw it coming, except for my aunt and me. Or maybe she knew all along and it was her unspoken fear that caused her to start acting so oddly. This gave her brother the cover he needed.' She looked away. 'God forgive me, but I was involved in deceiving her.'

'In what way?'

'I was her favourite niece. She had a childlike quality. Sometimes as a treat I was allowed to stay over and sleep in her bed. The pair of us whispering and giggling until her mother thumped the bedroom wall with her stick. My aunt's spirits sank when her brother got engaged. They told her she was just going to Dublin to see a doctor for a check-up. A few tests, maybe an X-ray. We'd leave her with the doctors for an hour and then call back for her. God forgive me for agreeing to go in the car, but I'd never seen Dublin and never thought that her brother would abandon her. And they knew she would make no fuss because she trusted me. Us holding hands in the back of Seamus Quinn's hackney car all the way to Dublin. We stopped at the Brock Inn near Finglas – the two men going in for whiskeys, sending out minerals for us waiting outside. Lovely countryside. The last view she saw not blocked by a wall. Grangegorman looked like a prison. High barred windows, a huge wooden door. I wanted to go in with them but my uncle told me to stay in the hackney. My aunt looked petrified. All I could do was squeeze her hand and say it would be fine. The doctors were educated men. They'd chat to her and realise that nothing was wrong, except that she was a bit down in herself. I don't know what they thought because my uncle was barely in the door before he ran back out like the asylum was on fire. I asked him what the doctors said but he told me to shut up and told Quinn, "Drive like fuck, man. Put your foot down and don't stop till we're safely back at the Brock Inn."'

'You never saw her again?' Fairfax asked.

The woman was momentarily silent. 'I'm not sure. What happened to her made me want to get away to England as soon as any Garda would forge my age on the form. Jem and I decided to marry in Dublin. A chance to let our families meet at Westland Row Church. We'd have a few drinks before folk saw us back onto the boat, but before that we'd have a slap-up wedding breakfast in a café across from the church. Jem would have sooner got married in London. He'd no wish to set foot in Ireland again. But I insisted and packed two dresses because my aunt and I were the same size. It was my wedding so I could invite whoever I wanted. Jem came with me to Grangegorman. He was so persuasive he'd have talked the knickers off a nun. He swore that, whatever it took, we'd get her released for just one day. I'd shame my uncle if he turned up because I wanted her as my bridesmaid. But when we reached Grangegorman I looked up at those high windows and saw a little scared face staring out from one. I'm sure it wasn't my aunt, with so many souls locked in there. But I panicked. God forgive me. In my mind she didn't seem like the aunt I knew anymore. It felt like she must surely be a mad woman if locked in that asylum. I didn't know what three years of captivity might have done to her. I hated myself for running away, but I couldn't stop, even when Jem offered to at least ask the doctors how she was. But I loved Jem and this was my first time to meet his people. Suddenly it wasn't about shaming my uncle. It was about not shaming myself by being associated with a lunatic. That makes me an unmerciful hypocrite.'

'It makes you human. I can write if you want and tell you how she is.'

She shook her head. 'How could I explain me knowing you if a letter arrived? My family would put the Spanish Inquisition to shame. But maybe you could check on her. Don't give her false hope by saying we've met. But show her some small kindness. It would mean a lot to me.'

'I will,' he said. 'But if you come to Dublin, I'll arrange for you to visit. It would be good for her and maybe good for you.'

Her manner grew abrupt as passengers began to disembark. 'I'll not have time. I'll be too busy being pregnant.'

'I didn't know you were pregnant.'

'I'm not,' she said. 'But I will be twice a week until I find the nerve to go back to London. I can only earn my keep in Castleblaney by thinning turnips in the fields or by smuggling. My two sisters cross the border into Northern Ireland three times a week, with a sack under their maternity smocks filled with flour or sugar or raisins. They flutter their eyelashes at the customs men before cycling to a black marketeer in Cullaville who swaps their smuggled goods for candles or paraffin oil. He's always trying to sneak a peep as they change dresses before cycling to a different border crossing where hopefully they won't be searched. For eighteen months I dreamt of donning a maternity smock. Now I'll look pregnant, not thanks to anything Jem did to me when alive but by his death.'

She took a step towards the gangway. He knew that when she disembarked she'd want him to hang back so that nobody would think they knew each other.

'What's your aunt's name?' Fairfax asked.

'Bridie Kerr.'

'I've just realised I don't know your first name.'

'Why would you know it? We Irish are good at keeping our secrets. I never saw you before and I'll never see you again.'

Then she was gone among the crowds of passengers; young women with cardboard suitcases struggling along the cobbles in the dawn light and young men entering early-house pubs crammed with dockers seeking news of work. Fairfax tried to follow her progress, but she deliberately removed her headscarf so there was no trace of the only person he knew in this unfamiliar country from which Charles always cautioned him to stay away.

One

Agnes

25 March 1941

Dillon looked so intense, lost inside his troubled thoughts, that his wife had to call his name twice before he averted his gaze from the window to peer fearfully at her in the bedroom doorway. It took a moment for his mind to clear sufficiently to recognise her.

'Agnes?' he whispered. 'Is that you?'

'Who else would it be?'

'What time is it?'

She kept her voice low, anxious not to reawaken the children. 'It's three a.m. and despite all your promises, you're at it again, like every night this past fortnight.'

'Three a.m. is when people are at their most vulnerable. They let their guard down. I, of all people, should know.' She took a step forward and he signalled for her to stop. 'Don't stray any closer to this window!'

Her nerves were frayed from lack of sleep but it was vital to stay calm. 'Francis, no soul will stir out there until the milkman and his horse start their round at six o'clock.'

'Just because a street looks empty doesn't mean it is. That's what I told my so-called comrades last week before they buggered off, concerned with saving their own skins. At one time they would have listened to me, back when their lives depended on it. I was the best intelligence officer Collins ever had.'

Her husband was two years shy of his fortieth birthday, but his face had grown so honeycombed with stress lines that some mornings, when she tidied him up enough to go to work, he looked closer to sixty. Just now, however, the way that he knelt by the moonlit window seemed to shave decades off him, reminding her of a scared boy. If she was gentle but firm, she might lull him back into a brief period of clarity when his paranoia lifted enough for them to properly talk.

'You've not been an intelligence officer for twenty years. You work for Joe McGrath in the Sweepstakes. It doesn't take much intelligence to pull the wool over the eyes of the US Postmaster General who breaks the law himself to secretly buy tickets for his mother. The only wars still raging are Hitler's one in Europe and the one being fought in your head. Now please, for my sake, get into your bed and not under it, where I found you shaking last night.'

She took a step forward to take his arm, desperate for some sleep in the few hours before she needed to rouse the children for school. But her movement was too sudden. She lost him again, his eyes panic-stricken as he shouted for her to stay back. It was too much for her, night after night. Any woman's patience would break.

'For God's sake, Francis, get up from the floor and lower your voice. You'll have the children in tears again if you wake them: the house in uproar. It's time to cop yourself on!'

'Keep a civil tongue when addressing a colonel,' he snapped back, but she sensed how her outburst had punctured the spell, causing him to feel a growing unease at upsetting her. She needed to bring him to his senses for as long as she could.

'You were a colonel for five minutes. Once you'd done all their fighting, the politicians drummed you out of the army.' She took a deep breath, knowing that she had to be gentle with him. 'It grieves me to say it but you're not the man I married,' she said in a softer voice. 'You once cut such an impressive figure. You still do on good days but they're rarer now. Don't get me wrong, Francis. I still love you deeply and the children love you. But they're scared when you get like this.'

Her words were enough for him to offer no resistance as she led him to sit on the bed. He looked up at her, slowly regaining his senses. His fingers grasped hers, at first with tenderness, but then more tightly, betraying his panic.

'You're a good woman, Agnes,' he said. 'Such a good woman. But I keep having terrible nightmares, even though these voices haven't allowed me to sleep in weeks. And please stop telling me that they're all in my mind.'

'The only voice that's real is mine, Francis. Here, in this bedroom we shared before you banished me to the box room with the baby, claiming I'd be safer there.'

'You're only safe if you stay away from me. On Bloody Sunday I saw wives wounded amid the pandemonium. And that was with honest volunteers doing the shooting, unlike the bastards coming for me.'

She tried not to wince at the pressure of his fingers squeezing hers. 'The only people coming are the bailiffs if Joe McGrath sacks you for being too agitated to do your job. I know you're scared, Francis, but with three small children, I'm scared too. I'm so scared of us starving that I get cross with them for no reason.'

'I know.' He sounded more like his old self. 'Your cross voice always reminds me of my sister. Only nine when she died, two years younger than me, but she ruled the roost. There's nothing I wouldn't have done for her, but nothing I could do to save her. I remember being allowed to sit up all night with Pop, keeping vigil beside her coffin in the parlour. Pop and I were never as close as during those hours sitting there with neither of us speaking.'

'You rarely mention your sister,' Agnes said softly.

He squeezed her fingers again, then released his grip. 'Talking is a sign of weakness. I don't want to end up like Vinny Byrne, gallivanting around race courses, boasting like he single-handedly plugged every spy Collins ordered us to shoot. For all his talk, all they rewarded him with was a carpenter's job in the Office of Public Works. Politicians needed men like me to do their dirty work. Now all they need me for is to take the blame.'

She took his hand back in hers. 'It breaks my heart to see you suffer. For years you never spoke about those times but it's like something has burst inside you. Why now?'

'I wish I knew, Agnes. Maybe I've grown weak or maybe I was always weak but was better able to hide it.'

'You were never weak. This isn't the man I married talking.'

He looked at her sadly. 'Go back to the baby. The boys will be up soon, demanding porridge. And look at the state of you, wandering around without even a dressing gown. You'll catch your death of cold.'

'And what will you catch your death of, shivering at that window?'

'When death comes for me, it won't come from a chill. I swear to you; I was settled in bed like you asked. I just took one final glance out the window and saw someone lurking in the shadows of St Columba's Church.'

'You saw wrong, Francis.'

'How can you be sure?'

'St Columba's Church is in Drumcondra. You live in Donnybrook now.'

He went silent, then slowly nodded. 'I do live here, don't I?'

'With a wife trying to mind you.'

He sighed. 'It's my responsibility to mind all of you.'

Agnes rose from the bed. 'Then get well for us.' She turned on the bedside lamp so she could fix the blankets for him.

'Turn off the light, please,' he pleaded. 'Don't give them a direct shot!'

She used her tone of voice for half-admonishing and half-cajoling the children. 'You have more chance of being strangled by a starched collar than shot by a sniper.' She pulled aside the lace curtain that covered the lower pane of the tall sash window and beckoned him. 'After all your brave deeds, don't tell me you lack the courage to properly look out this window. Tell me what you honestly see?'

He rose and stared out. When he spoke his voice was infused with unbearable sadness. 'An empty street of fine red-brick houses that are far grander than the streets where either of us grew up.' He looked at her. 'If I want to raise a family here I need to keep my wits, don't I?'

'Francis, I'm scared,' she whispered. 'Your head is so full of ghosts there's no room for the rest of us.'

'That's not true,' he assured her. 'Every day in work – whenever I can work – I worry about you all. But every night brings on a rush of panic. Panic is a virus that never leaves you. I'm scared that one night it will grip me so completely there'll be no way back.'

'Then promise to go and see Doctor O'Gorman for pills for your nerves,' she said. 'Not horse tranquilisers like the last ones that had you stupefied. Something that will ease your mind but still let you function at work.'

Dillon shook his head. 'O'Gorman is a diehard Fianna Fáiler. He'd sooner prescribe arsenic than anything that would cure me. And that's not just my paranoia talking.'

Agnes led him back to the bed. 'I know. They're the sanest words you've said in days. But surely Fine Gael has its share of doctors?'

'Donnybrook is awash with Fine Gael doctors,' he replied. 'Protestant and Castle Catholics. Doctors who play rugby and holiday in the Great Southern in Parknasilla. You can always spot a Fine Gael doctor: they send their fee notes in guineas.'

'But the Sweepstakes pays well, doesn't it?'

'A man's wage should be a private matter, provided he puts down enough money on the table for his wife to run the home.' She could have felt insulted at his secrecy. Instead she felt relieved to hear a stir of his old truculence.

'I'm just saying that Joe McGrath wouldn't see an old comrade go short of cash.'

He was mollified by her conciliatory tone. 'He's generous. But sometimes when he looks at me if I get addled, I know that, if I was one of his prize racehorses, he'd have me put down with a bullet.'

'Don't say that. Promise you'll find a Fine Gael doctor.'

'That's the odd thing about Fine Gaelers,' Dillon said. 'They only got a country to run because men like me saved it from toppling into anarchy.'

'I know,' Agnes said. 'I'm blue in the face hearing you say it. But we need you here with us.'

'I'm just saying we did what Collins ordered.'

Agnes coaxed him into bed and pulled up the covers. 'I wish Collins was alive. He was the last person you willingly took orders from.'

Dillon smiled. 'You didn't argue with Mick. Built like a bull and fond of settling arguments by getting you in a headlock.'

Agnes tucked in the blankets. 'Then pretend Collins has you in a headlock, forcing you to stay in bed.'

He patted her arm. 'First thing tomorrow I'll see Dr O' Gorman. Fianna Fáilers merely look at me with hatred. Fine Gael doctors look through me, like they want no reminding of their past. O'Gorman will see me right. He'll do more for me than my so-called comrades who promised to guard us.'

'Every curtain was twitching on the street last week, watching those men stand guard outside just to humour you.'

'I didn't summon them to humour me, but to protect us.'

She kissed his forehead. 'Who can protect a man from what's inside his own head? You need to start thinking straight.'

He closed his eyes, so exhausted-looking that it seemed sleep could only be seconds away. 'You're right,' he said. 'I wasn't thinking straight when I was wondering if assassins were coming for me.'

She switched off the light and had almost closed the door when he spoke again. 'But now that I *am* thinking straight, I know for a fact that they are.'

Agnes closed the door and stood on the dark landing, lit only by a red glow from the perpetual flame of the Sacred Heart lamp beneath the picture of Our Saviour. She prayed to St Jude and St Thérèse of Lisieux. How long would he stay in bed before being drawn back to the window? How long before Fox's greengrocers politely but firmly refused her more credit? How long before the Sweepstakes stopped paying her husband's wages? She had the number her local doctor had told her to phone when she could endure this no longer. How long more could she allow the nightmare to continue?

Two

Gus

25 March 1941

It's not my call as to when we make our move on him. For now, my job is simply to lurk on this dark street, unnoticed by anyone. I'm practised at this skill in ways that my superiors know nothing about. The secret of watching a man as twitchy as this poor bastard is to remain unseen, until I need to be seen, until I'm given the nod to act decisively. But until the order comes for a stampede of feet up the carpeted stairs and my shoulder to burst open a bedroom door, it's best to stay schtum, keep a watching brief and let sleeping dogs lie. Not that this blighter has got much sleep during the three nights I've spent observing him. From behind this lamppost, he is barely a silhouette at his bedroom window but I've learnt to spot his outline, crouching in whatever moonlight pools in through the lace curtains. He seems unable to stop himself from peering out, searching for any shadow stirring amid the quietude of this seemingly empty thoroughfare.

Not that Morehampton Road was so empty at night last week. A rota of armed ex-comrades – or men who assured him they were armed – silently took turns to station themselves at his gate. Their presence was intended to let him get whatever sleep he could, secure in the knowledge that the only men he could truly trust had rallied to offer protection, a first line of defence against enemies whom he claimed were tasked with executing him. But even while they reluctantly stood guard, looking foolish, he barely slept. I'm told he kept waking to creep down and check that the back door lock was not tampered with, anxiously pacing the darkened rooms of what was, until a few months ago, a happy family house, filled with the laugher of his three young children.

What do his children make of this stress, his shouts in his sleep, his paroxysms of terror brought on even by just a rattling letterbox when the postman delivers the bills that must be starting to mount up? I hear that his wife shields them as best she can. Three months ago he was an entirely different class of man. Self-assured, abrupt in tone, displaying the mannerisms of an ex-army officer as he set out every morning for his swanky job in the Sweepstakes. Always with a fresh shirt washed and starched and delivered to his house by a Swastika Laundry van. But such comforts will have to stop soon. It will only be a matter of weeks before his wife needs to take in laundry herself, to wash and iron, with more charitable neighbours paying a pittance to keep her afloat and less charitable ones silently gloating over her descent into poverty. Opinion will be split down the middle, based on the Civil War, as with everything else in this city. No doubt the neighbours who decide to help her out will do so in the discreet ways that the middle class employ to maintain the veneer of respectability. Their maids – box room Kitties, as they call them – will be ordered to use the back lane to collect the washing, minimising any public shame on this affluent Donnybrook street. It's a far cry from the Oxmantown two-up-and-two-down terrace where she was raised; with front doors opening directly onto the street as neighbours crowded onto their front steps to glimpse this infamous ex-colonel coming to court her. A man I drank with once told me how one elderly widow would aim a spit at his polished shoes whenever the engaged young couple passed her door to go walking in the Phoenix Park.

Maybe that story is just a myth. No one knows for sure what is true and false among all the stories told about him. No doubt his old army comrades know more than their prayers when it comes to those rumours, but in Ireland secrets stay kept. They stood guard because blood is thicker than water: not any blood that they share but the copious quantities they are rumoured to have spilt. However, old loyalties only stretch so far. Ever since they lost patience and abandoned him, I've been tasked to keep watch.

I'm told that the last straw for those former Free State army officers was when he insisted that every light in the house be turned out before he crawled up the stairs, fearful that snipers might shoot him through the landing window. His old comrades had begged him to walk upright like a man, at least while his scared children watched from their bedroom doorway. But his terror was so intense that his legs wouldn't take his weight. I wasn't told the details of the final argument between him and them. I just know that this was the night when they stopped standing guard outside his house, the night when they conferred in a pub before making the phone call to my superior that sealed their old comrade's fate. I am his fate. This is the cruellest joke. Because whatever face Francis Dillon keeps searching for on this darkened street, the one that he will least expect is mine.

Three

Dillon

27 March 1941

I knew the bastards were coming for me, I just didn't know when. I'll grant them that in terms of getting one tactic right. Always let the target stew, glancing fretfully over his shoulder at false alarms, until he gets so frazzled and fatigued from watching out for any sound that he lets down his guard for a briefest half second. A half second is all a killer needs. These bastards could bide their time, knowing this. They just didn't know they were playing chess against a veteran grandmaster.

By the age of sixteen I had learnt all there is to know about setting up a killing: how slow you must be in your methodical preparation and then the burst of speed when the killer falls into step behind his target on the street or barges in through a lodging-house door where some spy, in bed with a cheap hussy, shows pure cowardice by trying to use her body to shield him.

I was prepared to meet my killers head on this afternoon, despite shaking so much that I couldn't have pulled a trigger to defend myself, even if I'd had a gun. But I would be no coward, using anybody to shield me. This was why I locked Agnes into the box room after she came back from leaving the children with her sister. I had to block out her pleas to be released, her hammering on the door, the terror in her voice as if she had something to fear from me. *From me?* I was doing what any good husband is tasked with as head of the family. Protecting a loved one from danger. For days my nostrils had sensed death coming for me. Now a sudden banging at the front door proved that my instincts remained finely honed. The bastards were making a racket, smashing a pane of stained glass to sneakily reach in and turn the lock.

From the top of the stairs, all I could do was wonder why hadn't I thought to wedge the mahogany hall table up against the door. It was too late now, though I was surprised to see only two men enter the hall. Still, it only takes one finger to squeeze a trigger and it's easier for two assassins to flee than a whole gang. You drop your gun into a hedge, raise your collar, pull down your cap and merge into the crowd.

I had to give them credit for that. I'd have sooner given them the weight of my fists, if my fists had any strength left or my brain wasn't so scrambled. But my nerves were on edge after hours (or was it days?) of listening to Agnes's shouts from the box room. I wanted to call out for her to hush, for her own sake, to keep schtum and not reveal her hiding place. I didn't know what evil the two callous bastards staring up at me were capable of; what revenge they might mete out, acting like God on Judgement Day. Well, they could go to hell. The only judgement I cared about was that of God, seated in heaven with the Angel Gabriel and Michael Collins at his right hand.

I had to focus on how Collins trained me to overcome fear when I was a boy. My inner battle over whether to fight or to flee felt so intense that I was almost paralysed by indecision. Part of me wanted to crawl under my bed, but this was no time for cowardice. I had to keep my wife safe. So I lunged forward, charging down the stairs, legs stiff because I've no idea how long I'd been sitting on that top step. The scream emanating from me was not just primeval fear but an attempt to drown out Agnes's shouts from the box room. I needed to startle my killers into shooting me quick. Even after they had plugged me with several bullets I was determined to keep charging at them and scare them into fleeing.

But these bastards didn't intend to grant me the mercy of a quick death. Obviously they weren't just seeking revenge but information. But they could go to hell before I'd betray my secrets. Charging down the stairs had felt like plunging into an open grave. Instead I realised that I was being propelled towards a makeshift interrogation cell. They pinned my arms behind my back, holding my legs tight as they lifted me out the door into the fresh air for the first time in days. A grave awaited me at the end of this, but not one of my choosing, with a priest leading my old comrades in prayer and hopefully at least a few politicians having the decency to pay their respects. I was destined for a grave where nobody would find my body. Would their revenge extend to picking the lonesome spot in the Wicklow hills where Noel Lemass's corpse was left mutilated, at a time when there was no need for more blood-letting? The fighting had ended, our victory won, as I angrily told his killers when they returned to barracks, shame-faced and sullen after sobering up. But when the blood lust is up in some fellows, with whiskey downed by the neck to settle the jitters, you might as well try to hold back a flooded river.

But I would tell these buckos nothing because they were only untrained amateurs. They weren't even bothering to pull their hats over their faces despite every neighbour on Morehampton Road being alerted by my screams. They hadn't blindfolded me, which meant that I would see what route they took. But as they didn't intend me to live, perhaps it made no odds. Maybe they wanted to add to my torment by letting me see how they were deliberately taking me back to the same remote spot that I have spent twenty years refusing to revisit, except in dreams.

A van blocked the road. As they hauled me into the back of it, I spotted the intelligence officer in charge. He was calmly waiting to start his interrogation, being too big a cheese to do the kidnapping himself. I knew from the diffidence with which my abductors addressed him that he held a high rank in their ragtag army. I strained to lash out with my feet because I sensed, from his wheezy breath and a feebleness entering his grip, that one kidnapper was an old nag, past his best. But the other ruffian gripping my torso was like Hercules compared to him.

They must have a getaway driver too, because the van took off, swaying around corners, going so fast that it must be attracting attention, especially with petrol rationed. But this didn't seem to bother the intelligence officer, as he knelt beside me like a priest preparing to hear confession. I was about to tell him to go to hell in a handcart but something stopped me. A new fear started me shaking uncontrollably. I always thought that when they came, they would plug me quickly with a bullet. But this latchico pulled out something that glinted as it caught the light. It was the thinnest of blades as if intended to torture me methodically, slicing away my skin until I died from a thousand cuts.

'Fuck you all,' I screamed in terror. 'There isn't a man among you that Collins would have picked, even to send to the shops for cigarettes.'

The stocky ruffian holding my torso finally spoke. 'For the love of Jaysus, give it to him. This is like trying to have a hot date with a kangaroo. I hope to Christ it works.'

The intelligence officer raised his thin knife, only now I saw that it was a needle. 'Trust me, Gus, this would work on the lions in Dublin Zoo.'

'Well, after watching this fellow shake at his window these past few nights, I can tell you he's no lion,' the ruffian replied. 'So let's hope it knocks out lambs as well.'

Four

Gus

27 March 1941

It was madness to bring an attendant like old Finnegan on a job like this. His back is fucked and on cold mornings his chest sounds like an accordion played badly. Not that anyone fingers an accordion any other way. Da used to joke that the definition of a gentleman was someone who could play the accordion but didn't. But Da rarely joked much after 1923. He served out his remaining years in Guinness Brewery like a shadow of himself. The Guinness family run a tight ship in their fiefdom. They expect servitude. Workmen will rise before dawn when it snows, just to clear the paths in St James's Gate brewery so the Protestant directors can drive in and park their motors more smoothly. But they also reward loyalty, generally finding a job for the firstborn son of any worker. It was just my luck not to be the firstborn, though maybe I was lucky – seeing what happened to my older brother Eamonn. I suspect that a job would have still been found for me, like a consolation prize, when the dust from all the fighting settled. But if I had spent my working life rattling around the cloistered world of that brewery, I would have been forced to watch Da being unable to hide his grief any time he spied me clumsily making wooden barrels, trying to fill the shoes of my brother, who had seemed destined to become a master cooper.

That's why I wound up working in this asylum. The job is poorly paid but as secure as the brewery. The only certainties in life are that Dublin will never run short of Guinness and lunatics. Grangegorman is a job for life for those who can stick it. Few younger lads do now, with British munitions factories offering big wages. Old Finnegan remembers a time when staff were also locked in to sleep here at night, in quarters as tightly packed as sailors' bunks on ships. Back when attendants were called keepers and wore uniforms like peelers and carried cudgels. He once described his shock as a young attendant, when he was ladling out slops to three elderly patients, to discover that all three had spent decades working here as keepers, losing contact with their families. When the Chief Medical Superintendent eventually declared them too knackered to work anymore, they had needed to go through a humiliating ritual of being formally ordered to step out of the asylum, onto the street. They then had to wait ten seconds after the wooden door closed, before being permitted to knock on it and ask to be readmitted as inmates, having nowhere else to go.

Of course, that strict malarkey is long finished now. Finnegan has a tiny cottage at Dolphin's Barn but he also has a sick wife there, dependent on pills whenever the local dispensary doctor deigns to see her. Finnegan needs to keep bringing home a wage. That's why the rest of us cover for him, although with the asylum so short-staffed, the Superintendent turns a blind eye too.

But once we got Dillon in through the gates, with the injection having quietened him so that he stopped raising blue murder, I tipped Finnegan the wink to make himself scarce. The Super was showing a new English doctor around, the sort of well-meaning toff who arrives with noble intentions and is normally gone within a week. But with them watching, I needed someone more able-bodied to help me rouse Dillon enough for him to put one foot in front of the other in a half-stupor, while we held his shoulders and hoped the poor bastard was too zonked out to realise where his feet were leading him. As Finnegan wheezed his way towards the kitchens in pursuit of weak tea, I let out a shout for Jimmy Nolan in whatever corner of the courtyard he was lurking. Jimmy was never far away in any situation where he might mooch his way to a free cigarette.

All asylums have patients like Jimmy: sound as a pound when behind these walls but as jittery as jelly if forced to venture into the outside world. No patient here is more reliable than Jimmy, even if he's a confounded nuisance at times, following me around like a fawning sheepdog, desperate for any scrap of affection. *My little helper*, I call him, knowing that even this mockery grants him a status in his mind. Jimmy craves status as much as he craves cigarettes. *Your unpaid helper*, he retorts, if feeling cocky. Not that I mind a bit of cheeky banter, because he's a good, damaged soul, and I'd never take advantage of any man not keen to be of service. Doctors sometimes give patients a cigarette straight out. That's a waste; it only gives them a few minutes of pleasure. But give Nolan the hint of a cigarette and he'll draw a week of pleasurably nervous anticipation, from savouring the prospect of a gift to come.

I was right in suspecting that he was hanging around. I had barely called his name before Jimmy was snapping at my heels like a faithful spaniel. He instinctively helped me to stand Dillon upright because we have done this with other patients. But he looked surprised when I steered Dillon towards the door that leads to the corridor with our most private cells.

'I didn't get a gawk at this geezer,' he said. 'Is he a priest, like the last fellow we brought this way?'

'Jaysus, Jimmy. A bishop wouldn't ask me that. And before you ask, he's not a bishop either.'

'He's some bigwig,' Jimmy retorted. 'Your ordinary Joe Soap doesn't get escorted straight into the Ritz Carlton.'

I laughed. 'You wouldn't know the Ritz Carlton from the Morning Star Homeless Hostel.'

'I would so.' Jimmy sounded indignant. 'I saw my share of fancy-pants swanky hotels that time I was swanning around Hertfordshire. I only saw them from the outside, but I definitely saw them.'

'What were you over in Hertfordshire for?'

'The electric shock treatment in the Napsbury asylum. A tramp I'd met in a soup kitchen swore that it was as good a cure as a trip to Lourdes.'

'And was it?'

'Search me, I've never been to Lourdes.' Nolan shifted the weight on his shoulder as if to emphasise the effort he was putting in. 'This geezer is heavy,' Nolan said slyly. 'I reckon he weighs a cigarette and a half.'

As we reached the cell door I adjusted my grip to find the right key on my chain. 'Ah now, Jimmy,' I joked. 'Don't go mistaking me for Santa Claus.'

Either the way that I gripped his shoulder again or Jimmy's laugh brought Dillon to whatever part of his senses he still possessed in his disorientated state. I had barely opened the cell door before he began to struggle, summoning a fury that seemed to stem from pathological terror.

'Bastards!' he shouted. 'You can rot in hell before I'll say a single word! Shoot me if you're going to! I've stared down the barrels of guns held by tougher bastards. I've seen ...'

He stopped speaking while we manhandled him onto the narrow wooden bunk. His eyes followed the heavy handcuffs I produced, watching like a man being hypnotised as I dangled them above him.

'This is the stroke, pal.' I kept my voice kind but firm. 'I don't want to use these, but I will if necessary. In here one size of handcuffs fits all, so if they're too tight it's not a pleasant sight. Now you can huff and puff or settle yourself down on this bed and get some kip. Trust me, you're as safe in here as you'll ever be.'

I don't know if it was the dangling cuffs or the horse tranquilliser kicking in again, but he ceased to struggle so that I no longer had to hold him down. This was just as well because Jimmy Nolan was staring at Dillon, his face contorted by a rage I had never previously seen.

'I recognise this bastard,' he said. 'Please, Gus, let me give him one good dig. Just one. Nobody else need ever know.'

I needed to grab Jimmy's fist as he raised it. 'For the love of Jaysus, Jimmy, you're bang out of order. Swing that fist and I'll have you back on a locked ward.'

'I don't care.' Jimmy struggled to release his clenched fist. 'Just one punch for everything that he got rewarded with when I got nothing.'

I maintained my grip until I felt the strength drain from his arm. Jimmy stared around the cell as if more shocked by his rage than I was.

'Jesus, Jimmy. What did this fellow ever do to you to deserve that?'

Jimmy was trembling uncontrollably, so cowed and lost in his own thoughts that if I had offered him an entire packet of fags he'd have barely noticed.

'His sort did nothing to me, but nothing to help me either. That's the goddamn truth. They simply forgot I existed.'

Dillon had remained quiet during Jimmy's outburst, as if trying to decipher what was happening. Now he roused himself. I needed to hold him down as he shouted, 'You murdering cowards! Snatching a man from his home.'

Jimmy leaned in with an accusatory whisper. 'At least we didn't snatch boys off the street. Boys found dead the next morning.'

These words seemed to engage Dillon. 'I'm damned if I'll be executed for that blasted lie spread about me.'

Dillon's eyes were manic, yet I'd never seen a patient look so exhausted. I pressed down his shoulders and he lacked the strength to resist. 'You are damned,' I said quietly. 'Every patient is, once the doctors dump you in here. Settle down and get some shut-eye. You're doing a lot of jigging about for a man who is going nowhere fast.'

My words had some effect. He lay quietly after I took my hands away, yet his eyes were still distrustful. Stepping away, I beckoned for Jimmy to follow me to the cell door.

'What got into you, Jimmy?' I whispered, more concerned than annoyed. 'You're normally quiet as a mouse.'

'Please don't tell the Superintendent, Gus,' he pleaded. 'I'll do any task for nothing. Just don't let them put me back on that locked ward. I lost the head for a moment. This man and me have history.'

I snorted. 'History has the fucking lot of you in here.'

'I just felt such jealousy that I'd have given a month's wages for one punch.'

'You've not earned a wage in years, but you earn privileges that can get be taken away just like this.' I clicked my fingers to emphasise the point, although Jimmy looked so distraught that he would have knelt to lick my boots if asked. I let him suffer a few seconds longer, then added, more kindly, 'Whatever happened outside this asylum stays outside. In here, you are all equal. Equally fucked.'

A sound disturbed us both: Dillon had rolled over to land on the hard floor. Jimmy went to help him, his anger replaced by compassion. I held him back.

'He didn't fall,' I said. 'He's where he wants to be. Where he feels safest.'

Dillon lay still for a moment, as if absorbing the impact of having hit the floor. Then he crawled underneath his bunk. Jimmy blessed himself, saying a silent prayer as I ushered him out. I turned the key. I don't know if Dillon heard but I knew enough by now to know that he would remain under that bunk all night, hiding from the phantom executioners inside his brain.

Five

Fairfax

27 March 1941

It was the smell that got to me first, apparent from the moment the Medical Superintendent unlocked the outer door into a long corridor. The growing clamour of shouts and sobs did not affect me as much. I had learnt over the years to tune out such sounds, not from indifference but to let me function as a doctor without being swamped by the avalanche of distress that greeted my arrival into any psychiatric ward. But this cloying smell of sweat, shit and stinging disinfectant was unnerving. I balanced an almost primeval impulse to flee against my determination to prove Charles wrong about me being too soft for this place.

My tour so far had included being shown into the epileptic ward, where the only incident that staff had to report on was one patient having a fracture of the left scapula arising from muscular contractions during one of his regular fits. The cramped facilities for treatment in the small tubercular ward had seemed distinctively primitive, with one urinal obviously unusable, although I'd kept such observations to myself. I had seen the packed kitchens, where three copper water-boilers were squeezed in such a small alcove, with no ventilation and only inches between the roof and boiler tops, that a perpetual cloud of steam enveloped the patients who assisted the cook there. I had toured the mattress-making workshop, where work seemed to consist entirely of patching up old mattresses; the busy carpentry and shoemaking workshops, where the only complaints were about shortages of wood and leather; the brush-making workshop, where ingenuity was employed in making brooms from the leaves of cordyline trees that grew in abundance on the remote coastline at Portrane, where a sister hospital was located; and the cobbler's workshop, with such holes in the wooden floor that patients moved with great caution while attending to allotted tasks.

In fairness to the Superintendent, he had deliberately made no effort to hide such defects: from the linoleum being so badly torn in the main hall of the Male House that I tripped on it; to the recreation area allotted to the female hospital being so overgrown, due to a lack of petrol for the motor mowers, that patients were not allowed to walk there until a competent patient, practised in the use of a scythe, could be found and sufficiently trusted to use such a dangerous implement to tame this wilderness. The refractory ward, by its nature, had been clamorous and manic due to the unmanageable nature of many patients there, with some imbeciles boxed in by benches for their own safety. But I had prepared myself for that ward.

So why then did I need to steel myself as the Superintendent unlocked the door into this general ward? The stench was even more overpowering, but I forgot it in my astonishment at the number of beds crammed into one vast room. It seemed impossible that so many patients could sleep here at night, if they did sleep, in bunks so tightly bunched that there was little space for personal possessions, beyond the sets of rosary beads and scapulars wound around some chipped bedsteads. The luckier patients, with bunks in the centre rows, would be fortunate enough to glimpse a shaft of sunlight through the high windows on a clear day, but the men confined to beds next to the bare walls were forced to live in constant shadow. It was hard to tell how many such patients were bedridden, following strokes or other ailments, and how many had lost the will to bother rising from their straw mattresses. Indeed, I found it hard to tell anything amid this maelstrom of misery and mania.

Leaving the Superintendent to confer with a nurse at the bedside of one elderly patient who seemed close to death, I walked to a chimney breast in the centre of the room. It looked as if no fire had been lit for months, but a man of indeterminable age was kneeling beside a wicker basket that had been placed in the cold hearth, growing increasingly upset while rifling through a pile of discoloured, misshapen sets of dentures in the basket. I leaned over to see if I could help.

'Are you seeking your false teeth?'

The man glanced up, surprised at being addressed or having any attention paid to him. He didn't reply, but his suspicious stare was both timid and truculent at the same time.

'Which set of teeth is yours?' I leaned lower, speaking slowly so as not to scare him. 'Can you not recognise them?'

The toothless mumbled reply was in such a thick accent that I could barely distinguish the words. 'Sure, they're all bloody well mine and none of the blasted things are mine. I've not seen my own teeth in years though some smug bastard in here will be munching his stew later wearing them. You'd need to be up early to find your own teeth when they all get dumped in this pile. In the old days I scrambled to find my teeth first, but nowadays I make a beeline for the clothes pile. It's one thing to wear another man's teeth in your gob, but you get a right pain in your hole if you stick your hand in the basket to grab a pair of clean knickers and find that they weren't washed properly. You're fucked entirely then.' He broke into such a fit of bronchial coughing that it took him a moment to get back his breath. 'You're forced to wander around all day like a buck eejit, with another man's skid-marks rubbing against your arse until you finally get a chance to have a lucky dip when another clothes basket comes around.' He glared suspiciously at me. 'What's it to you, anyway? Haven't you your own teeth, unless those are my ones in your gob?'

'I'm just trying to help you.'

'Pray to St Apollonia.'

'Who is she?'

'The patron saint of dentists. She had every tooth pulled from her during her martyrdom. Do you know nothing, you heathen Protestant?'

'How do you know I'm a Protestant? Is it my accent?'

'You didn't need to open your gob. I'm not so daft that I can't spot that a fox is a fox before it barks. Now fuck off and let me find a set of gnashers that won't cut the jaw off me.'

The patient turned away to sort through the remaining sets of dentures. I re-joined the Superintendent who had been watching us.

'You're after meeting John-Joe, I see. I hope he kept a civil tongue for once, Dr Fairfax.'

'What's his diagnosis?'

'Cantankerousness mainly, although if I check his file I'm sure they found a medical term to admit him. Mania, I suspect. John-Joe doesn't belong here but he's here for so long that the poor sod doesn't belong anywhere else.'

'Has he family?' I asked.

The Superintendent shrugged. 'If he has they are gone to ground. At times I feel like I'm running a lost property office here, with the public eager to deposit their stray possessions but nobody eager to claim them back. After a year behind these walls a patient has only a one in ten chance of seeing the outside world again. After two years, the chance falls to one in twenty. That's what makes this place as packed as Noah's Ark.'

We both looked around at the chaotic ward for a moment before he spoke again.

'When I took over from my predecessor I had many good intentions. I spent weeks going through files, to weed out patients with no proper reason to be here. I learnt my lesson. There were two brothers in here for years. Harmless codgers. Sane but feeble-minded. I thought it was time to give them their freedom. Five weeks later, a policeman requested me to formally identify their bodies. It was in the yard of a slum house off Dorset Street that doesn't possess a front door. At night vagrants wander in to kip down on the floorboards on each landing. But there's a hierarchy at play, the survival of the fittest, as Darwin would say. The building was served by three foul-smelling privies in the yard. One toilet had been broken for years so nobody ever set foot in that cubicle. I don't know how the two brothers squeezed in there, but it was the only space they could find. I wouldn't mind so much if they died from the cold, because there was a hard frost that year, but the coroner confirmed that they died of starvation. I hadn't given them their freedom; I'd given them a death sentence.'

'You were trying to do the right thing,' I said.

The Superintendent nodded. 'The longer I'm here, the more I realise there is no right thing. Their deaths taught me that I no longer have the luxury to see myself primarily as a doctor. I'm an administrator, first and foremost, a dictator when necessary, because this beast of an institution must be somehow kept going, day in and day out. Too many people depend on it. I try to devote half my time to making informed medical decisions, but other problems elbow their way in. I spent this morning authorising the use of penicillin sodium.'

'For what type of patients?' I asked.

The man gave a low mirthless laugh. 'For cows. I'm trying to cure an outbreak of chronic streptococcal mastitis in our herd at Portrane Asylum. I need a hundred and eighty gallons of milk delivered here each day for these patients around us.'

We gazed around at the crammed ranks of beds. Some patients lay motionless, while others were trying to squeeze through the narrow spaces between bunks as if seeking their way out of a maze. I noticed how the general hubbub had lessened, with every patient growing watchful, aware of the Superintendent's power to reward or reprimand. The Superintendent was aware of the charged atmosphere too.

'Look at them staring at me.' He nodded towards the patients, but only a few felt sufficiently emboldened to nod back. 'They've all gone beyond the stage of looking to me for miracle cures. Now they just pray that somehow I summon up more food for them and enough gas to cook it. They're praying for the miracle that just for once their stew won't be so watery that they feel as famished after wolfing it down as during the hours spent yearning for it. But maybe this once I can help. Everything in Ireland is strictly rationed, but today I've done a favour for Seán Lemass, the Minister for Supplies. If I keep a minor scandal under wraps, he may do us some favours in return. Extra rations would be nice, but I'd settle for a supply of rubber sheets or even stoppers to replace the broken ones in the earthenware troughs in the operating theatre.'

He turned to me as if to offer reassurance. 'Don't get me wrong, Dr Fairfax. I've not abandoned the Hippocratic Oath. I care deeply for every patient here.' He stared down at the elderly patient whom the nurse was tending to. 'Look at this poor soul. He only has another night or two in him. Yesterday he could just about speak, although he didn't know his own name. Today, as you see, he has already slipped into a stuporous condition.'

'How many years has he been here?' I asked.

The Superintendent nodded to grant the nurse permission to reply.

'It's not years,' she said, 'it's days. He arrived by stretcher from the Royal Hospital for Incurables in Donnybrook. They nurse old soldiers mainly. He had suffered a cerebral haemorrhage, but they said there was nothing more they could do for him. The men who brought him here kept loitering as if worried about him. Then I realised they were just anxious to get their stretcher back.' She turned to the Superintendent. 'I'll check on him, Sir, as often as I can, and ask the night nurse to do the same. God willing, he'll have a peaceful death and someone with him at the end.'

The Superintendent nodded his thanks and led me out of the cramped ward, down the corridor and into the fresh air. I took a deep breath, realising just how hard I had been trying not to breathe in the stench back there. I sensed the Superintendent eye me, as he had been doing since he commenced this tour of the asylum.

'Well, have you seen enough?' he asked.

'Enough for today or to stop me ever coming back? I can't help but get the impression that you are trying to put me off working here.'

The Superintendent stopped to watch as an ambulance sped up the long driveway as the gates were closed again. It parked in the yard near us. The back door opened and an elderly attendant clambered down and sheepishly scurried away. A second attendant – a striking-looking man in his forties – leaned out to call someone's name. The Superintendent turned back to me.

'Rest assured, my wishes are the opposite. I'm just trying to give you the lowdown, fair and square, on the difficulties we face in this cauldron. You impress me. Your curriculum vitae states how you have also trained as a psychoanalyst. I don't agree with such ideas but maybe that's just my suspicion of all entrenched ideologues.' He patted my shoulder, anxious not to give offence. 'Not that I accuse you of being an ideologue. But I have seen the harm that blind faith in any ideology can do, especially when that ideology splinters into factions and feuds.'

'Caused by what Freud called "the narcissism of minor differences",' I replied. 'Trust me, I'm no ideologue. I steer clear of the virtual civil war between Kleinian and Freudian psychoanalysts.'

'The Civil War I saw caused by ideological splits was not virtual,' the Superintendent said. 'It was vicious and bloody. It lives on, like a virus in the blood, to this day.' He nodded towards the ambulance where a scrawny figure was now helping the burly attendant to lift down and drag a semi-conscious figure towards a door into another part of the asylum. 'There are men still fighting it inside their heads eighteen years after the last shot.'

'Are you referring to this patient being admitted?'

'I see no new patient.'

'I'm not sure I follow you.'

'I just see an eminently respectable citizen coming in for a brief rest. Will he need treatment? Definitely, yes. Does he need the shame of public exposure? No. He is what we call a good patient. It doesn't mean he's less mad than most patients. In fact, this new patient you just saw arrive is more delusional than most of those whom we term to be bad patients.'

'What makes him a good patient then?'

'He has good contacts on the outside, including – rather surprisingly if you knew their tangled history – our Minister for Supplies. The colonel has a good job with the Sweepstakes and a good home if we can quietly patch him up enough to let him shuffle back there.' The Superintendent watched the ambulance drive away. 'Are you familiar with the Irish Hospitals' Sweepstakes, Dr Fairfax?'

I laughed. 'I'm not much of a gambler, but I see stories in the papers after each draw. I have also sensed a fair degree of surreptitious activity in England, with hospital porters acting as illicit ticket-sellers.'

The Superintendent chuckled. 'The thrill of the illegal bet. It has spread across the globe, especially in America. It's ironic that America boasts of being the home of the free and yet they are not free to gamble. That's lucky for us, I suppose, with thousands of dollars pouring into Ireland by circuitous and circumspect routes. The Sweep is a marriage made in heaven – one shrewd bookmaker and a tightknit bunch of ex-IRA men who were close to Collins. After being trained to smuggle in guns from America, smuggling in counterfoils and dollars would be a cinch, if it weren't for the sheer scale of the gambling.'

But I was only half-listening now, ambushed by grief. I could steel myself against big landmarks, like the fact that Charles's forty-fifth birthday would occur shortly. But random memories hurt the most. I was recalling the first and only time we attended a motion picture together, when we had yet to see each other naked. A newsreel was showing footage from Dublin of the first Sweepstakes draw. Two live elephants, hired from a circus, led the procession. They were followed by an open-backed truck, on which the organisers had mounted an enormous, elaborately-decorated wooden elephant, inside of which was crammed all the tickets for the draw. Lines of girls had marched behind this, through streets sodden with rain, clad in the traditional bridal costumes of the countries where tickets had been purchased. Some cinema-goers tut-tutted at Charles's uproarious laugh when the commentator announced that the carnival atmosphere made Dublin feel like Rio de Janeiro. 'Carnival atmosphere, my backside,' Charles had proclaimed loudly, indifferent to disapproving glances around us. 'Look, it's pissing rain. It's always pissing in Dublin. All I remember are buckets of rain and buckets of blood.' An admonishing patron was tapping his shoulder when the footage switched to rows of nurses in gleaming uniforms picking winning tickets from a gigantic drum. The commentator explained how the lucky winners included a man in a Welsh village who was banned from partaking in Holy Communion by his local Methodist church for gambling and denounced for having engaged in such moral debauchment. This phrase caused Charles to laugh so much that an usher asked us to leave, to Charles's amusement. I had felt awed by this man's self-confidence and excited when Charles whispered as we crossed the foyer: 'It's time you saw my flat. If we can't find a Sweepstakes ticket, we'll just have to make our own kind of moral debauchment.'

I became aware of the Superintendent watching me again. 'You disappeared on me there,' he said, 'lost in your own world.'

Discommoded, I nodded towards the door through which the attendant and his helper had carried the newly arrived patient.

'I was just wondering why you haven't shown me that part of the asylum.'

'I was saving the best for last. That wing contains single cells for solitary confinement. Not as a punishment, but for discretion. It's in better condition than the other wings. The British army paid to use it during the Great War as a war hospital for shell-shocked soldiers. They even installed a new sanitation unit in the exercise yard so their soldiers wouldn't need to piss alongside other patients. Some soldiers were so traumatised that they're still with us, in ordinary wards now. But the majority recovered. They were treated like celebrities at first, with women in Kingstown knitting socks and officers arriving in motor cars to whisk them off for jaunts. Easter 1916 changed all that, but then again, it changed everything.'

'Can you remember any of the officers?'

The Superintendent gave me an inquisitive glance. 'Why?'

'I recall meeting an officer once who visited patients here. I think his name was Willoughby. Charles Willoughby. An acquaintance of my brother.' Protective white lies were kicking in, with their sting of betrayal; a shield I needed to hide my life behind.

'I just remember a succession of moustaches – handlebar among the old officers, pencil among the younger – and orders being barked out, even when visiting the sick. And one chap with an annoyingly uproarious laugh who seemed to overstay his welcome. But the army mainly kept to themselves,' the Superintendent said. 'It made that wing feel separate. Maybe that's why we still use it for patients whose presence we wish to keep quiet. But feel free to explore it, if you stay. You can even meet our newly arrived Free State ex-colonel – not that you'll get much sense out of him. Neurasthenia wasn't confined to the trenches. It doesn't take a bombardment of shells to lose your reason. Administering, or seeing a bullet administered, to someone's head can have the same effect, though it may take years for the trauma to kick in.'

'Did he administer the bullet or see it administered?'

The Superintendent shrugged. 'It is not our business to ask. Our job is to get him well enough that when he returns to work he can remind the Hospitals' Sweepstakes that Grangegorman is a hospital too.'

'You get nothing from all the dollars pouring in?'

The Superintendent shook his head. 'Where the money goes is a closely guarded secret. Apparently there are backhanders to be paid to the clandestine ticket-sellers and smugglers, and other unspecified expenses. The general hospitals benefit, but you will see no psychiatric nurses photographed pulling tickets from that drum. Our patients don't rank among the deserving poor. They just have us and we're so short-staffed that I won't think ill of you if you decide on an Irish divorce.'

'I didn't know one could get a divorce in Ireland.'

The Superintendent opened his cigarette case to offer me one. 'A lot of Irishmen do. They tell their missus they are popping out for fags and never come back. Your qualifications are almost too impressive. Even in Ireland you could find a better job elsewhere.'

'I knew that when I applied here.'

'Then why apply?'

I exhaled a slow breath of cigarette smoke. 'Look, if you don't want me, just come out and say it.'

'Trust me, I'm so desperate to have you that I feel like locking you in, Dr Fairfax,' the Superintendent replied. 'I'm trying to understand why you applied. Excuse my bluntness, but are you running away from this Hitler war?'

'No.'

'Then what are you running away from?'

'In London my father is a famous surgeon. In Ireland I am nobody. At times in any man's life he just wants to be nobody.'

'You wish to be T. E. Shaw.'

I smiled in acknowledgement of the pseudonym adopted by T. E. Lawrence when he wished to retreat from public view, burdened by the fame of his heroics in capturing Aqaba. Not everyone would get the reference. By the way he used it, almost as a test, I could sense how starved of intellectual stimulation the Superintendent was, burdened by the daily drudge of keeping this asylum running.

'My past deeds are somewhat less heroic.'

The Superintendent smiled, as if something between us had been settled. He opened the locked door that led, up steps, to his office. 'That's no bad thing. My patients are befuddled enough without having Lawrence of Arabia prancing among them. Join me for a whiskey.'

'I'm not much of a drinker,' I explained.

'Nor am I.' The Superintendent led the way. 'But trust me, the one thing you will need after any shift here is a stiff Irish whiskey.'

Six

Dillon

Asylum time

I had never felt more alone and abandoned than in that cell after those two scoundrels locked the door, leaving me there to await execution at dawn. But no mother deserts her son. Mama somehow found her way in or else she had been waiting in a corner until the bastards were gone. Even though I was under the bed, I knew it was Mama. I knew the sound of her footsteps anywhere. I knew her good shoes when they entered my line of vision and I knew the posh - though by now shabby - dress she always kept as a reminder of her early life in America. Her life before Pop decided to bring his young family home to the Ireland from which his own father was forced to flee during the Famine. Pop could have been a big cheese if he'd stayed in his native Boston. His best friend back there, Crooked Joe Kennedy, is now American ambassador to the Court of St James. But Pop was always as straight as Kennedy was slippery. Pop was a true patriot, passionate about an Ireland he'd never seen until the liner carrying him and his wife and my big brother docked in Queenstown.

This homecoming occurred before I was born, though when I learnt the facts of life and counted back the months before my birth, I realised that I had been conceived somewhere out on the North Atlantic, amid the gales and swells of that ocean, midway between the Land of Opportunity and the land of Pop's forefathers. Perhaps Mama was wearing this same dress when she turned towards him in their Second Class cabin, having finally got my older brother asleep, so they could savour their own time together. The smallness of the cabin, his silent thrusts so as not to waken my sleeping brother, Edward – named after the patriot Lord Edward Fitzgerald. They were deliberately reversing the thousands of journeys made by starving Irish people on those same waves, braving shipwreck and starvation and cholera in similar hopes of a new life. On the voyage I must have become Pop's seed of hope, his different future, the carrier of his dreams inside Mama's womb.

Obviously they never spoke to me of such intimacies, but there had to be a reason why Mama kept this dress for all those years. A reason why she was wearing it again now as she leaned down by my bed in this godforsaken cell, tenderly reaching out a hand, beckoning me to risk venturing forth from my hiding place. I crawled out across those cold stone flagstones, able to see more of her body in the half-light. I was not yet close enough to see her face, but I knew her smell. I had known it since I was in the womb. The smell of safety. The scent of La Rose Jacqueminot perfume, distilled in Paris from Provence rose and jasmine, a gift from Pop every year on her birthday.

Her whispering voice soothed me as I gazed up at her dim face. 'My poor, poor son,' she said. 'What have they done to you? What class of animals would leave you like this – you, the gentlest child ever? I remember such a hard labour with you and then, after all my shrieks, when the midwife placed you in my arms, you didn't even cry, as if ashamed of having caused me such pain. I think you always carried this guilt inside you. Because you never caused me grief again, even when other boys were running wild in Drumcondra.'

I crawled a few inches towards her and she moved slightly back, as if encouraging me to fully emerge out from under the bed.

'Only once did I have to scold you for being late home for tea and then I discovered you had been doing the Stations of the Cross for my intentions in St Columba's Church. I loved your gentleness and goodness, and yet I feared for you being so soft. I prayed lest the Black and Tans found you on the streets after curfew and beat you into a pulp. I prayed every time I watched a coffin pass our window during the afflicted days when the Spanish influenza took hold of the city. I prayed to the Blessed Virgin to protect you from every danger I knew of. But there were dangers I didn't know of, neighbours we trusted, Devils who walked amongst us, hiding in plain sight.'

By stretching out my fingers I managed to touch the hem of her dress. 'Hold me, Mama,' I begged. 'It's so long since I've been held in your arms. I'm so lonely and scared. Please, just hold your son.'

The woman leaned down so that I finally recognised her face. 'Why would I hold you when you're not my son? I have no son. Someone shot him dead in a remote quarry. An unarmed child, left riddled with bullets after being snatched on Clonliffe Road with two pals. How could you be my son when you're still alive? I know whose son you are. I know your Yankee seed and breed because we lived on the next street to your parents.'

Her hate-filled stare brought me to my senses. How could I have thought that this woman was my mother, when Mama was no longer in Ireland?

'My daughter was sweet on you when she was twelve,' the woman continued. 'She used to wait on the corner to snatch your school cap, hoping to get an innocent chase. You played football with my older son, who had to identify his brother in the city morgue. With our other neighbour there, poor Mr Hurley barely able to recognise his son after a bullet tore away most of his skull. And Edward Healy's older brother crying in that morgue, needing to formally identify Edward's corpse because his parents were too much in shock. The Healys were once a prosperous family, but

Mrs Healy had to stop giving piano lessons after her son's murder. Music was never again played in their house.'

What if this harridan had left the door unlocked, when sneaking in here to spread her lies? My killers could be waiting out in that stone corridor.

'It wasn't only piano keys heard in the Healy house,' I replied defiantly, trying to conceal my fear. 'Neighbours heard the clank of their son's printing press spewing out lies every night.'

'Neighbours?' The intruder snorted. 'You lost the right to call us your neighbours when you decided that a few handbills were enough reason for three boys to be snatched under cover of darkness and slaughtered. Mrs Healy didn't just lose her son that night, she lost everything. Her husband gave up his job to mind her. She couldn't be left alone, with her nerves gone. I was broken too, but I hid it better. I couldn't let my other chislers see how broken you had left me.'

'Those deaths had nothing to do with me.' I no longer cared if my raised voice betrayed my location to the killers searching for me. 'For twenty years I've been unable to walk down a street without hearing strangers whisper this falsehood or seeing women cross the street like I was the Devil incarnate.' I raised myself onto my knees. 'Why blame me for you being crazy enough to let your son go wandering at night, amid the mayhem of a civil war? You let him paste up vile posters declaring that my fellow army officers were a murder squad who should be shot on sight.'

'If you weren't a murder squad, why was he riddled with bullets? Don't deny you picked him up in your army car on Clonliffe Road. You were seen, strutting like a peacock in your shiny new uniform and boots! You knew you'd be recognised because we all lived within yards of each other. Not that you'd been home to see your parents in weeks. You and your cronics too busy drinking and torturing folk in Wellington Barracks. The Black and Tans were saints compared to you.'

'I took those boys into Wellington Barracks for their own protection,' I protested. 'Twenty minutes later I set them free. What happened after that is anyone's guess.'

'Try telling that to your mother. She had to run away from the shame of it, back to America where she belonged.'

'My parents ran away from nothing. Pop spent years supporting Irish causes. I'd see him come home, exhausted from meetings, and be barely in the door before another knock came for help. And when the Black and Tans came, they didn't knock, just kicked the door in, looking for his sons. Every stick of furniture smashed, poor Mama trying to put the house back together. Pop had to go cap in hand to the Bank of Ireland after his offices were ransacked. Yet, for all his sacrifices, he needed to start all over, a broken man forced to return to America.'

'He left because your actions tarnished his good name!' The harridan stepped back to slouch against the cell wall.

'He left because a Protestant clique of bankers foreclosed on his loans once the Civil War ended.'

'Who says it ended?' The woman formed her fingers into the shape of a gun aimed at me. 'Maybe your parents couldn't face their neighbours after what you did.'

She raised her hands to her lips and blew softly as if after firing a shot. Then she raised them above her head. I couldn't stop watching in horrified fascination because, by using some cheap vaudeville trick, she made it seem as if her fingers were disappearing into the stone wall behind her.

'I was friendly with your mother,' she said, 'though I rarely saw her after my son's murder. But if hunger forced me to visit the huckster corner shop that gave credit on tick, we'd sometimes pass without speaking. She always kept her face bowed, because even though I'm too much of a Christian to spit, she could taste the phlegm I wanted to leave dripping down her face.'

I could barely speak for fear, watching her shoulders start to disappear into the wall.

'The coroner's inquest exonerated me of any involvement,' I said.

She snorted. 'Call that farce an inquest? A simple country doctor in Clondalkin bullied by hotshot government lawyers sent to sort out your mess. Your old neighbours read the verdict in the paper but we read between the lines and knew the truth. Hide behind the law all you like, *a stóirín*. But you can never hide from me, not even in this madhouse.'

Then her entire body disappeared through a gap in the wall that closed over. Moments before I had asked myself how she managed to slip in through the locked door, but I'd been asking the wrong question. These walls were porous, the bricks no stronger than gossamer. Maybe this cell also had a trick floor? What if there was a lever, like a hangman uses, that could make the floor tilt? I would be rolled forward, unable to stop myself from following her through that gauze wall to land in whatever room lay on the far side. A torture cell, perhaps, or the recreation of an innocuous bedroom in a lodging house, with flowery wallpaper behind the bed about to be splattered with blood, when the footsteps of men came pounding up the stairs.

Seven

Superintendent

27 March 1941

After we entered my office I unlocked the filing cabinet where I kept my whiskey hidden. Pouring two good Irish measures, I replaced the bottle, relocked the cabinet and carried the glasses over to my desk.

'Hiding whiskey is a little joke on my most trusted attendant,' I confessed. 'Gus has worked here for twenty years. He knows every secret. I take it for granted that this includes where I hide my filing cabinet key, but any whiskey he pilfers at night must taste all the sweeter for him thinking I'm unaware of its theft. Every Superintendent needs one attendant like Gus, who can do things on the QT; things that would have to be written into the reports to the governors if a medical professional were involved. It's why I cut him considerable slack. If you want to know about anything that moves about this asylum or this city, Gus is the man to ask. Just don't ask him directly because he'll rarely give a straight reply. I can ask him about this Willoughby chap you mentioned if you like.'

'There's no need,' Fairfax said, so hastily that I took note of his unease. 'I barely knew the chap.'

I nodded and we clinked glasses. Fairfax took a seat as I sorted through piles of envelopes on my desk and then looked up.

'Don't be mistaken, Dr Fairfax, when I talk of being forced to mainly devote my energies to being an administrator. I still try to introduce medical innovations here, though I've abandoned my predecessor's method of inoculating patients with malaria to treat general paralysis of the insane.'

'Did his treatments work?'

I shrugged. 'All treatments are trial and error. He was a distinguished physician. Generally, after the malaria took hold of the patients, the quinine he administered to cure it also improved their general mental state.'

'Are you saying that he sweated away their madness?'

I tut-tutted in soft reproach. 'My predecessor did not invent malaria therapy. That honour falls to a Dr Wagner-Jauregg in Vienna. But from your curriculum vitae I suspect that you value certain Austrian physicians over others.'

The Englishman acknowledged my discreet rapier thrust. 'Dr Freud has never, to my knowledge, deliberately infected anyone with malaria.'

I nodded, still sorting through my correspondence. 'Wild ideas can be just as parasitically dangerous. Your record as a psychiatrist seems exemplary. However, your dalliance – and in Ireland that is all it will be seen as – with psychoanalysis is your own business. I'll hold no man's beliefs against him, be it in Freud or clairvoyants or seventh sons of seventh sons. Perhaps a miraculous cure can be unlocked for a chosen few through the interpretation of dreams. But the only miracles I have time to focus on involve loaves and fishes. My predecessor infected patients with malaria, but in an evidence-based way. No three-card trickery. Most patients improved or rarely endured anything worse than jaundice. His notes mention two deaths caused by seizures, but death is ever-present here.'

I paused, having found the envelope I was seeking. Opening it, I scanned the salient points of the single-page consultant's report inside it:

I have personally examined Francis Dillon who is now a patient in the Richmond Asylum in Grangegorman. I find him to be at present completely and permanently insane. Mr Dillon has delusions of being shot and executed and that all around him are conspiring to kill him. He hears voices urging his destruction and his whole delusional state is definitely linked to his previous military experiences during the War of Independence.

In my opinion the experiences this man endured during his military service at that time and particularly his own active part in certain violent events, including Bloody Sunday, have preyed on his mind and conscience so that in recent times he has been gradually losing his reason. At present time, I therefore unequivocally attribute his present incapacitated state to his military service and I consider him to be totally and permanently disabled.

I enclose my standard fee note for five guineas and decline your request on the telephone for any deduction of same.

I passed the page with the embossed letterhead to Fairfax. 'Don't say we are not prompt. Here is the external report commissioned by the Military Service Pensions Board on our newest patient.'

'But he has only arrived,' Fairfax said. 'When did this examination take place?'

'Note how the consultant never says that it actually occurred in the asylum. Ideally Dillon would be examined here tomorrow but the consultant has a golfing tee-time in Woodenbridge that he was most insistent on not missing. In fairness he's been on standby for three days, so it's partly my fault. I've had Gus watching Dillon's house. I should probably have admitted him earlier but I kept hoping for some improvement, while dealing with the delicate matter of shifting a monsignor from the cell I intend using. There are always sensitivities when dealing with a public figure. The report could have waited but speed is of the essence and Dillon was recently seen privately by this same consultant, though hopefully not at five guineas a pop.'

Fairfax handed back the letter. 'His verdict is fairly unambiguous. The man doesn't seem to hold out much hope of treatment.'

'Treatment is our job,' I replied. 'His job is to be unambiguously bleak. Ambiguity is not a commodity highly rated by the Irish Civil Service. They like black and white reports, decisions so clear cut that no civil servant need take responsibility. Seán Lemass told me to submit this report at once and leave the rest to him. It will earn Dillon's wife an emergency pension while we try to patch him up. A vengeful man might have let Dillon's family starve, but Lemass has taken a personal interest, which is very decent.'

'Why?'

'Lemass's older brother was kidnapped and tortured after being assured he was safe to return to Ireland when the Civil War ended. I'm not saying that Dillon was one of the Free State officers involved, but let's just say that he shared the same bathwater in the same barracks as Noel Lemass's killers.'

'I take it that in your Civil War this Lemass chap – what was the expression my new landlady used last night – dug with the other foot?'

'That expression covers religion,' I said. 'Our Civil War involved Catholics fighting Catholics: each side competing to outdo the other in viciousness and piety. The present government were on the losing side.'

'Then why are they in power?'

'Whoever won the Civil War was bound to lose in the long term. The winning side needed to stump up and deliver a functioning country. No Ireland that either side could deliver would ever live up to the grandeur of a rebel marching song.'

Fairfax picked up a file on Dillon and read through the details I had entered in advance.

'This says he was a colonel at nineteen. How do you get to be a colonel so young?'

'Join the IRA at fourteen. It also helps if you're among the chosen few that Collins trusted enough to pick for his Squad.'

'I know of Collins, obviously, but who were his Squad?'

I sipped my whiskey and remembered the sole occasion that I met Collins. In 1920 I received a message to meet an unnamed man at the corner of Prussia and Aughrim Street. I spied a young lad checking that I was alone before a man appeared with a scared young woman who looked little more than a child. I recognised him by his aura of quiet authority, although he never said his name. 'This is Lily,' Collins said. 'She has suffered a violation. Two drunken Tans. Blasted savages, although I shouldn't speak badly of the dead.' I asked if they were dead and he shook his head grimly. 'They soon will be. Lily's in shock. She needs sanctuary. Here are two ten-pound notes. One is for the asylum because I hear you're short of food. The other is for her. Hand it to her the day she's well enough to leave. Her family won't take her back; they don't want the disgrace. But when she feels ready to leave, you personally walk her down the quays and onto the boat. Any questions?' When I shook my head he placed a hand on my shoulder. 'A wise man asks no questions. I heard you are wise. Don't disappoint me.'

I still had the second ten-pound note locked away. Lily remained the quietest patient on her ward, with *melancholia due to shock* written on her file. Every year since then I had asked if she wished to leave, reminding her that I had money for her fare. Her reply was always the same: 'I disremember, Sir.' I was wise enough not to ask what she chose to disremember – being led by Collins down Aughrim Street, her violation in a tenement room, or the life she led before then that they stole from her.

'Collins was a scarlet pimpernel,' I told Fairfax. 'Your army sought him here and sought him there. They just never thought to seek him when they stopped a broad-shouldered man on a bicycle at checkpoints and laughed with him after they asked his name and he'd reply with a wink, "Sure, lads, I'm Mick Collins himself."'

'I saw a newspaper photograph of him entering Downing Street during the Treaty negotiations and thought him a very striking assassin,' Fairfax said. 'In the next photograph I saw he was in uniform in a coffin, having been shot by his own kind.'

'Having died in the arms of Dillon's older brother,' I replied. 'And I'd advise you against calling Collins an assassin while you're in Ireland. Collins ordered men's deaths, but never pulled the trigger, he only pulled the strings. His Squad did the killing. Such a Squad needs cold-blooded killers, but also innocent-looking lads to collect intelligence. Collins picked Dillon because he looked like a schoolboy. You must feel truly special if singled out to be part of an elite group like that. You might feel shock at doing and seeing terrible things, but you are carrying out orders that Collins tells you the country needs. However, when peace comes, it is a far greater shock to discover you're not needed anymore. Collins's Squad were like a fizzy lemonade that he shook up, but with his death the cork popped off and nobody could control what came fizzing out.'

Fairfax scanned the details of the file. 'Dillon's military career seems to have come to an abrupt halt.'

I nodded. 'A colonel at nineteen. Unemployed at twenty-one. Lads like him are indispensable in a guerrilla army but lack the skills to administer a peacetime one. After the government promoted more experienced officers over his head, his army career ended with a half-arsed attempt at a coup. By then, several of Collins's Squad needed psychiatric help, but most preferred to seek it from a whiskey bottle. However, in Ireland we like strong mythical heroes, which is why we generally prefer our heroes to be dead. The public like to think of the Squad as an elite band of brave volunteers, anointed by Collins. It would damage that myth if one of them was known to be a quivering delusional patient in here.'

'Is that why Seán Lemass is keen to help cover up this patient being admitted?'

I shook my head. 'The Minister is a practical man, disinterested in myths or vengeance. Nothing is being covered up. He is just making sure that a former comrade's family is looked after. As Lemass said to me on the phone, terrible things were done on both sides and there is nothing more that needs to be said.'

Fairfax went quiet, lost in thought and, I suspected, some sort of grief. I wasn't sure who he had lost and I strongly suspected he wasn't going to tell me.

'Terrible things are done in all wars,' he said at last. 'Done to the victims and – although they might not admit it, even to themselves – terrible things are done to the perpetrators' souls, if we possess souls.' He paused. 'I am not sure if you are religious.'

'Atheism would be a luxury in Irish public life,' I replied, thinking of the endless masses I needed to attend. On the church steps, as members of the congregation greeted each other, even the most taciturn of higher civil servants could never decline my request for a quiet word as I lobbied for a new nurses' home. 'But I take your point. If I didn't believe in invisible wounds, I would have remained a general practitioner.'

Fairfax nodded. 'And I would have become rich, as an ear, nose and throat specialist, like my father.'

'There's money in ears, noses and throats,' I said. 'More than we'll ever make.'

It was the first time I heard Fairfax laugh. The whiskey seemed to allow him to relax. 'You've stolen my father's mantra. I am a disappointment to him, in more ways than one. He is highly qualified in the business of making money. There is money in throats, he frequently told me as a boy. And a job waiting in his practice once I qualified as a doctor – a natural progression interrupted by the final months of the war.'

'You were in France?' I asked. 'I wouldn't have taken you for a military man.'

He smiled ruefully. 'I wasn't there long enough to pick up any mannerisms, just long enough to catch a glimpse of the horror. My company was mainly held in reserve. But I'm still haunted by the memory of a petrified Irish boy under my command. He surely lied about his age to enlist, to get away from sleeping three to a bed, or so he could send home money to his mother. By the time I encountered him, the sights he endured in the trenches had rendered him mentally defective. He should have been sent to somewhere like here. Instead he became separated from his unit, by accident or design, wandering on his own for days until spotted by another officer. This constituted desertion. Desertion only has one sentence. Most death sentences were commuted, but my commanding officer felt that Irish soldiers needed extra discipline. He decided to make an example of this boy to instil backbone in the ranks.'

He paused. 'The British army have strict rules for executions. Prisoners to be stood upright, feet tied twelve inches apart. Six inches of rope left between their bound hands and the post to avoid unsightly chaffing of their wrists. Often the guards plied condemned men with so much drink they could barely stand upright. But this Irish lad had taken the pledge before enlisting, so he was convinced he'd go to hell if he drank. I had often seen my father administer morphine to patients.' Fairfax glanced at me. 'Am I unwise on my first day to confess to being a rule-breaker?'

'Not if they involve British army executions,' I said. 'It's not a practice we're fond of. I was a staunch Home Ruler before they started shooting prisoners at dawn here. By the time they finished there were no Home Rule supporters left.'

'It took a certain degree of subterfuge to get my hands on morphine,' Fairfax said, after a pause. 'The boy was so deranged that he was unaware of me administering it. He shook so much I had to hold him in my arms while embarrassed guards looked on. I can still feel him clinging to me, beads of sweat on his chest even though the cell was freezing. Then, when the morphine kicked in … his eyes were still wild, but his body shook less and when he looked at me again it was the first time I ever saw his face at peace, like he felt safe in my arms, until the guards prised him away to kit him out. It wouldn't do to have a soldier not properly attired on the occasion of his execution. Not that he knew where his guards were leading him at dawn, past sullen mutinous comrades, ordered to line up and watch. I never felt such unspoken hatred as when passing those men to take my appointed place. The firing party were so rattled that they all missed his heart. It was my task to administer a shot to his head to put him out of his pain. That morning my father's practice lost his chosen successor and I lost my innocence.'

I walked over to the filing cabinet to retrieve the whiskey and refill our glasses. I could sense Fairfax watching, wondering how I would respond. I raised my glass. 'Here's to subterfuge,' I said. 'And to that poor lad's soul.' I took a sip. 'I trust you did not become a psychiatrist just to assuage your guilt.'

'No.' Fairfax took a drink. 'I have my own reasons for not wanting to emulate my father. That young boy in France should not have been shot. He was no longer fighting the war there; he was fighting the war in his head. I've met hundreds like him in asylums ever since. For them their war never ends. It haunts me that I can't simply cure their affliction, like my father breezes his way through ears, noses and throats. But just occasionally I can lead them out of their recurring nightmares, if they let me into them by talking.'

'Surely you had enough such patients in England to keep you busy?'

'The asylums there are crammed with forgotten men and will be twice as full when this current war ends, unless Hitler wins and euthanises them all. I could have re-enlisted after Dunkirk and become a field doctor. But I am more attuned to fighting invisible battles, one to one. I left England because …'

He paused. I knew he was struggling. Again I felt a grief below the surface that he could not speak about. I suspected that there were more things he had no wish to mention, but every man is entitled to not just a public and a private life, but a secret life too.

'I left England,' he continued at last, 'because we must live by our own moral code. I accept that moral codes are flimsy things, creaking with contradictions, because our personalities are held together by contradictions.' He paused. 'In the most recent asylum I worked in, a conscientious objector was assigned to us as an orderly. He got the worst jobs, cleaning latrines or working in the violent wards where some patients are so demented that they are shackled for their safety. He did his work without complaint, accepting the abuse of ex-soldier patients.

'But verbal abuse wasn't enough for some veterans. They exacted retribution. The official report states that he fell from an attic window, but I heard the gleeful shouts of patients as he was pushed. My fellow doctors developed a collective deafness – not liking what had happened but denying hearing anything. I had grown to admire the conscientious objector. It takes moral courage to be true to yourself, to refuse to be part of something you don't believe is right, knowing you'll be ostracised for following your conscience.'

'How do you know he was pushed?' I asked.

'I saw him pushed,' Fairfax replied. 'When I insisted on submitting my own account of his death, it became clear, by how other doctors shunned me, that my services were unwelcome there or in any other London asylum who heard that I was ... to use a term you Irish love to hate ... an informer. So you could say that I'm in a self-imposed exile.'

'Is that the only reason why you are in Ireland?'

'Was it St Thomas Aquinas who said that if you possess one valid reason for a course of action, you don't need two?'

'Touché.' I knew not to push any harder but I also knew for sure that he was holding something back.

'In England I specialised in working with patients suffering from trauma,' he added. 'You have such patients too.'

'Trust me, we have patients suffering from everything and from nothing.'

'I'm here to work but also to learn. I will of course follow your methods of treatment. If you allow me to engage in any psychoanalysis, it will be on my own time. I visited Berlin in 1933 and glimpsed the world that Hitler would impose on us. I hope he can be defeated, but I know how the men now fighting him will return with mental as well as physical wounds. By the look of his file, your latest patient might make an interesting case study. Maybe you might let me try to work with him. I might not succeed in helping him. But I hope at least to learn more about men traumatised by war, so that, when I feel welcomed back in England, I can help with the next wave of traumatised men who will be packed off to asylums when this war is done.'

'I've promised Seán Lemass to get Dillon back on his feet as soon as I can,' I said. 'To be honest, I think that his psychosis and delusional insanity is so severe that neither insulin injections nor electroconvulsive therapy may work, but I will try both.'

Fairfax nodded. 'He looks like what he needs is rest first. Will you let me visit him on my own time? All I will be doing is trying to get him to talk.'

'About what?'

'Whatever memories are tormenting him.'

'Well then, for God's sake, don't mention a place called the Red Cow.'

'What did Collins order him to do there?'

'Collins was dead by then. His Squad were on their own. The genie was out of the bottle and nobody knew how to get it back in. As an intelligence officer, Dillon specialised in keeping secrets. I have two thousand patients. I'm sure that I can find you others equally traumatised on which to practise whatever you do.'

'Can you find me others who committed acts of violence?'

'Why?'

Fairfax went silent. He has been badly hurt by somebody, I thought, mentally or physically. He is not just looking to cure others; he's come here to try and cure himself. I was allowing a wounded man to join my staff. Ireland was no safe place for an Englishman to ask probing questions. It was only two decades since the last British troops left a trail of atrocities in their wake. There was no harm in Fairfax but he had no idea of the harm he might do by stirring up the past. I neither understood nor trusted psychoanalysis, but if Fairfax wanted to try it I wouldn't stop him when I so badly needed another doctor. Still I would get Gus to watch him like a hawk. If anything else was going on I trusted Gus to sniff it out. I knew that I wasn't getting the full truth here. The curriculum vitae that accompanied his application for this job, which I had been unsuccessfully advertising for months, was so impressive that I had phoned several colleagues in London.

His story about a conscientious objector dying in suspicious circumstances was true, but Fairfax had resigned from the asylum where that happened in 1940. Until ten days ago he had been a slightly reserved but highly regarded doctor working in an upmarket private asylum in London. Nobody there knew why he had suddenly resigned and was swapping that comfortable post for a public asylum that paid a fraction of his former wage.

He finished his whiskey and declined a refill. I locked the bottle away in my filing cabinet and turned. 'We've been drinking Bushmills. A staunchly Protestant distillery, but when it comes to whiskey I am ecumenical. It sounds as if your digs are not entirely comfortable.'

'They are adequate to my needs.'

'I suspect your room would feel brighter with a good bottle of Bushmills. Let's have a wager, Dr Fairfax. I will wait a fortnight to let our new patient regain his strength before I start electroconvulsive therapy. A bottle of Bushmills says that you won't get a word out of him about what ails him before then. I wish you luck, but I think you will be buying the whiskey. Have we a deal?'

Fairfax nodded. Gus would drink half the bottle after I won my wager, but I intended to make sure that Gus earned it first, as my eyes and ears.

Eight

Gus

Asylum time

As a rule, I have learnt to take men in here as I found them. From the lunatics to the mentally infirm; from simple imbeciles to the moral imbeciles who combine mental defects with criminal or violent propensities; from the feeble-minded, who might be capable of earning a living outside if they could manage their own affairs, to epileptics who could swallow their tongues at a moment's notice. And then the unwanted souls, whose families view them as a hindrance to social advancement. A simpleton in the family was not as damaging to the prospects of a good marriage as a history of TB. But few of the gentle souls incarcerated in here ever get out. Even the saner patients, if unwanted, have more chance of winning the Hospitals' Sweepstakes than walking out of here to stand as free men on the North Circular Road, watching cattle being herded down to ships on the quays and maybe fleeing on those boats themselves.

This was a sad but useful fact for us attendants. We were so overstretched that without unpaid help from reliable patients, daily life here would collapse. Not that I ever took advantage of any patient unwilling to do a task. I wasn't like O'Sullivan, a bastard attendant who nearly broke a patient's jaw after the patient refused to leave his bed one night to help carry out a coffin bound for the paupers' plot. That patient would empty spittoons or unblock latrines without complaint, but we all knew he had a phobia about dead bodies. O'Sullivan was bang out of order. Not that the patient dared complain or any of us grassed. No man wanted to be known as an informer. But O'Sullivan could never grasp why, for months afterwards, other attendants kept offering to fetch his cocoa, taking turns to piss into it first.

Like I say, I took men as I found them. But I was perplexed as to why an English psychiatrist would voluntarily apply for a position here. The Superintendent was suspicious too, for reasons he didn't care to reveal when giving me my orders. I had encountered my share of Englishmen keen to sit out the war in Dublin, during my excursions to certain Dublin pubs whose clientele tried to cultivate a literary or vaguely revolutionary ambience. Usually they were pacifists or claimed to be artists or writers who dropped hints about military exploits against the Generalissimo in Spain. Just occasionally, if I went for a discreet ramble with some British drinker, I found that many were as poor as church mice. But others seemed intent on spending their lavish inheritances in advance on any pleasures that Dublin could provide.

Dr Fairfax seemed a different kettle of fish. For a start it was strange that, with England needing doctors badly, he had secured a travel permit to work in Dublin. He lacked the flamboyant Bohemian air of many of his countrymen who were regularly fleeced for free drink by liggers in those pubs. Indeed, if I ever had a reason, or the money, to visit a doctor, Fairfax seemed like the man I'd want to see. So far he had taken a compassionate interest in every poor soul locked up in here.

This morning an incident had occurred in a female dayroom, when one patient, who had been admitted with severe depression but seemed to respond to treatment, was allowed to enter the toilets on her own. She smuggled in a cup which she broke into pieces and used one shard to inflict a severe gash on her throat. When Dr Fairfax was summoned, and I was asked to show him the way, the nurse who had discovered the patient seemed equally terrified by fears of the woman bleeding to death and by fears of the Superintendent's wrath if he deemed her neglectful in her duties. But as she told Fairfax, she had a hundred patients in the dayroom and was told that the woman no longer needed special observation. Fairfax had calmed the nurse and the patient, whom he sedated before stitching the wound himself, reassuring her that he had been in the army medical corps before training as a psychiatrist.

After the situation was under control he had asked the nurse to take him to see another patient, Bridie Kerr from Castleblaney, who seemed initially flustered but – once Bridie's nerves settled – pleased to find someone taking time to acknowledge her presence. Fairfax had spoken to her at length and with kindness. I didn't inquire how he knew of her existence because my rule is not to ask questions.

Now, with his long shift already over, he wished to see our latest patient. Over the past two days, every staff member had wanted to glance in through the peephole at the ex-colonel, while wanting nothing more to do with him. Dr Fairfax was the first doctor, apart from the Medical Superintendent, to ask me to unlock the cell door. We entered the cell and I watched him studying Dillon who was curled up on the floor, half hidden beneath his bunk. Fairfax's stare had the professional detachment all doctors possess, but it was impossible not to also sense his compassion.

'So this is the patient all the staff are talking about?' he said.

'Or not talking about,' I replied. 'We Irish have ways to navigate around embarrassment. Generally, we say everything that needs to be said by saying nothing. You'll get used to it if you actually stay, Doctor.'

'What makes you think I will hightail it back to England?'

'You've queer notions of doctoring, even for a Protestant. No disrespect.'

'None taken.' Opening his silver cigarette case, Fairfax held it out. 'Cigarette?'

I accepted one with a nod of thanks. 'You're a gentleman. I'm gasping for a fag.'

He lit one himself and proffered the match, but I shook my head, placing the cigarette behind my ear. 'I'll be gasping even more for one later on tonight.'

He exhaled, the aroma of rich tobacco wafting through the cell. I wondered if Dillon smelt it in whatever drugged state he was in, because his nostrils twitched slightly.

'Your name is Gus, isn't it?' Fairfax asked. 'Is it short for Augustine?'

'It's short for Gussy. What's Fairfax short for?'

'I'm not sure I follow your meaning?'

'Your accent makes you sound like you were born with a double-barrel name.'

Fairfax smiled. 'My surname got amputated during the Great War.'

'Was it painful?'

He laughed, not in the least put out, and knowing that perhaps I was testing him. 'Only for my father, who took great offence at my wanting to disassociate myself from him. But he has always taken a rather dim view of me. I saw men in the trenches lose a lot more than just a hyphen.'

'War affects men in different ways,' I replied, diplomatically. 'Any man who came through it with only half their surname blown off did okay.'

He watched me carefully, curious to see how far I would push him.

'Attendants in English asylums tend to be less ... how shall I put it ...'

'Forward.'

'I was going to say less inquisitive.'

'More servile.'

'More respectful. Far too respectful of my accent. I prefer honesty.'

'You've come to the wrong city. Ask a Dubliner a question and you'd need to get Military Intelligence to decode the answer.'

'Is telling the truth so difficult?'

I shook my head. 'No. But it mightn't always be advantageous.'

He laughed again, a rueful quiet laugh, and reopened his cigarette case. 'Would it be truthful to say that while you may be gasping for a cigarette later, you're also gasping for one now?'

I took the cigarette gladly and this time lit up. 'It would be a statement of fact made without mental reservation,' I said.

'You're a curious fellow,' he replied. 'The Medical Superintendent hinted as much.'

'I'm the exact opposite,' I replied. 'I'm deeply incurious. I mingle in pubs to stave off lonesomeness, but, if I'm honest, most of humanity bore the bejaysus out of me.'

'Yet you seem curious about me?'

'I can't get all the parts of you to add up.'

No Irish doctor would let me get away with such impertinence, but he just nodded thoughtfully, then looked towards Dillon. 'Are you curious about him?'

'I feel sorry for him, which isn't the same thing. The Super had me watching his house in case he did anything to put his wife and children in harm's way. I should probably have phoned the Super earlier to tell him it was time to act. But Dillon has powerful friends, though they probably now regard themselves as merely powerful acquaintances. When gunmen become pillars of respectability, they dislike scandal. It is one thing to commit crimes against an occupying army in your youth, but another to commit crimes against respectability when you can now afford to buy your wife a fur coat from Mr Barnardo on Grafton Street. Dillon's old comrades humoured him for as long as they could but sympathy can be a surprisingly shallow well.'

'They were only postponing the inevitable,' Fairfax said. 'This man is in pain. I'm surprised he wasn't admitted sooner.'

'If he was an ordinary Joe, he'd have been admitted long ago and into no private cell. The Super told me to use my discretion in deciding when his situation was becoming impossible.'

'How could you make a call about his mental condition?'

I shook my head. 'You don't get my drift. The Super meant when his condition became impossible to hide from his neighbours. At that tipping point, we whisked him away. A patient whose discretion I trust helped me to get Dillon acquainted with his new lodgings. I'd be stumped without the likes of Jimmy Nolan to help out at times. It also gives him a sense of responsibility.'

'And gives the asylum an extra pair of unpaid hands.'

I nodded. 'Sadly, the labourer who must sell himself piecemeal is a commodity, like every other article of commerce, exposed to the vicissitudes of competition and fluctuations of the market.'

He stared at me quizzically as the quotation registered.

'You've read your Marx.' He sounded impressed.

'Also my Catholic Truth Society pamphlets and an odd copy of *The News of the World* if someone manages to smuggle that newspaper off the Liverpool boat.'

'What would Marx say about this situation?'

'That Jimmy should be rewarded for his labour. Possibly with a cigarette ... if I have another to spare.'

Taking the hint, Fairfax proffered his cigarette case one final time. 'Take one for this Jimmy chap and don't ask me again. I'm not a tourist to be fleeced.'

I accepted gratefully. 'You're a gentleman twice over and most definitely not cut out for medicine in Ireland.'

He nodded towards Dillon. 'Should we not lift him off the floor?'

'If you want,' I said, 'but sometimes we do people harm by trying to do them good. The Super gave this poor blighter an injection for agitation, which he is sleeping off. Place him back on the mattress and he may harm himself when he rolls off, trying to crawl back under his bed where he feels safest.'

'The consultant who wrote his external medical report holds out no hope for him.'

I shrugged. 'You'd need to discuss that with the Super. What would I know?'

'You know …' He paused, trying to recall a phrase. 'What was it my landlady said about a fellow lodger last night? *"That lad knows more than his prayers."* The other doctors I've met here are good people, keen to ask about best practice in England and the results in asylums that use electroconvulsive therapy. They're honest about this asylum being overcrowded, with hundreds of senile cases surrounded by hopeless dements. The Superintendent says that only a few hundred patients here are capable of responding to any treatment. I suspect that he and his fellow doctors think that none will respond to the sort of treatment I espouse. But I don't know because at some point in every conversation with Irish people I feel an invisible shield come down. They remain polite, but use words to lock me out.'

'And you think I'm different?'

'I can't make you out. My father would call you an impudent little bugger.'

'I look forward to meeting him.'

'I don't expect paternal visits. He's not fond of the Irish. Don't take it personally. He's not overly fond of me either. I was always eclipsed by my older brother.'

'I know the feeling.'

'You have an older brother?' he asked.

'Let's just say we all lost something in the violence here two decades ago.'

'Were you yourself involved in those events?'

I shrugged. 'A bishop wouldn't ask me that.' I liked Fairfax and I wondered if he had yet figured out why he liked me. All the qualifications in the world can still blind you to what's in front of your nose – or what you mightn't mind being dangled in front of your nose, if prepared to risk imprisonment and ignominy to satisfy your needs. If he couldn't make me out, it hadn't taken me long to twig him. Was this why he left England, I wondered, though I wasn't foolish enough to ask. Instead I said: 'My only way to earn the trust of the poor sods in here is by being neutral on political matters. I tell patients I was in England during the Civil War. Subterfuge and silence are the weapons of the Dublin working man. The patients think me a political eunuch. Ireland remains split in two. I keep my own counsel. Nobody came out of those times unharmed. Just look at Dillon here. Finding yourself being made a colonel at nineteen is like a kid finding himself with his first erection: overawed by the sudden power but clueless about to how to use it.'

I wanted to make Fairfax blush and was amused by my success.

'An interesting analogy.' He was unable to hide a speculative glance at me.

'That also explains him being an ex-soldier at twenty-one.'

Fairfax nodded, as if collecting his thoughts. 'The Superintendent mentioned something about a rather shambolic coup.'

'The less said the better,' I replied. 'I'm not saying that Dillon is guilty of everything he's accused of. But if I was accused of half of it, I'd get paranoid, looking over my shoulder. The problem with secrets is that you never know who's also keeping them.'

'Have you many secrets to keep?' His tone was casual, but it was his first overt remark, though it might sound innocuous to an eavesdropper. I decided against pushing my luck further, disinclined to play the teasing word games that I occasionally got drawn into at closing time in Bohemian pubs when talking to French or English exiles whom I knew I could avoid encountering again.

'I'm too poor to have secrets. Not like Dillon here, the child soldier.' I gave Fairfax a direct stare, knowing that I would be grilled by the Superintendent, though I hadn't any intention of telling him all I had gleaned. 'What makes you so interested in him?'

'His war in Dublin was very different from the war I saw in France, but maybe his trauma is similar. I specialise in war trauma.'

'What drugs do you use?'

'None, if possible. I'm not saying that drugs are not a necessary evil. Often they are essential to give some poor devils peace of mind. But in other cases – and it's a slow process – one can see extraordinary progress in patients if they are afforded the time and space to simply talk.'

'Maybe you're right,' I said. 'But maybe we all have certain things we cannot say because of the impossibility of unsaying them. You may see being an asylum doctor as being like a father confessor, but I see it more like being a boxing referee. When a boxer gets knocked down he should stay down for the count of eight. He needs the referee to shield him, not engage him in a tête-à-tête. The Super is under pressure to patch up Dillon. Grangegorman is a scrapyard for people that nobody wants, but in every scrapyard you can inject new life into certain engines by using a high enough voltage.'

Fairfax approached the unconscious Dillon on the floor and, careful not to wake him, took the pillow from his bunk and carefully positioned it under his head. He looked up. 'Have you ever seen a patient receive electroconvulsive therapy?'

I nodded. 'I wouldn't even wish it on whatever bastard murdered my older brother in the Civil War.'

This made him pause. 'I'm dreadfully sorry.' He straightened up. 'What side was your brother on?'

'Terrible things were done by both sides. That's all I'm willing to say.'

'It's not always easy to forgive and forget.'

I gave him a cold stare and jangled my keys. 'Did I say that I forgave or forgot? Subterfuge and silence are my weapons in every aspect of my life.' I led the way out of the cell. 'You're wasting your time if you think you'll get Dillon to talk. You mean well, but you'll only stir up a hornets' nest in this poor bastard's head. Still and all, our chat has been rewarding.'

'Why is that?' the doctor asked in the freezing corridor.

I locked the cell door. 'I'm three cigarettes richer. And not Woodbines either. I like what I can't afford and I always enjoy a posh fag.'

Nine

Dillon

Asylum time

I was being held for so long – though I wasn't sure how long – in this prison that I began to suspect I wouldn't be shot after all. If my captors planned a Noel Lemass job, my body would already be decomposing in a ditch in the Featherbed Mountains, after they used rifle butts on my face so that not even my wife could identify me. Nor were they willing to grant me a proper soldier's death, with a firing squad to defiantly stare down. These curs planned something else for me. Every time I woke I heard a gnawing. At first I thought it was enormous rats scurrying under the floorboards, their teeth seeking any weakness in the rotten wood. This was so terrifying that I was almost relieved to realise that the sawing must be a carpenter at work in the next cell.

This could only mean the ultimate humiliation. They planned to hang me like a common criminal. If they were building a gallows in the adjoining cell, they must be waiting for one man to disembark from the Liverpool boat. Any passenger who recognised him would pretend not to. Albert Pierrepoint must have left his grocery shop in Oldham to take the boat and resume his role as hangman. I'm told that a space always clears around him on deck as he asks his assistant curt questions; triple-checking his victim's weight and height to calculate the exact drop required. Tasking his assistant to kneel and rapidly bind his victim's legs with a leather strap, Pierrepoint generally gets his business done, with the criminal's neck snapped, in under a minute.

Despite all the killing that occurred in Ireland, all the zealots working themselves into a frenzy to commit atrocities, our government could never find a citizen willing to assume the post of official hangman. Before every execution, the latchicos who applied for the post, lured by seemingly easy money, all shook so violently or primed their nerves with such strong drink that the governor in Mountjoy Jail would send them away and dispatch a telegram requesting the services of the British hangman. A taciturn Englishman who learnt his trade by assisting in a long-established family business of grocers, vintners and hangmen. A barber on Capel Street who had to open early to shave Pierrepoint, after prison warders collected him from the boat, once told me he risked asking, 'Do you not need a whiskey before the task?' The gravel-faced man had quietly replied, 'If you can't do this job without whiskey, you'd best not do it at all.'

Lying in my cell and examining my conscience to prepare my defence – should those blaggards intend to give me a court-martial – I had to admit that while whiskey wasn't involved before every killing I witnessed, whiskey or some other class of madness was used to shake off the aftershock. The drinking mightn't occur for weeks afterwards, but some sights and sounds would haunt you unless expunged by a bender. We killed for such passionate love of our country that we often found ourselves mired with the jitters afterwards. But what class of cold creature must Pierrepoint be, to be able to kill dispassionately; focused only on calculating the required length of drop; perfecting his glorified carpentry tricks with a hand steadier than the barber who shaved him before dawn on Capel Street?

Maybe I was about to find out when he and his assistant stormed into my cell to place a black hood over my head. Had

Pierrepoint been spying on me for days through the Judas hole in my cell door, slyly judging my weight before making miniature adjustments and testing his trapdoor again? I still wasn't certain that he was in the next cell, fine-tuning his gallows, until I saw evidence of the drop being measured.

Don't ask me to explain how he somehow used my cell windowsill as ballast when testing his trapdoor, because I was only a fair to middling scholar in O'Connell's School before school got interrupted by my fight for Irish freedom. I had never learnt enough geometry or trigonometry to grasp what I was witnessing. I couldn't tell if it was a hallucination, a nightmare or another trick being played to torment me by my captors. But Pierrepoint must have pulled the lever to test his trapdoor, because his rope somehow caused the high window in my cell to plunge downwards until the sill came to rest near the floor.

I was in no fit state to explain such sights. I just felt drawn, against my will, to approach the window, hoping to gain some sense of where they were holding me. I went to kneel down but was suddenly afraid to, when I saw that a young figure already knelt there. I studied his features and grew perplexed, because I knew this boy and he was only a boy, no matter what he thought. I knew his every thought, his burning hopes and secret fears. His greatest fear was rats. I was right when I thought I had heard them gnaw under the floorboards of my cell. But since then they had endured a terrible drop, tumbling out through a crack to fall two storeys into the enclosed yard of an abattoir. I knew where I was now. I even knew the date, though this made no sense. I wanted to tell my younger self to stop fretting as he knelt there. This daring raid he was helping to plan would succeed. But as I knelt beside him he didn't notice my presence. His gaze was too fixated on the hordes of rats fighting over every scrap of rotten meat in that yard, their bodies bloated from this nightly feast of offal and bone. As

I followed his gaze, those rats still scared me, although twenty-two years had passed since this sight was first implanted in my mind.

I turned to gaze again at his features, but my younger self was no longer beside me. He had moved inside me or perhaps I was inside him. This made no sense, except for a brief second of clarity when I sufficiently regained my reason to remember that I was insane. No hangman had visited my cell to measure me. It had been a Medical Superintendent, reassuring me that I had nothing to worry about. I was mad but the necessary papers had been signed to ensure that money would flow. Flow to whom? When I tried to remember, my sanity deserted me. I became seventeen years old again. I knelt there, so petrified by watching those rats attack each other in the yard below, that I barely heard a young woman approach until she stood behind me in whatever moonlight came through the grimy window. Her voice broke my thoughts. Its teasing, girlish quality made her sound younger than she looked as I turned to stare at her in a white nightdress, with an old coat thrown over her shoulders. Her face looked gaunt with stress, but this did not dilute my unexpected surge of desire. Or maybe this surge was caused by me knowing so little about women, having rarely been alone indoors with one so late at night before.

'What has you so agitated, young fella?' she asked.

'Those rats must cannibalise each other when they run out of scraps of meat,' I heard myself say. 'If we don't exterminate rats they'll overrun the country.' I couldn't stop myself admiring the contours of her figure, barely concealed by her husband's cast-off coat. 'How can you bear to live in an abattoir?'

'I don't.' Her tone betrayed how her pride was hurt. 'I live in a house attached to an abattoir. Do you think I like that sight or am not frightened for my baby in his cot? But jobs are scarce as hen's teeth in this mayhem. My husband is lucky to still be employed here, though he spends half his time on the run, with me terrified that the Tans will wreck these rooms, searching for him and maybe doing God knows what to me. It's not easy to be a woman left on her own and it will be even harder if suspicion falls on me. I want freedom too but I've two small children to think of. When the IRA swarm the yard, make sure to tie me up and lock me and the babies in my bedroom, you hear? Do it proper. Have you ever given a woman a clatter?'

'I've never hit any woman,' I protested, 'nor ever would.'

'That's very chivalrous, but it would be best to give me a dig, not hard but hard enough to leave a convincing bruise. My children will be out on the street if the abattoir owners think I played any part in whatever the proper IRA men are planning here at dawn. It's not just rats you want to exterminate.'

I was a proper IRA man too, I pointed out. We were not murderers and under instructions to kill nobody in this raid. My role was to watch until dawn, when an armoured car would arrive from Marlborough Barracks. Her window had a clear view of the abattoir yard. It was also high enough up for my comrades, loitering out on the street, to spy the handkerchief I would wave when all the soldiers left the armoured car to enter the abattoir and collect their meat ration. At this signal, my comrades would rush the yard and hijack the armoured car before the soldiers realised what was happening. If it went to plan, my big brother was waiting, wearing the army uniform he wore when awarded a medal for gallantry at the Somme. He would enter Mountjoy Jail in the hijacked armoured car, impersonating a British officer as he presented forged documents stating that a volunteer under sentence of hanging was to be transferred into his custody for interrogation. If our plan worked, we would cheat Pierrepoint out of five guineas for another snapped neck. As always, my brother was taking the greatest risk, bluffing his way into the belly of the beast. The volunteers who would dart into the abattoir yard were risking their lives too. My role as a lookout was small. Yet everything depended on me judging the exact second to signal to them.

My nerves jangled at this responsibility until I remembered that, of course, this had already happened years ago. I was a delusional 42-year-old man, standing again outside of my younger self, watching him blush as he realised how aware this young mother was of him being unable to stop gazing at the contours of her nightdress. He was mesmerised by the actuality of being alone with someone so beautiful. Pull yourself together, I tried to tell my younger self. You're a soldier, not a corner boy. But he couldn't hear me because I couldn't hear myself either. I found myself being absorbed back inside his body, with no thought anymore of what it felt like to grow older; no thought of anything except how to hide my embarrassment at being caught staring at her. But she seemed amused as I looked away.

'Listen to me,' she said softly. 'Asking you had you ever given a woman a clatter. I'm glad you never have and hope you never will. I bet you've never even kissed one.'

'I have.' I felt myself blush even more.

'Who did you kiss?'

'The typist in my father's office.'

She smiled, enjoying teasing me. I couldn't blame her. It must have been lonesome on her own every night. 'Did you threaten to have your rich father sack her if she refused? I had a boss like that once, too loose and fancy-free with his hands.'

'My father isn't rich.'

'What is he then?'

'He owns a small insurance business. He's comfortable.'

'Comfortable sounds rich to me. Did this typist want to kiss you?'

'I don't know for sure,' I confessed shyly. 'She kissed me for Ireland, I think.'

The woman threw back her head, convulsed by a laugh that made her breasts quiver against her nightdress. She looked at me quizzically. 'You IRA boys have queer notions about how a girl should best serve Ireland. How old are you?'

'Seventeen ... and a bit.'

'You don't look it.'

'It's best if intelligence officers don't look threatening. The less attention people pay me, the better I do my job.'

'Intelligence officer, my backside,' she replied, amused.

'Michael Collins himself appointed me to this rank.'

'Did he now? And was it Collins who told you to kiss the typist?'

'No. That just happened.'

'As kissing does. Was it enjoyable at least ... kissing her?'

'I'm not really sure,' I confessed. 'If I'm honest, I was a bit too afraid.'

She laughed again, good-naturedly. 'You obviously haven't mastered the art of kissing. You can't swallow her tongue or you couldn't in my day.'

'When was your day?'

She sat on the one good chair. Even in the half-light I saw how tired she looked. 'It feels like yesterday, but after two babies it also feels like decades ago. What made the kiss so scary?'

'It's a long story.' I was reluctant to go into it, with her husband on the run and no guarantee that he'd ever be the same man again if he was picked up and tortured.

She lit a half cigarette she had been keeping to savour when her day's work was done. 'The armoured car never arrives before dawn,' she said. 'I could do with hearing a voice that isn't my own. We've all the time in the world to talk, and that's all we'll be doing, so get no notions.'

'I have no notions,' I assured her.

'I know but I need to say it anyhow. You're still an innocent lad, but I've met my share who weren't, starting with my ex-boss who only stopped his groping when I stuck a hatpin into his palm. Forget those rats and tell me about your first kiss.'

'It's not very romantic.'

'First kisses sometimes aren't.'

'It happened the afternoon that Collins ordered us to track down a vicious thug of an RIC detective named Igoe. Igoe raised blue murder when stationed in Galway before being moved to work out of Dublin Castle. Did your husband ever mention him?'

'No.'

Her voice was serious now. I didn't want to say too much about Igoe building up a squad of rural RIC officers who had committed such heinous acts that it wasn't safe for them to stay in their own part of the country. Like a Pied Piper, Igoe lured them to Dublin, not just for their own safety but because they could identify the IRA leaders in whatever county they fled from. Igoe's henchmen didn't wear uniforms on their daily walks through Dublin. This meant that we never knew where they were until they pounced on some country volunteer stepping off a train at Kingsbridge or the Broadstone; a lad summoned up to a meeting with GHQ that he would never reach because Igoe's bowsies were discreetly scanning every passenger to see who they might recognise. We couldn't plug them all, but if we killed Igoe, his spy ring would fall apart. Igoe pulled the strings, but rarely involved himself in the arrests. He would just be another face amid the onlookers, who only came into his own in Dublin Castle, where nobody could witness his murderous rage except the poor bastards at his mercy.

'You've gone quiet.' The woman almost scorched her fingertips as she extracted one last drag from her cigarette before stubbing it out. 'Do you think I don't know the dangers my husband is facing? I'm no innocent Bridget. Go on with your story.'

'We didn't know what Igoe looks like, so a Galway volunteer offered to come up and identify him. I met up with this volunteer. Within half an hour he'd pointed out Igoe walking up Grafton Street. Once I saw Igoe I could spot the other peelers, fanned out on either side. They had that walk drilled into peelers. I knew all the train timetables and thought that Igoe must be headed for Harcourt Street Station.

'I sent a runner to tell the other Squad members to meet us there and we'd plug him. But I made a bad guess or else Igoe sensed he was being followed. He suddenly turned back, with the half dozen men with him also turning. I was never so scared. I didn't know whether to run and risk a bullet or brazen it out by casually walking past him. The Galway volunteer pulled his hat low and we had passed Igoe when he stopped.

'Maybe he caught a glimpse of the Galway lad's face but I think it was because he smelt my fear. He nodded for his henchmen to shove us down a lane for questioning, with passers-by making themselves scarce. I bluffed and said the volunteer was a stranger who'd stopped me for directions. This was the lie Collins trained me to tell, but it felt like betrayal. I could hardly breathe with fear that he'd bundle me off to Dublin Castle, kicking my teeth in so badly that I'd beg for a bullet. But I escaped scot-free. The volunteer sacrificed himself to save me. He saw me shaking and shouted, "I know you, Igoe, you black-hearted bastard, and you know me too, so leave this passer-by out of it. Or have you gone so soft you pick on schoolboys barely out of short pants?"'

I looked up at the woman, ashamed. 'I should have done something to save him ...'

She touched my shoulder kindly. 'What could you have done, child? Igoe's G-men are armed. I bet you didn't even have a gun on you.'

I shook my head. 'It's better if intelligence officers go unarmed. Other Squad members use their guns. I use my boyish looks to persuade maids in lodging houses to steal the contents of wastepaper baskets, so I can piece together torn up letters and discover why strangers are really in Dublin. My boyish looks made Igoe let me go, thinking me just a scared kid. But I didn't know whether Igoe was only toying with me. I tried not to run until I reached my father's office. I begged his typist to walk with me to the hideaway where I sleep at night. I was terrified of being followed. When we saw two policemen walk towards us on Wicklow Street I shook so much that the typist pinned me in a doorway and kept kissing me like we were courting until the peelers had passed.'

It seemed to grow dark in the room, the stub of the single candle on the table flickering, its wick almost drowned in hot wax. 'What happened to the Galway volunteer?' she asked, her voice so soft that I knew she was fearful for her husband.

'After Igoe finished beating him in a police cell, he shot him four times in the legs, claiming he was trying to escape. He would have bled to death if a DMP man wasn't so disgusted that he called an ambulance. When he gets out of hospital he'll be crippled for life.' I looked at her in bewilderment. 'What turns a man like Igoe into a sadistic bully, drunk on absolute power?'

She shivered. 'A certain type of man gets excited by power. Often a hen-pecked one who previously never had power. I steer a wide path, but that doesn't mean I've not encountered them. If there are no rules to stop a man doing anything he wants, then God only knows what evil he'll do, if power goes to his head.'

The candle on the table flickered one last time and went out.

'I could never be like that,' I said.

My tone was so earnest that she leaned down over me. 'I know that. Just like I know that my husband isn't cruel, though whenever he turns up I never ask what he's done.'

'I've seen things I wish I hadn't seen,' I confessed. 'Necessary things, don't get me wrong. But freedom comes at a price.'

'Freedom had better be worth it,' she said. 'You're a nice boy, so get off your knees at that window and just lie back.' Her body came so close to mine as I lay back as instructed that for a moment I thought she was going to lie beside me. Then I realised that she was actually arranging a blanket over me. 'Mick Collins sent you here on an act of reconnaissance, not an act of penance. Now sleep.'

'Do you know Collins?' The bare floorboards no longer felt hard because there was such comfort in that blanket covering me.

Her smile reminded me of my mother on the nights when I was just a year or two younger and she used to urge me to stop talking and simply go to sleep.

'In this city a woman needs to know more than her prayers,' she said. 'There has been many a night Mick hid out in my father's house on Richmond Road. Only once did Da try to turn him away. My kid sister Lizzy was in a bedroom on her own because she had the Spanish influenza and we were all told to stay away from her. We didn't know if she would live or die. Just twelve years old. My father didn't want Mick to risk being under the same roof as her and Mick isn't a man to stay in any house where he's not welcome. "I'll go and not disturb you when there's sickness in your home," he told my father. "But I'll not go until I say goodnight to Lizzy." None of us could stop him going up to Lizzy's room, despite the risk of infection. He knew Lizzy was mad about him. He spent an hour holding her hand and chatting. Then he slipped quickly back down the stairs and disappeared without a word.'

'My own sister died young,' I said. 'Did Lizzy ...?'

I hesitated. She tucked the blanket tighter around me in the dark.

'Lizzy is alive and bold as brass. Maybe the worst of the flu had passed before Mick visited her. But try telling that to Lizzy or my mother. They're convinced Mick is a walking saint with miraculous powers. I'm not convinced, but whatever he is, he's a good man and I'd do anything for him. He told me to be nice to you, but not too nice. So like I say, don't get notions in the night. I'm no typist.'

'I've never taken advantage of any woman,' I said.

She kissed my forehead lightly as I lay there. 'I'm more afraid of people taking advantage of you. Mick has given you a grand title but robbed you of the chance to just be a boy. So let me tell you one thing. Next time a girl pins you in a doorway, she wants to be kissed back. Now get some sleep. I'll wake you before dawn. The baby will have woken me.'

Then she was gone, though I never heard her footsteps move away. I felt cold and went to pull the blanket tight around me. But the blanket wasn't there and nor was the low window. I realised I wasn't seventeen anymore. I was a grown man being held prisoner under sentence of death. My jailors must have got Pierrepoint to readjust his trapdoor because the pulleys had raised my window back up to its original height. I crawled along the floorboards, making for the sanctuary of lying under my bed because, from down here, my high window now looked like a guillotine ready to fall.

Ten

Gus

Asylum time

Dillon was still lying on the floor when I turned the key in his cell door. He glanced up fearfully but at least he was conscious of my presence, unlike on other mornings when whatever the Super had him sauced on meant that he was barely aware of anything. This was my fifth time in his cell, though I sensed that he had no idea who I was. That didn't bother me. I knew exactly who he was. Not that I was here to judge. Nor was I here to cure him enough to get his moxie back. That was the Super's job. I was simply here to feed him and, when I felt sure I could trust Jimmy Nolan again, this wouldn't even be my job anymore. I felt sorry for the poor bastard lying there, but pity isn't a useful therapy. The only treatment I could provide was a dose of reality.

'The dead awoke.' I placed a wooden bowl and spoon on his small table. 'And just in time for grub, though don't ask me what's in it. It's Grangegorman stew. The same pot has been on the boil since 1815. There's not much meat floating in it but the hundred and twenty-five years of accumulated grease adds to the flavour.'

Dillon eyed me cautiously. He hadn't risen from the floor but at least he hadn't backed away. He reminded me of a nervous old dog who used to live wild near the canal at Rialto. Any sudden move and the scared mutt would disappear into the weeds and bushes. But if you spoke for long enough in a calm tone, then while he still mightn't trust you, at least he'd gradually let you come near him. This same approach worked with certain nervous men who also lurked on that canal at night, although at least with the old dog you knew that the worst he could do was bite you.

'If you don't mind me saying, you'd be wise to get up off that floor. You wouldn't lie there if you knew how often it's covered in piss and jizz and vomit. I've seen acts performed on them floorboards that you wouldn't see in a circus or it would be closed for indecency.'

'I don't know what the hell you are,' he replied, 'but I'm not like that.'

'I don't judge anyone for what way they are,' I said. 'Especially not the men who only come in here to dry out. It's natural for any man to go on an occasional bender and we can't all traipse off for the cure to Mount Melleray monastery where a sanctimonious Holy Joe weaning himself off the gargle might remember your face and blow your cover afterwards. It's different in here. All men are equal and equally forgetful when they leave. I'm fine with the drunkards and dipsos but spare me the incurable wankers. I don't mind mopping the floor after them, but with some repressed craw thumpers you'd need to mop the ceiling too.'

I had Dillon's attention. I could sense him straining to make sense of where he was.

'You're a lucky geezer,' I said. 'A cell all to yourself. Normally only priests get this cell, though we have to pretend that we don't know they're priests. Collective amnesia is a useful ideology, the only useful ideology. Forgive and forget. And if you can't forgive, then at least the doctors here have ways to make you forget.'

Dillon addressed me directly for the first time, trying to sound authoritative but unable to conceal a quiver of unease. 'I'll ask a straight question and deserve a straight answer. Have you come to kill me?'

'Me?' I tapped the spoon against the bowl, hoping that hunger might lure him to the table. 'Listen, pal. I'm not the cook. If you die of poisoning, then tell your ghost not to come back blaming me. I have to eat this same blasted stew every day too and it's a wonder any of us are still standing.'

My jocular tone coaxed an edgy smile from him. Dillon cautiously rose, careful to keep his distance. 'Another straight question. Where the hell am I?'

I tried to keep my tone light. 'Let's put it this way. You're not in the Ritz and this food wasn't sent over from Jammet's. You're in Grangegorman Mental Hospital, pal.'

'Don't call me "pal". I dislike overfamiliarity.'

'What would you prefer? Francis? Frankie?'

'You could try "Colonel Dillon".'

'Well, Colonel, you're confined to barracks after the doctors signed a committal order. Your wife was in a terrible state when you locked her into a bedroom. Do you not remember?'

I saw him try to make sense of this. 'I'm not saying I believe one word you say.'

'Well, you're now a ward of court, whether you believe it or not,' I said. 'You'd be in a public ward if the Minister for Supplies hadn't intervened to ensure they found you a discreet billet.'

Dillon looked puzzled. 'Seán Lemass? Are you saying he intervened?'

'I would have thought you two were sworn enemies.'

The more we spoke, the more conscious Dillon was becoming of his situation. He shook his head groggily. 'What did they inject me with? I've never felt this sluggish.'

'You'd need to ask a doctor. The last time I saw a needle so big, a pal was sticking it into a greyhound who won a race in Harold's Cross and then slept for forty-eight hours.'

'You're not a doctor?'

'An attendant. Call me Gus.'

'At one time Lemass and I were like blood brothers. But we've not spoken in twenty years.' He paused. 'If you're my jailor, surely your job isn't just to me keep me locked in, but to keep people out. Why do women keep visiting me here?'

'I doubt if they do. Grangegorman is a kip but not a Dolly Fawcett kip, crammed with khaki wacky jive bombers.'

He drew himself up to his full height, adopting a military bearing. 'Are you calling me a liar?'

'I'm saying you're either a certified lunatic or the Military Service Pensions Board has been defrauded out of five guineas.'

He took a step closer, trying to stare me down.

'Move away from that door. I have an office job I must go to.'

'No disrespect, but you'll find no red carpet waiting in the Sweepstakes office. You might find a straitjacket though.'

'Mind your tongue. You're addressing a colonel.'

'I'm not losing my job by letting you out this door, pal, so don't snap your cap at me,' I replied firmly. 'You're just another unfortunate soul stuck in this antsville. The patient who helped me escort you to your cell got surprisingly agitated about your military rank. Normally not a violent bone in his body, though he hardly has a bone not kicked into an unnatural shape that God never intended. I usually let him bring meals to our more select patients. But I thought it wise to bring you your stew myself until I'm certain that he has calmed down enough not to spit into it.'

Dillon's voice lost the imperious tone he had tried to summon. My words sank in, triggering a memory. 'I remember now. I was kidnapped. You were the chief bottle-washer. Then at the end, some little runt with rage in his eyes ... rage like Igoe's.'

'Who is Igoe?'

'I demand to see your superiors.'

I tapped the spoon against the bowl. 'They've all been to gawk at you through the spyhole. If this was a peepshow, I'd make a fortune. You should eat. Don't be afraid of not liking the taste, because it's tasteless. But you'll get used to it.'

'I'm not hungry.'

I opened the door, on my guard in case he tried to make a break for it. 'You'd still be wise to eat it. There are rats under the floorboards. The asylum is so old we can't keep vermin out. Generally they leave you alone but I wouldn't leave food hanging about to attract them because these are the biggest rats you ever saw. So snaffle your grub before the rats do.' I paused to take a last look at him as he sat down and tentatively stirred the tepid stew. 'And trust me, I didn't spit into it. I wouldn't do that, no matter what evil bastard murdered my brother.'

Then I closed the door and left him to his purgatory.

Eleven

Dillon

Asylum time

This time that latchico of an attendant Gus didn't arrive with the slop that passes for dinner. He sent his sidekick, the stooped figure who had helped haul me into this cell. I had only vague memories of my kidnapping, but I could recall his rage and how he would have done me harm if Gus hadn't intervened. Today he looked so timid that he barely dared to glance at me. I suspected he might drop the bowl of stew and mug of weak cocoa if I'd said boo as he placed them on the table. He stared at the uneaten slop I had been served for breakfast, wondering whether to take it away, and was about to leave my cell when I summoned him back.

'I know you possess a tongue. Do you not speak anymore?'

He turned. 'Who would listen?' He nodded towards my untouched breakfast. 'This is the fifth morning you've not eaten your stirabout. You need to keep up your strength. If I bring that back to the kitchens it will be snaffled up, cold and all, because most patients would kill for an extra portion of anything.'

I rose and examined the stew he had brought in. Its smell made me both nauseous and ravenous. Yet distrust prevented me from eating anything.

'How can I be sure it's not poisoned?'

'You can't be. But look at the state of you, man, you must eat.'

He sounded genuinely concerned, but it didn't mean I could trust him.

'What concern is it of yours?' I asked brusquely. 'Last time we met you wanted to lather me with punches.'

He shrugged apologetically, looking so emaciated that a puff of wind might knock him over.

'I just lost the head. We don't normally get the likes of you banged in amongst us.'

'The likes of who?'

'A colonel. Even if stripped of that title.'

'My comrades and I never left the National Army,' I replied. 'It was the army who left us. But our bonds remain strong. One old comrade visited me last night to ask for my instructions. I told him to station a trustworthy man on this corridor and have another one patrol the exercise yard.'

'Did you now? And were your instructions written or verbal?'

I disliked the hint of impertinence entering his tone. 'What difference does that make to you?' I said.

'I've crossed that exercise yard ten times today and saw no ex-gunmen patrolling. Just the usual lines of broken men shuffling in circles. You've had no visitors last night or any night.'

'How would know? You're no doctor. You're a nobody.'

He nodded. 'Nobody pays attention to nobodies. That means nothing gets past us, especially in this place.' He sounded cockier. 'But I was once somebody. We met back then. Do you not remember my face, Colonel?'

The way he took a step forward alarmed me. I stepped back, maintaining my distance, eyes alert for sudden movements.

'I never saw you before. Try to draw a gun and I'll ring for the attendant.'

'You have no bell and I have no gun.'

'If it's a knife you have, I'll fight to my last breath.' I tried to sound fearsome but was shaking so much that I knew he could see through my bluster. He didn't attempt to come nearer. Instead he turned his empty pockets inside out.

'Can't you see, you paranoid fool? I've no knife, no gun, I've nothing. Gus lets me fetch and carry and throws me an odd cigarette in return. That's all I have to show for forty years on this earth. If I'd been sent to kill you, you'd have been dead by now. You know enough about killing to know there's no advance warning. Shoot quick and vanish. Mick Collins's mantra.'

'What do you know about Collins?' I asked.

He stepped closer, palms open to show he was carrying nothing. But the words he kept repeating rattled me. 'Drip. Drip. Gurgle. Gurgle.'

'Quit your blathering,' I ordered.

'It's not blathering.' He drew closer. 'It's gurgling.'

'Whatever it is, I don't want to hear it.'

'I remember a night when you couldn't stop hearing it, though the rest of us couldn't hear a sound. The gurgle of blood in a dying man's throat. A little brook still bubbling up even after he was shot dead.'

I had stepped so far back that my shoulders were pressed against the wall. 'I don't know who the hell you are, but stay away.'

'None of us could figure out why you were still haunted by that sound, hours later in the hideaway. Surely you remember me? We're old comrades.'

'I doubt that,' I said. 'I remember faces.'

'Then have the decency to remember mine.'

My eyes were closed but the faces I was remembering didn't belong to him. I was back inside the mayhem of a boarding house on Pembroke Street on Bloody Sunday. I was remembering the silence as we snuck in, hoping our boots would encounter no creaking floorboards as I led Paddy Flanagan and another lad upstairs and pointed at the doors of two adjoining third-floor rooms where our targets were probably not yet awake. I was remembering the startled look of both men, ordered out of bed in their pyjamas and told to face the wall, before Paddy fired at the base of their skulls and they fell without making a sound except for a gurgling of blood in one of their throats as his body gave a last involuntary shudder. The shots caused such ringing in my ears that I barely heard Paddy telling me to get the hell away as I tried to explain how, as an intelligence officer, I was meant to search for incriminating documents. Then I was alone on the third floor as the others ran down to where panicked British officers had emerged from their rooms, held at gunpoint on the staircase by other volunteers, while their wives tried to shield them, screaming that we were murderers and scum.

But everything occurring on those lower floors seemed to be happening in another world. I felt paralysed in that bedroom, knowing that Collins would want any letters, but unable to move. I was hypnotised by the gurgling sound that continued in that officer's throat even though he was dead. I might never have found the strength to flee if I hadn't heard my name called from the doorway. I turned to see the young maid there, not just with a look of shock on her face but of absolute betrayal. For weeks I had courted her as instructed, coaxing morsels of information about what room each lodger slept in, assuring her that the IRA simply planned a raid to gather papers. These corpses gave the lie to that. They turned my endearments in darkened doorways into lies too. Her eyes told me that she felt as used as if I had violated her body.

As she turned to flee back to her attic bedroom, the shouts and shots below me became real, the screams of an English wife as a bullet meant for her husband passed through her arm. I could no longer control my impulse to run. My orders had been to oversee the assassination of these two spies. What was happening on the stairs was the responsibility of other volunteers. But there were not enough of us or else there were more officers than expected because we should be gone by now. I couldn't see everything that was happening as I ran down, amid the smoke from gunshots and falling plaster where bullets went astray. I saw two volunteers try to hold another volunteer's arm steady as he closed his eyes and fired shots through the jaw of an officer charging towards him. Then I was out on the eerily quiet street, dodging down lanes to catch the dockers' ferry across the Liffey to the North Wall Quay. Once news leaked out about all the shootings due to happen that morning, every bridge would be closed off, every passer-by questioned. Only when that ferry docked and I could mingle with church-goers making their way into Mass did I feel able to breathe again. I could remember all this vividly. The only face I couldn't recall was the one confronting me in this cell. I opened my eyes, determined to show that I was not intimidated by him.

'Whoever you are, take my breakfast and go. I want no truck with you. I'll only talk to the doctors.'

He shrugged. 'You'd be better off talking to me. What you say to me stays with me. I'm not a doctor deciding whether to put you into convulsions with insulin or run electric volts through your brain. I'm your only comrade left. The others have washed their hands. It's Saturday afternoon.' A slyness entered his voice. 'They're probably teeing off now at the Hermitage Golf Club.'

I studied him suspiciously. 'How do you know that I play golf there?'

'By accident,' he replied. 'Patients in here fight over the smallest task, like who gets to empty the doctors' wastepaper baskets. Copies of *The Irish Times* are like rolled gold. Not to read but to smoke. Roll a scrap of newspaper tight enough and you'd swear you were smoking Woodbines. Some years ago I was tearing a strip off a page of an old *Irish Times* hidden under my mattress when suddenly there you all were before my eyes. A report on the

Hospitals' Sweepstakes Golfing Society's inaugural outing at the Hermitage, with you elected Honorary Secretary. You were lined up for the photograph: all the success stories. Big Joe McGrath, lording it over everyone, and Frank Saurin, the best dressed volunteer on Bloody Sunday, and Joe Dolan, now a picture of respectability. You stood beside your fellow intelligence officer Liam Tobin who helped you plan Bloody Sunday and later helped you kick the shit out of prisoners in Wellington Barracks. But all that was in the past because there you all were, gentlemen golfers with spats and plum jobs, whereas I'm left with nothing. Is it any wonder that I flew into a jealous rage at the sight of you?'

'It was a harmless golf outing.' I was suddenly defensive. 'We work hard in the Sweepstakes. It's a tricky business, trying to hover just above the right side of the law in America. What's so wrong with a game of golf?'

'Nothing for the class of folk who can afford it. But they weren't the class I broke my health fighting for. I remember when golf courses were just handy places to execute informers.'

I know who he was referring to: a fellow intelligence officer, Vincent Fovargue, who we had left dumped on a fairway in Middlesex with a note: *Spies and traitors beware – IRA.*

'Fovargue signed his own death warrant by letting the British turn him under torture,' I said. 'Sam Maguire fired the shot into his skull but it was Collins who gave the order.'

'And you all danced to Collins's tune. Including Maguire – another one of us who died penniless.'

'Fovargue knew the price for talking,' I said. 'And you know too much about things that aren't good for you. What are you really doing here?'

'Bringing you your stew. Enjoy the privilege while you're still a celebrity in here. You'll lose this cell once the new English doctor stops taking an interest in you. You'll queue for meals like the other two thousand of us.'

'What English doctor?' I asked, nervous suddenly. 'I've met no English doctor.'

He sensed my anxiety, because he adopted a placating tone.

'He's called Fairfax. You've not seen him yet, but Gus says that every day he makes a pilgrimage to spy on you through that peephole. He's biding his time until he thinks you're sufficiently compos mentis to wheedle secrets from you. Accept the advice of a fellow Bloody Sunday volunteer and act doolally for as long as possible.'

'I knew every volunteer on Bloody Sunday,' I said. 'You weren't one of us.'

'Really?' The man sat down uninvited on a stool. 'Then why in dreams do I still hear the screams of the wives and children of the three men I helped shoot dead on Morehampton Road? And why do the screams only get louder, twenty-two years later?'

'I've never met you before. I want you to leave.'

He rose and approached me, making those sounds again with his throat, 'Drip. Drip. Gurgle. Gurgle.'

'Stop,' I said. 'You're trying to work me up into a state of agitation. I won't stand for it.'

'You didn't need us to work yourself up into that state on Bloody Sunday night. We needed to calm you down in that hideaway, with you convinced you could still hear blood gurgling in a shot British officer's throat.'

'I knew the lads in that hideaway. You were not among us.'

He nodded. 'Normally not. I was just a rank-and-file volunteer, drafted in because the Squad needed extra hands to hit every lodging house at the same time. You were given Pembroke Street. I had Morehampton Road. My C.O. warned me not to go home that night. The Tans were on the warpath. Seán Lemass kept assuring you that you were just hearing a tap dripping. We all claimed to hear it too, because you were like a scared child needing to be told fairy tales. Do you not remember two men risking their lives, breaking curfew to walk you along deserted streets and calm your nerves?'

'I remember Lemass walking with me. There was someone else but I can't recall who.'

'That's because I let Lemass do all the talking. You were shaking so badly I didn't know what to say.'

I tried to think back to a night that I had spent years training myself to forget. Eventually the semblance of a name came to me.

'A young lad, so quiet we were startled to hear that he went crazy and got himself arrested later. Nugent or Nolan.' I gazed at him, trying to reconcile this stooped figure with my memories of that night. 'Jimmy Nolan.' I paused in disbelief. 'Jimmy? Is it you? You look much older. Though I probably look older myself.'

'You were seventeen years old that night. I was twenty.'

'You served time in an English jail between the Truce and the Treaty. Lincoln?'

'Dartmoor.'

'After that I thought you emigrated. To be honest, it's years since I thought of you.'

He didn't take offence but put a hand on my shoulder.

'Don't feel bad for saying that. It's what the friends of most patients in here gradually come to say. People are so busy getting on with life that it's years since anyone thought about most of us.'

He removed his hand. 'On Bloody Sunday night I thought I knew the true meaning of isolation in that hideaway above the dispensary. All of us crammed in, frantic about rumours that Dick McKee and Peadar Clancy had been picked up and were being tortured in the Castle; stunned by news of the slaughter of spectators in Croke Park; yet elated about the killings we'd committed. That hideaway felt so cut off – though in the heart of the city – with us fearful that the Tans might come looking for us. Grangegorman is in the heart of the city too – Dalymount Park just a spit away – yet this place feels far more cut off because nobody is coming looking for us. I remember us arguing that night about what shape the future would take. We never imagined a future shaped by asylum walls.'

'You and I are not the same, Jimmy.' I felt a need to put a distance between us. 'I'm only here temporarily, for safety's sake, because men were coming to kill me.'

He shrugged dismissively. 'The only killer in here is TB, working its way through wards so packed there's barely space to breathe. But we're all breathing in each other's stale sweat. TB may come for you here but nobody else will.'

A memory returned to me, not of Nolan's arrest but of Collins's furious reaction to it, hours before the Truce came into force. The news reached us during the meeting when Collins was ordering us younger members of the Squad to get a boat out of Dublin and take a holiday. With the fight done – or paused until further orders – the last thing he had needed was a volunteer being needlessly arrested.

'You went crazy,' I said. 'You tried to single-handedly hold up a truck packed with British troops at the Customs House. You're still daft because I know that enemies have been stalking me for months.'

Nolan gestured dismissively. 'Nobody gives two shits about you anymore. Who would be bothered killing you? After Collins died, you were all headless chickens, too pumped with drink and ego to know your time was up.'

'Mind your tongue! I held the rank of colonel.'

He nodded. 'And I held the rank of Prisoner number 4271 in Dartmoor. The screws didn't let any truce curb their enthusiasm for kicking the shit out of me. Did any of you even notice that I went on hunger strike for nine days to protest about the treatment meted out to us prisoners in English jails? I carried on the fight by my only means left. When Terence MacSwiney was on hunger strike, papers around the globe covered his sacrifice in Brixton Prison. I was afraid the screws would force feed me. It's how they killed Thomas Ashe.

'Instead the governor entered my cell with the Irish newspapers, saying nothing as I read them and realised there wasn't one line about my hunger strike. Finally, he spoke: "It's time you gave up this lark, old chap. The world hasn't time for amateur theatrics. I see from your bruises that the warders gave you a ragging. I'll put a stop to it. I've examined your file. Fifteen years' hard labour for holding up a Crossley Tender. The act of a deranged man. No wonder your side has no interest in you. You're fighting a war that's over. So eat something, for God's sake. You need your strength because you seem to be fighting it on your own."'

'We did think of you,' I replied. 'We thought you were crazy for waving a revolver at that army truck. It was a miracle the Brits didn't shoot you.'

'I hadn't been thinking straight for months,' Nolan said, 'though I followed every order I received, taking part in street patrols, raiding a railway depot for armour plating. Following orders stopped me having to think for myself. My unit never noticed anything wrong because I could play the good soldier with them. I only went to pieces when alone. I kept reliving the screams of the women on Morehampton Road after the men begged to be taken into a different room so their families wouldn't have to watch us shoot them.'

'Those men were spies who had it coming,' I said.

'But were they?' Nolan asked. 'We only had your word. The English officer we plugged was a spy who deserved what he got.

But what about the second lad? A blacksmith, just arrived from Scotland to seek work because his father couldn't get him a start down the pits.'

'He was going to seek work with the police.'

'That hardly makes him an elite spy, trained in espionage, like we were told. Or the landlord we shot for simply renting them rooms.'

'Those men were guilty of collusion, even if they hadn't got around to colluding yet.'

'And was that sufficient reason?' Nolan asked. 'I'm not after medals or praise, just peace of mind. I need to know if the men I helped kill deserved to die.'

'Both Collins and Cathal Brugha checked our list of targets. They considered every man on it to be a legitimate target.'

'But were they right?' The anxiety in his voice perturbed me, the enormity of his question.

'I was only seventeen, Jimmy,' I said. 'Why are you asking me?'

'Because Collins and Brugha ended up shot and we ended up in here. And I've nobody to ask.'

'Two weeks before Bloody Sunday, Lloyd George was talking about having murder by the throat,' I said. 'Two weeks later he put out feelers for peace talks. The operation was a success. History hasn't got time for incidentals. Even if some men weren't spies, we scattered the real spies who scurried from their hidey-holes to seek refuge in the Castle. Any butchery that day was done by soldiers massacring match-goers in Croke Park. My conscience is clear. If yours bothers you, that's your problem.'

Nolan gave an ironic salute. 'Yes, Colonel.'

'Don't get snide with a superior officer.'

'You lost that rank when O'Higgins and Cosgrave kicked you out of the army. You won the Civil War for them, but proved you couldn't be trusted.'

I needed to ask the vital question. 'What side did you take in that Civil War?'

Nolan stepped back. 'Who says I took any side?'

'Everyone had to.'

'Half the men who were out in Easter Week took no side. I was in no fit state to pick one either.'

'If you took no side, why should anyone on either side trust you?'

'Because I trusted you on Bloody Sunday.' He paused. Any animosity in his voice was gone. 'After being drummed out of the army how did you make a living?'

I only had to close my eyes to recall the bare stairs up to the tiny office in Capel Street where I tried to start an insurance business like my father's because it was all I knew. The ill-fitting suit that felt cheap after wearing an officer's uniform. The typist trying to look busy while waiting for the phone to ring, who wisely found a new job before I ran out of money to pay her. That phone never rang because nobody wanted to have anything to do with me.

'It wasn't easy,' I admitted. 'Not until Joe McGrath rounded up some trusted comrades to help break up strikes by troublemakers among the workers building the Ardnacrusha Dam. After that, he kept us on when he started the Sweepstakes.'

'It's a pity he didn't think to ask me. I don't mean for a fancy job. I'd have been happy to just be allowed sweep the floor.'

'Maybe McGrath didn't know where to find you, Jimmy.'

'I'm easy to find if anyone bothers to look. I tried coping outside but I always end up back here, except for one time when I tried the Napsbury asylum in England. Napsbury was no picnic but had better food than Dartmoor.'

'Did their treatment work?' I asked.

He looked down at his clothes, washed so often that they were the colour of nothing. 'What do you think?' He picked up my breakfast. 'Gus will be wondering where I am. Hopefully he has some jobs for me because I'm dying for the butt of a fag.' He nodded towards the stew. 'That's cold, but you have to eat. It's the one thing you can learn from me. Don't endure a hunger strike only to discover it's all been for nothing.'

He had reached the door before I called him back.

'What is it?' he asked.

'You and Lemass took a risk by helping me on Bloody Sunday night. Thank you.'

He nodded bashfully, unaccustomed to thanks. 'I'd have done it for any comrade.'

'Then let me ask you something, comrade to comrade. My own doctor once said that I'd be right as rain if I tried the insulin shock treatment. Have you had it?'

Nolan weighed up how to reply, then stared at me. 'Do you intend having it?'

'I don't know. One minute I can think clearly; the next minute I barely know where I am. We're old comrades. Should I let them give me insulin?'

'If you're thinking of taking insulin, it's best to know nothing about it.'

'Why is that?' I asked.

'If you knew anything about it, you wouldn't go through with it. I have to go. If Gus revokes my status as a bowl collector, I'm nobody in here, Colonel.'

He stood to attention and did his best to salute properly. Then he locked the door, leaving me alone with a cold bowl of stew and the ghosts rattling around my head.

Twelve

Gus

3 April 1941

There was no need for me to be present during their first encounter. Fairfax knew this but said nothing as I unlocked the outer door that led into a corridor with walls painted with a mishmash of any remnants from various tins of paint left over after painting more public parts of the asylum. The Superintendent knew I wasn't needed here, but it was he who insisted on my presence. He'd given me no verbal instructions but a coded look I possessed enough street sense to decipher. In theory I was present to save the doctor if Dillon became violent, but in reality the Super wanted me to save Dillon from himself if he grew overly talkative. The Super relished the stimulation of intellectual jousts with this English doctor. But I sensed an unspoken suspicion. Fairfax was too well connected to be reduced to applying for a position in this shabby backwater.

Fairfax was sufficiently astute to sense that he was under suspicion. He paused as we reached Dillon's cell and looked at me.

'I really don't need a chaperone.'

'Think of me more as your batman.'

'My army days were brief and best forgotten.'

'But you served?'

'Is that why half the staff here seem to think I'm a spy?'

'I can only speak for myself.'

'What do you say?'

'Generally, as little as possible.'

'This war in Europe is damnable. The moment that Hitler's stormtroopers land on Dover Beach I'll be on a boat to England to fight with my bare hands if necessary. But for now, as someone once said, "I will not serve that in which I no longer believe, whether it calls itself my home, my fatherland, or my church."'

'Jimmy Joyce said a lot,' I replied. 'I drank with his father on occasion. You had to buy old man Joyce whiskey because he regarded porter as a drink for jarveys. Mind you, this never stopped him buying porter when it was his round, because he was on his uppers more often than not.'

He nodded. 'I'm impressed you recognise the quotation.'

I shrugged. 'If we didn't read banned writers, we'd have shag-all to read.'

He smiled as if to say touché. 'You're a strange chap. I don't quite know what to make of you.'

'I'm not strange,' I assured him. 'Life is strange. It leads you into strange places. And, because you're asking, I don't think you're a spy.'

'What do you think I am then?'

I thought him devilishly handsome but didn't say it. I thought there could be worse ways to spend a dark night than playing back-seat bingo with him in a Model T Ford parked beyond Finglas, if petrol wasn't rationed. But I wasn't going to say that either.

'I think you're leaving it late in the evening to visit a patient. Did the Super advise you not to mention the Red Cow?'

He nodded. 'I was previously unaware of that oddly-named location.'

I put the key in the cell door. 'Then stay unaware. It's a quarry in the arse of nowhere, conveniently located just beyond the Dublin City boundaries.'

'How is that convenient?'

'If an inquest is needed on anyone found dead out there, the responsibility falls on a country doctor for whom excitement is more normally treating two cases of lumbago in the one week.'

I opened the cell door and let him enter first, hanging back to remain as unobtrusive as possible. Dillon wasn't curled in a ball on the floor tonight. He sat on a stool, staring at the far wall as intently as if it was a screen in the Metropole cinema. He didn't turn, but I knew from how his fingers gripped the stool that our approaching voices had worked him up into a frenzied state, which he was expending enormous amounts of nervous energy in trying to conceal. Dr Fairfax only spoke when he realised that Dillon was too scared to turn around.

'Mr Dillon?' he inquired politely. 'Do you wish to know who I am?'

'You've an educated accent,' Dillon replied. 'At least it means they've not sent an ignorant guttersnipe to shoot me.'

'What reason would I have to shoot you?'

Dillon started to shake slightly. 'My enemies never had the common decency to notify me of the alleged charges. You'd be surprised how many men get court-martialled in absentia. Stop trying my patience. If you've come to do it, just do it!'

The doctor placed a hand on his shoulder. 'Mr Dillon, turn around, please.'

Dillon recoiled from the touch. 'When I witnessed my first killing, the volunteer's hand shook so badly after seeing his victim's face that he made a dog's dinner of it. Blood and guts everywhere. So focus on my skull and aim. It's the coward's way but effective.'

'I'm here to kill nobody, although this is not the first time I've been called a coward.'

Dillon was sufficiently intrigued by the remark to relax his grip on the stool. 'How come?'

'If you have a big brother whose shadow is impossible to escape, you will always be viewed as the family coward. Last year, after my brother George was wounded at Dunkirk, having refused to leave that beach until every man under his command escaped on a small ship, the army added another bar to his Military Cross received in the Great War. A sane man of George's age would secure a safe posting, training recruits, but he needs to be in the thick of things. I don't know where he is though. Letters get censored. Since arriving in Ireland, I find that everything gets censored.'

His story engaged Dillon enough to make him turn and study the doctor's face. He gave me a dismissive glance, but I knew that my presence was helping to root him back into the reality of his present situation.

'Excuse my manner of welcome,' he said. 'I was miles away.'

'So I noticed,' Fairfax replied quietly.

'I was expecting a different type of caller.'

'Do I disappoint you?'

'All younger brothers disappoint. I also have a big brother who earned a Military Cross for gallantry in France.'

'I'm surprised,' Fairfax said, though I knew he wasn't. It was in the file that I had seen him study in advance. I knew it was there because I had taken the liberty of reading it myself two nights ago. On cold nights it was useful to know where the Superintendent kept the keys to his cabinet of files, because he also kept an opened bottle of whiskey there. 'I was told you are from an IRA family.'

'Much good it did us,' Dillon replied. 'My brother and I had barely finished fighting to restore peace when the Irish banks swooped on loans my father took out to keep his business going during the Tan War. After all his decades agitating for Irish freedom, the banks packed him back to America as a broken man.'

'One can accuse banks of many things,' Fairfax said. 'Sentimentality is rarely among them. Tell me about your brother.'

'Why?'

'Both our big brothers fought in the same war.'

'My brother fought in three wars.' I could see Dillon beginning to compose himself. 'Firstly as a British army captain enduring the horrors at the Somme. Not fighting for your empire, you understand? Fighting for the right of Ireland and all small nations to govern ourselves.'

'I don't doubt it.' Fairfax cautiously sat on the other stool, close to Dillon.

'You'd be wise not to,' Dillon warned him. 'My brother's fight for freedom never changed. Only his uniforms changed. He came home from France with a revolver that I took the liberty of relieving him of when I was fourteen. In the Tan War, Mick Collins made him Director of Intelligence and he was bloody good at it. In our Civil War he was a major general until he resigned, sick of the whole business.' Dillon stared belligerently at the doctor. 'So I win in any big-brother poker stakes. You English may have a king, but in needing to live up to a brother who fought in three wars, I hold three aces.'

'I yield the floor,' Fairfax conceded, though he would have agreed to anything to keep Dillon talking.

Dillon seemed mollified by his tone. 'Afterwards the politicians appointed him Clerk of the Dáil, but they didn't want him there. They just didn't know what else to do with him or any of us who had done their actual fighting. He could have enjoyed a sinecure for life if he'd stayed but you can't expect a panther to become a lapdog and so he just quit.'

Dillon paused as if the memories pained him.

'Do you know what he was doing the last time he set foot in an Irish barracks?' he asked. The doctor shook his head.

'He was bamboozling the Duty Officer at the Curragh Camp to buy a set of encyclopaedias for use in the Officers Mess. Imagine such a decorated officer being reduced to selling encyclopaedias door to door to feed his family! That night in the Curragh he could have sold a dozen sets, with so many old comrades turning up to get sozzled and buy him drink and recall old times. But his decency stopped him taking their charity. He slipped away before the black dog of drink took over.'

I didn't say a word but I could remember drinking in pubs in those uneasy years after the Civil War fizzled out and seeing Edward Dillon out on the razzle most nights, suffering from mood swings and jitters as he frequently cleared bars by waving a loaded gun that no one dared take off him.

'How is he now?' the doctor asked.

Dillon gave a laugh. 'That's the irony. He went off the rails at the start but is now as sound as a pound. My brother got lucky by managing to drink the madness out of himself. He drank himself stocious, then drank himself sane. He weaned himself off whiskey and got on with his life. But that's the way with big brothers; we never catch up. He has a big job in film distribution now, whereas I – who just tried to build an ordinary life for my family in those early years – ended up in here. Still, at least I know why I'm here. Apparently I'm insane. What's your excuse?'

'Perhaps I've come to kill you,' Fairfax said. 'Some minutes ago it's what you thought.'

Dillon shook his head. 'My thinking gets clouded when I'm sitting alone. I drown inside my own fear. You're no killer. You're English for a start.'

'Why would that stop me? You created your share of English widows.'

'I never pulled the trigger. My job was to finger the target.'

'Does that exonerate you?'

The enquiry was mildly put but I knew that Dillon would take umbrage.

'I don't seek exoneration. I did whatever Mick Collins asked of me. If you were Irish, like the latchico loitering in the doorway, I'd be more worried.' He nodded towards me. 'We Irish nurse our grudges. You English are a peculiarly forgiving race. You're not here to seek revenge. You're another posh doctor seeking a fee in guineas.'

The doctor drummed his fingers on the table. 'I could use five guineas. I suspect my lodgings on the North Circular Road were last painted during the Crimean War.'

'Where you lodge doesn't matter a damn,' Dillon replied. 'What's important is the location of your consulting rooms.'

Fairfax smiled. 'As it happens, I possess none.'

Dillon glanced in my direction again as if accusing me of bringing an amadán into his cell. 'The first thing any doctor needs is rooms. Preferably in Merrion or Fitzwilliam Square. Size doesn't matter as much as the address. I once tried to sell insurance but my business failed because I lacked the right address.'

He may have been suffering from mental aberration but Dillon's businessman's acumen remained spot on. I was thinking of William Coleman, a dodgy electrician I used to drink with before he served three years in the Joy for arson and fraud. Coleman was now using the veneer of a respectable address in Merrion Square to set himself up as a medical practitioner, specialising in curing venereal disease, masturbation, superfluous hair growth, inferiority complexes, impotence and constipation – all of which was a cover for his real business as a clandestine abortionist.

Dillon was staring at the doctor in puzzlement. 'How do you hope to get patients?' he asked.

'My patients are here,' Fairfax explained. 'I'm not in private practice. I've come to Ireland to work solely in this asylum.'

Dillon glanced over, as if inviting me to share his incredulity. 'But why?'

'Because I'm a psychiatrist.'

Dillon's own afflictions seemed forgotten. His tone became that of a man of the world. 'The Hippocratic Oath contains no vow of poverty. I'm told that the consultant who declared me insane was affronted when asked to reduce his fee. He refused because he's a doctor first, but a shrewd businessman second.'

Fairfax nodded, as if accepting this reproach. 'Perhaps I lack his acumen. That man certainly won't starve.'

Dillon's voice lost its purposeful tone and grew fretful. 'But my wife and children may. I was a good provider until my enemies started to close in.' He glared at me. 'Either come in or go, but stop blocking the doorway. I want the door locked.'

'Mr Dillon,' the doctor said. 'You are safe here. I've heard of people trying to break out of asylums, but I never heard of anyone trying to break into one.'

'You don't know the men who want me dead. They will go to any lengths.'

'Do you know them?' the doctor asked. 'Do you know their names?'

'I'll know their faces when they come.'

'Trust me, Grangegorman is harder to break out of – or into – than any jail.'

'My brother broke into a jail once and barely escaped with his life. We tried to rescue a friend, using a hijacked armoured car.'

'Did you succeed?'

Dillon gave him a cold stare. 'Englishmen who ask too many questions in Dublin often have one thing in common.'

'Which is?'

'They end up shot.' But Dillon's tone was more defensive than confrontational. He sighed as if even the act of talking exhausted him. 'No offence. I'm not partial to questions. I'm just saying that walls are more porous than you think.'

'Not these walls, Mr Dillon. They seem to me to have been built not to keep assassins out but, as a woman said to me on the boat here, to keep secrets locked in. Why not judge for yourself? How often have you stepped outside your cell?'

'I feel safer here,' Dillon replied. 'No disrespect to my fellow lunatics but they're not a social circle I wish to mix in. A man needs to retain some dignity.'

'He also needs to stretch his legs. Please, walk with me. It will help to orientate you to your surroundings.'

'I've no need to. I don't intend staying long.' Behind Dillon's protestations I sensed his fear of any situation he could not control.

'I hope you're not here for long either,' Fairfax replied. 'But getting your physical bearings may help you regain your mental ones. Shall we risk a short walk? Even just to look out at the exercise yard. Gus will be with us. There's no need to be afraid.'

'Who says I'm afraid?'

Fairfax had deliberately struck a nerve. Whatever about backseat bingo, I decided I wouldn't fancy playing him in chess. Dillon pushed past me to glance with some timidity down the empty corridor.

'It's late in the evening, Colonel.' I addressed him for the first time. 'Most patients are in their wards. Grangegorman is never quiet, but this is as silent as it gets.'

He seemed to be trying to decide whether he was being led into a trap, then summoned the courage to step out into the narrow corridor. He tried to strike a jovial tone. 'Lead on. We'll inspect the troops, even if they're unfit for battle.'

I walked ahead, unsure of where Fairfax intended us to go or if the Superintendent would approve of this excursion. But it wasn't my place to intervene, just to observe. Dillon's footsteps grew hesitant as we passed a row of cell doors. I wondered what memories such corridors conjured up? The interrogation cells in

Wellington Barracks, when he and his friends ruled the roost, using boots and fists during the Civil War? The basement of Oriel House – headquarters of the Criminal Investigation Department – which acquired such a reputation that people crossed to the far pavement on Great Brunswick Street to avoid passing it? These had been places of interrogation where Dillon was in total control. Here he lacked control. This seemed to cause deep unease. I suspected he would have bolted back to his cell except that he didn't want to lose face in front of this Englishman.

I unlocked a door into a wider corridor. The air was fresher here, although nowhere in this asylum could you escape from unsavoury smells and the distant cries of patients. There was dampness in the air but also an odour of dread like a foretaste of purgatory. I unlocked a door that led into a dimly lit yard. Dillon peered out, reluctant to venture further.

'I got the shivers the first time I set foot in an asylum,' he said.

'Where was that?' Fairfax asked.

'Portrane. Two months after Bloody Sunday.'

The doctor sounded surprised. 'Your file doesn't indicate that you were ever a patient there.'

'I never said I was. Mick Collins ordered me to slip out and quietly bring five Squad members back to Dublin.'

'What were they doing in an asylum?'

Dillon stared out into the yard. 'Dancing. Or at least at first just dancing. People forget how young we were. Young men like to dance with girls but we'd have been fools to go dancing in Dublin when our descriptions were circulated by Dublin Castle spies. You never knew who might be watching or when you might fall into the clutches of Eugene Igoe.'

'I've heard that name before somewhere,' the doctor said.

Dillon turned. 'You heard him called a different name, when your daddy scared you with tales of the bogeyman. Igoe was a bastard detective who liked inflicting pain. Some nights he haunts my sleep still. It was to get away from Castle savages like him that Joe Dolan and four other lads gate-crashed a staff dance at Portrane Asylum. Just for devilment. Portrane is a godforsaken spot, but it felt safe, miles from anywhere. They could let their hair down and try to get a wiggle on with the nurses. Joe was a ducky shincracker on the dancefloor. He was cooking with gas with some girl when an attendant got shirty because she was his mot and Joe lost his rag. I'm not saying who was to blame. Joe had nerves of steel when needed, no better man to sidle up behind a target and pull a trigger. But he had a temper when he let down his guard. The asylum staff tried to give him the bum's rush and Dolan took it bad. Too much whiskey involved, downed by the neck. Not that I knew much about whiskey back then. I never touched a drop until after the Truce.'

Fairfax risked provoking him. 'Your file suggests you took to it with a convert's zeal.'

I saw the change in Dillon's manner.

'My drinking is none of your business.'

'My business is to make you well.'

Dillon shook his head. 'Insulin injections will make me well. Your job is to keep me safe.'

'From whom?'

'Those who want me dead. You don't understand. You never lived through a Civil War.'

'I only arrived in France not long before the Armistice but I saw my share of horror. Twice as many men died there on any given day as during your entire Civil War.'

'The Great War was different. Your enemies weren't friends whom you once thought you could trust. The Great War was barbaric, but at least you knew which trench your enemy would come from.' Dillon turned to me. 'For the love of Jesus, close this door. You have us framed like sitting ducks for any sniper.'

I bolted the door without a word, intrigued by where this conversation might lead. The doctor addressed Dillon.

'If you're not safe in here, where are you safe?'

'Nowhere. How do I know that a gunman didn't get himself admitted as a patient, instructed to smuggle in a weapon and await his chance?'

'Yesterday I visited the attics here and saw what patients bring in and what they leave behind when they die,' Fairfax said. 'Handbags, crammed with rosary beads, Miraculous Medals, photos of children, letters beseeching families to visit. I've found every type of heartache when I looked through those handbags but I've never found a gun. If you don't believe me, come and look for yourself.'

I'm not sure who was more surprised at this suggestion – myself or Dillon. I knew those attics well. They were my retreat when I wished to be alone with someone special. Otherwise I avoided them, because while I had grown immune to the overcrowded bedlam in the wards, something about those silent attics unnerved me. I saw how the thought also unnerved Dillon.

'Are you saying you're mad enough to risk going up there with a certified lunatic?'

'I'm not mad,' the doctor replied calmly. 'Nor, I believe, are you.' He turned to me. 'Have you a key for up there?'

I shook the keyring attached to my belt. 'I've a key to everything except Betty Grable's heart. It's a bit of a climb, however.'

'That shouldn't be a problem.' He turned to Dillon. 'You're a young man still and it won't be the first time you climbed a flight of stairs.'

This was an unfortunate choice of words or Fairfax was a sly bastard, I thought as I led them down a passageway to the backstairs. All of Dublin knew that on Bloody Sunday Dillon had guided two assassins up several flights of stairs in a lodging house in Pembroke

Street. But I could not tell what memories were triggered for Dillon by our steep climb up the bare attic stairs. We reached a door, which I unlocked, and flicked the light switch. The attics were lit by two bare lightbulbs. Dust-laden shelves stretched in all directions, so that it resembled a vast library. But instead of books, the shelves contained rows of handbags, each containing the remnants of a life. I'm not superstitious. I've enjoyed sex on summer nights in Goldenbridge Cemetery, knowing it's a spot where I am unlikely to be disturbed. The dead don't frighten me, but even though I use these attics for my own private purposes, their melancholic aura was such that my instincts urged me to flee. The doctor ran his finger over a layer of dust on one handbag and asked Dillon to open it.

'I will not.' Dillon seemed equally rattled by the gloom. 'I'm no grave robber.'

'You're a trained intelligence officer,' Fairfax replied. 'Well versed in piecing clues together. So open it and tell me if its owner was mad.'

Dillon opened the bag slowly and spread out its contents: two sets of rosary beads; a tiny bottle that once contained cheap perfume and a faded photograph of three children, although the image was so wrinkled from being constantly held in someone's hand that it was hard to distinguish their features. There was an unfinished letter, beseeching someone to visit and, most poignantly of all, a door key. Fairfax watched Dillon lightly finger it.

'There's always a door key, isn't there, Gus?'

'I couldn't rightly say,' I replied. 'I'm never up here. We take people's personal possessions when they are admitted and promise to return everything when they're discharged. It would be heartless to suggest they bin their front door key because they'll probably never use it again.'

Dillon was reading the unfinished letter. The childlike handwriting showed signs that the writer was crippled by arthritis.

Reaching deep into the purse he produced a tiny set of discoloured silver teaspoons. He looked at me. 'How can you say you're not heartless if you work here?'

'The system is heartless,' I said. 'That doesn't mean the staff are. We do our best, knowing our best isn't enough.'

I didn't bother explaining how we rarely took away people's rosary beads, but there was little room on the wards for anything else that might be stolen or cause confusion over who owned it. Possessions on any ward got mixed up. Amid the daily chaos it was deemed best for bags to be stored up here when patients were admitted, where nobody could rifle through them. Often many were only ever opened one more time, when some attendant needed to add in any small personal effects that patients had on them when they died. I recognised this set of teaspoons as belonging to a Mrs McGrath, originally from Rathmines. Her last of many addresses was a flat in Buckingham Street, as her husband drank his way through her small savings. These teaspoons were the last wedding present she managed to hold onto, after he pawned every other possession. She had kept them hidden away in her clothes when he had her committed. I used to occasionally sneak them down to her ward because she found a curious comfort in caressing and polishing them. Families had a right to claim these bags, but very often – like her husband – they didn't even bother claiming their relations' bodies. I was not obliged to attend funerals but I made it my business, out of respect, to attend my fair share over the years here, each one lonelier than the last.

Dillon uneasily put the set of spoons put back in the bag. He pointed at shoes on the shelf beside it. 'Are these this woman's shoes?'

'I don't know if they started off as hers,' I told him. 'But they were her shoes when she died.'

Dillon looked at the doctor. 'Why did you bring me up here?'

'To show that I don't think you are irreparably insane. If I did, would I risk it?'

'Are you saying that the doctor who declared me mad defrauded the government?'

'I'm saying you're suffering from a delayed response to deep trauma. It may not be irreversible. Temporary insanity can be cured. That doctor's stark diagnosis let your old comrades appease their conscience by ensuring your family doesn't starve. But how often do those comrades visit you?'

Dillon was silent for a moment. 'Not every night. Often they come in such numbers that there's barely room for them all to fit in my cell. We have great chats, such lucid conversations about the merits of the Peter the Painter Mauser pistol over the Colt .45 that I ask myself, why am I locked up? Then I look around at their young faces and realise that every second man there is dead. So, you see, Doctor, I have moments of great lunacy as well as this present moment of clarity. I have no real idea who has been to see me. Most days I'm as confused as the patients in Portrane on the night Collins sent me there and I saw something I could scarcely believe.'

'What was that?'

'The true face of insanity.' Dillon paused, as if still stunned by the memory. 'But not from the scared cowering inmates. I saw it in five young men whom I'd trust with my life. Like I said, there was whiskey involved when they gate-crashed the staff dance, but this went beyond drunkenness. Joe Dolan was the ringleader. Normally cool as a cucumber. I remember him killing a British officer outside the Wicklow Hotel and strolling into the hotel an hour later to eat lunch. But he could fly off the handle too. We saw it on Bloody Sunday when Joe's target wasn't in his lodgings in Ranelagh and the only person in that British officer's bed was his mistress, cowering half naked and begging for mercy even before Dolan started to beat her to within an inch of her life. She was just a strumpet and she was lucky that Joe only stole her jewellery. But he was so enraged that he set fire to other rooms in that house, filled with women and children. Volunteers had to drag Dolan away and start a water-bucket chain to stop the place burning down. He was out of order on Bloody Sunday, though I could excuse his behaviour then, because he was psyched up to kill.'

He looked around at the stacks of possessions left over from forgotten lives and shivered. 'Why the hell am I telling you all this? I demand to be returned to my cell.'

'Gus will bring you back when you wish,' Fairfax assured him. 'But it's good to talk. At least tonight you know you're talking to people who are real.'

'Do I?' Dillon shook his head. 'What was your phrase? Temporary insanity. That's what I witnessed in Portrane. Joe's behaviour there was different from Bloody Sunday. Ordinarily the Squad never drank: you need teetotal discipline to be alert to danger. But maybe that constant stress only hits you when the pressure is off. Joe and the others had just been throwing shapes at first to impress the nurses. But it spiralled out of hand, the nurses so terrified that the lads had to be bundled into a padded cell. By the time I reached Portrane, the lads had slashed the walls of that cell with their knives. Gazing through the spyhole I barely recognised my friends because, just for one night, the stress we lived under drove them stark raving mad.'

The doctor opened his cigarette case to offer Dillon a fag. I made a slight movement, knowing this would cause him to offer me one, though I resisted the urge to smoke it now. I wondered how much of this conversation to relay to the Superintendent. None, I decided. Fairfax waited until Dillon took a long drag before he spoke.

'How was your friend, Mr Dolan, afterwards?'

'Joe?' Dillon looked up. 'Oh, sound as a pound once he sobered up. He has an important job now. A pillar of society. All the Squad did well for ourselves, except poor Tom Cullen, found drowned in a lake, and Frank Teeling, who served jail time in '23 for shooting a man dead in the Theatre Royal bar, although Teeling claimed it was in self-defence.'

'Was the man in the theatre armed?'

'In a manner of speaking.'

I said nothing as I savoured the rich smoke from Dillon's cigarette and hid my unsmoked fag beside a distinctive handbag where I would be able to find it when I had the privacy to visit these attics again. Other treats were also secreted away here. It wasn't my place to tell the doctor that the only thing the murdered man in the Theatre Royal had been carrying was a bag of tomatoes to which Teeling had inexplicably taken exception. His frayed nerves had already made him such a loose cannon that he had accidentally shot dead a fellow Free State officer two months before the Theatre Royal murder.

'If Teeling served jail time it was his own fault,' Dillon added. 'The government had already offered him a gratuity to disappear to Australia and dry out on the voyage. We'd paid a high price to establish peace and you couldn't just go around shooting people at will.'

'Unless they were Jews.' The words were out before I realised I'd spoken aloud. Dillon glanced at me sharply.

'I'm not addressing you. I'm speaking to the doctor, who is an educated man.'

'Sorry, boss.' I focused my gaze on my boots. But Fairfax picked up a tension in the air.

'What Jew are you referring to?' he asked me.

I shrugged, knowing I had strayed into dangerous turf. 'I spoke out of turn. If you wish to stay here talking, I may need to leave, Sir. I've other duties to attend to.'

'No one leaves till we all leave.' Dillon glared at me. 'You'd better not be accusing Commandant Jimmy Conroy of murder. He was never found guilty of any crime.'

'Who am I to accuse anyone of anything?' I replied guardedly.

Dillon studied my face. 'You're too fond of giving lip and you remind me of someone. Have we ever met outside of here?'

I shook my head. Mollified, Dillon turned to the doctor. 'There was a lot of heavy drinking after the fighting stopped. None of us were sure if the Civil War was over or not. We didn't know what to think. Up to then we'd never had to think about things, we just felt them. War is terrifying but the smouldering quiet after one is more unnerving, with nobody sure what comes next. This blaggard here is wrong to accuse Jimmy Conroy of deliberately murdering Jews. By 1923 Jimmy didn't know who he was shooting at. He and his father fought in Easter Week and few volunteers were as close to Collins. If a few Jews were accidentally shot, Jimmy's mind was astray by then. We snuck him away to the States. He was part of Collins's Squad and we looked after our own.'

'Even by letting someone get away with murdering an innocent Jew?'

Dillon shrugged defensively. 'They crucified our Lord and Saviour.'

If they did, it wasn't on the tiny streets of Little Jerusalem off the South Circular Road, I thought to myself, but stayed schtum.

'I'm no theologian,' Fairfax said. 'But I thought our Lord and Saviour was a Jew.'

'Being born in a stable doesn't make you a donkey,' Dillon retorted. 'Our new archbishop in Dublin has preached that you'll find Jews engaged in practically every movement against Our Divine Lord and his Church. Archbishop McQuaid is a learned scholar. He has preached that the Jews are in league with the Freemasons, but you're probably a Freemason yourself.'

The doctor shook his head. 'In another disappointment to my father, I've never worn Masonic garb or spoken on the square. How does your archbishop's sermon explain away what your friend Conroy thought he was doing?'

'In ambushes you haven't got time to think,' Dillon said.

'Are you saying that a Jewish man ambushed him?'

'Yes, although not personally.'

Fairfax looked puzzled. 'I don't follow your meaning.'

'A Jewish dentist ambushed a lady friend of Conroy's. Ambushed her sexually.'

'In what way?'

'Jesus, do you need every sordid detail? The dentist didn't come across with the agreed cash following an intimate transaction. I had no interest in the class of women Conroy went with, but I don't judge how another man takes his comfort. He wasn't the only man in Beggar's Bush barracks she went with. Some of them got affronted on her behalf. They just took things too far and blamed every Jew for his behaviour.' He glanced sharply at me. 'I've forgotten the details but I bet this blaggard remembers.'

'I never read about it, boss.' My tone was deliberately non-committal. I wasn't going to mention the night in the Palace Bar when the artist Harry Kernoff told me about leaving a little Jewish club with some friends after a night playing cards. Two National Army officers had appeared behind them, shouting vile names before opening fire. Harry fled down a lane but his friend

Emmanuel Kahn was shot dead, trying to run down Stammer Street. Another friend was left scarred, by a bullet in his shoulder and a paralysing fear of venturing out at night again. Kahn's murder occurred two weeks after another Jew was shot dead when three army officers on St Stephen's Green asked him his religion. His brother, who escaped later, found three bullet holes in his coat, which had been flapping open. Harry Kernoff only spoke to me once about those events, but every Jew knew that Conroy was involved, with another army officer who slipped away to New Zealand before his case came to trial. 'I only ever read the sporting pages in newspapers,' I said. 'And only then if St James's Gate go on a cup run.'

'The newspapers got it wrong,' Dillon said. 'I doubt if Conroy remembered anything after he sobered up. After Collins's death Jimmy was constantly drunk, imagining ambushes everywhere. He was a gladiator. When killing needs doing, you need gladiators. When peace comes, they fester, frustrated they're not allowed do the one thing they're trained for.'

'So you just ship him off to America?'

Dillon shrugged uncomfortably. 'He did more than his share for Ireland, plugging so many men that Collins could see how Jimmy's nerves were falling apart. Collins sent Conroy to America to rest up. But the Clan na Gael Yanks we entrusted him to couldn't handle his drinking. They shipped him home to us and we were glad to have him back when the Civil War started. He was with my brother in Béal na Bláth when Collins was shot. I think that's when he lost the head entirely. Collins was the only man he looked up to. He took a few pot shots at Jews during a drinking spree, but that's all it was: a spree and not a pogrom. No one was more disgusted than his fellow officers, but we couldn't let the police arrest him.'

'Why not?' the doctor asked.

'Arresting him would have been a political decision. The Squad were above politics. We despised politicians. What Ireland needed to rebuild its self-respect were heroes. The public loved to think of us as an elite squad. If one of us was exposed as a drunken gurrier, how might people see the rest of us? Some volunteers on Bloody Sunday had the shakes so bad that bullets flew everywhere. The public don't want such details. Our deeds brought an empire to its knees. That's how it had to stay in the public mind, even if it meant sneaking Conroy back to America for the second time to let the Yanks dry him out. To do anything else would have caused scandal. And Conroy was an exception. Maybe the Devil got into Joe Dolan that night in Portrane, but even the best of us sometimes need a spree to clear the head.'

The doctor glanced around at the shelves of unclaimed keepsakes. 'This strategy doesn't seem to have worked for you.'

Dillon shrugged. 'Not for lack of trying. Are those cigarettes rationed?'

Fairfax opened his case. I took the opportunity to procure another fag without waiting to be asked. With the doctor focused on watching Dillon inhale deeply, I hid mine beside the first one.

'Maybe I'm not cut out for heavy drinking. Lads like Joe Dolan, trained to pull a trigger, could release their tension on sprees. I was trained to keep secrets in.'

'It didn't stop you writing a book about your exploits.'

Dillon shrugged. 'I wasn't long married and thought it might somehow be therapeutic, help me rid myself of stuff bothering me. But it wasn't because you can't write about such things. I also thought it might earn a few bob. But people prefer to read the book that some woman ghost-wrote for Dan Breen. More blood and less intelligence. There's no money in books unless you're good at killing.'

'And were you?'

It was cold in the attics before the doctor's question but the guarded look in Dillon's eyes seemed to plunge the temperature below freezing. He stubbed out his cigarette.

'My life is none of your business,' he replied icily.

'You're my patient.'

'A doctor is not a confessor. You deal in drugs, not absolution. I wish to be taken back to my cell.'

I rose to leave, anxious to end this conversation and get away from there. But the doctor wasn't done yet.

'I borrowed your book from the Superintendent,' he said. 'It ends in triumphant euphoria the week the Truce is signed. You and other Squad members go on a holiday to the Isle of Man, where you can let yourselves be carefree young men at last. The weight of war is off your shoulders; the funfairs and amusement parks are glorious, the victory you have achieved is glorious and on the last page you paint a future destined to be glorious.'

'That was how life felt that week.'

'Your book ends there but the fighting doesn't. After the Treaty it gets more vicious, with you fighting among yourselves.'

'Not Collins's men,' Dillon insisted. 'We stayed loyal to Mick.'

'Collins dies in your brother's arms. Why doesn't your book deal with that?'

Dillon glared at him. 'Who would thank me for writing about that? Nobody wants to read about a civil war. The glorious things I wanted to remember I put in my book. Anything I wanted to forget I stowed away in a cardboard suitcase in an attic inside my mind. But it feels like rats have got in, because every night I hear them scurry overhead, gnawing through the cardboard, letting the bad memories spill out. That's all I'm going to say.'

'Maybe those memories need dealing with?' Fairfax suggested. 'Maybe keeping them secret is what has you in here?'

Dillon glanced at me. 'I'm here because this bastard kidnapped me from my home.'

I'd had enough of this. 'I don't mind being called a bastard,' I said, 'but I object to being called a kidnapper. It makes me sound like the men who abducted Noel Lemass when he was peaceably walking down a Dublin street.'

'I'll not be interrogated by a guttersnipe.' Dillon turned to the doctor. 'Nor by an English pacifist, dodging the Hitler war by skulking off to Dublin like a scared dog.'

Fairfax stood up. 'Insult me with any slur you like. My father will have already beaten you to it.'

'I may be mad,' Dillon replied, 'but I made my father proud. I served my country. I won my war.'

'But lost your peace of mind. I see a soul in torment.'

Dillon rose to his full height. 'You see a colonel.'

'The government clipped your wings,' the doctor said. 'Demoted to being an adjutant at Baldonnel Aerodrome. Which is more forsaken: Portrane or Baldonnel?'

'They shafted every man loyal to Collins,' Dillon said bitterly.

'Despite everything that you did in their name?'

Dillon nodded.

'But what exactly did you do?'

Dillon stared at Fairfax. 'I'm here for medication, you sly bastard, not interrogation.'

Fairfax shrugged. 'If that's what you want, you can be drugged to your eyeballs and released to sit at home like a zombie. Medication blocks things out until you've almost forgotten your own name.'

'Maybe I've things I want to forget. If so, they're my own business, so go to hell.'

The doctor put a hand on Dillon's hunched shoulder. 'Mr Dillon, I'm trying to take you out of your private hell.'

'Only God decides who goes to hell.'

Fairfax glanced at a heap of unclaimed rosary beads. 'Maybe God is no help to you in here.'

Dillon snorted. 'That's great. So you're an atheist too. And a Protestant one.'

'I'm just saying, sometimes we end up imprisoned by mental chains that only we can free ourselves from.'

'How the hell would you know what I feel?'

The doctor nodded. 'That's a valid point, Colonel. You risked your life to earn your rank. They commissioned me as a Second Lieutenant the day I left public school. My social class was deemed sufficient to put me in charge of men who knew far more about life than me.' The doctor paused. 'If you don't mind me saying, your Bloody Sunday executions were rather haphazard.'

'We had to get in and out fast,' Dillon replied. 'I make no apologies.'

'I saw a young Irish lad executed at dawn for cowardice in France, with his killing carried out according to the rule book. The prisoners stood upright, feet tied twelve inches apart. But he was no coward; it was the horrors of war that caused his mental derangement. I lost my faith in all armies on that day. I now fight invisible battles with afflicted men like you, nightmare by nightmare, ghost by ghost.'

'You're saying you became a psychiatrist to assuage your guilt,' Dillon replied. 'Well, assuage your guilt on someone else.'

Fairfax smiled. 'Maybe that's our difference. You can't face your guilt.'

'I've nothing to feel guilty about,' Dillon retorted.

'You nurse it so deep inside that all you have left is guilt. Your knuckles are white from gripping on it.'

Dillon switched his focus to me. 'Why did you bring me up to this attic?'

'I didn't,' I said. 'The doctor did. To show you that no guns are hidden here.'

'There's more than one kind of trap. Tell him I don't blab to British spies.'

'Why don't you tell him yourself?'

'I'm speaking to you because you work here. This gadfly is just a fly by night.'

'I look through your spyhole and I see a curled-up ball of fear,' Fairfax said. But he was addressing Dillon's back as the patient unsteadily made for the steep stairs. 'What harm can it do to talk to me?'

Dillon beckoned me. 'Tell this man to dig up Vincent Fovargue's corpse and ask it what talking leads to.'

The doctor walked behind us, trying to reason with him. 'Mr Dillon ... Colonel ... the Superintendent wants to fry your brain. But I've seen electroconvulsive therapy turn men into zombies. Is that what you want?'

Dillon turned at the top of the steps. 'I want to be treated as a prisoner of war. I'll tell you my name, rank and number. Nothing else.'

'Your war is in your head. I want to help.'

'How do I know you didn't bring me up here to try and stage my death?'

Dillon trembled as he spoke. I stepped in front so that I would be the first man descending the stairs. If he fell and broke his neck there would be hell to pay with the Superintendent, though I knew men who would feel that he had got his just desserts. But I was taking no chances because I lived by my own moral code. I made no claims to being a good man. I kept my eye out for anything that could be filched or any pleasure that could be snatched. But even if only a cog in this asylum, I felt a duty of care to the souls in here. I was relieved to feel Dillon's trembling hand reach out to grip my shoulder as we made our descent in that dim light, leaving Dr Fairfax standing at the attic entrance, staring down. Dillon kept murmuring the same phrase, though I couldn't tell if he was addressing the doctor or me or himself.

'How can I be sure of anything anymore?'

Thirteen

Nolan

Asylum time

The Colonel may have been asleep when I entered his cell. I've seen men sleep in here with their eyes open and others not seem to sleep at all. Colonel Dillon was slumped upright. Either he had dozed off like this, his back to the door, or he was staring at an unseen figure who he imagined to be standing against the far wall. I had to cough twice before he turned to take in my presence, holding a bowl of stew that I had covered with a pilfered dishcloth to try and keep it warm. He nodded, as if slowly coming to his senses. I placed the bowl on the table.

'I entered the kitchens to ensure no funny business. If this is poisoned, then we're all doomed because I saw the cook ladle it himself from the pot.' I sniffed at whatever aroma wafted up. 'It's some class of stew ... well, the usual class of stew.'

'Thank you,' the colonel said. 'Just leave it there.'

'I'd like to see you eat it.'

He gesticulated impatiently. 'What difference does it make to you?'

'None, but ...'

'But what?'

I could envisage him in his prime, dismissive of any underling who dared question him.

'It's just ...' I struggled for words to not make my request seem like an impertinence. 'Before you arrived I felt totally alone in here and I'll be alone when you leave. But having you to talk to makes me feel like I'm someone again, a man who served his country. Nobody in here sees me like that, but you knew me from way back, if only in passing. We're both veterans. It would mean a lot if you showed enough trust to eat the food I bring you.'

He nodded. 'It's not that I don't trust you, Nolan, but I'm beyond hunger.'

'Just try a few spoonfuls, Colonel.'

I could see how ravenous he was, how torn between hunger and paranoia. He sat on the stool and steered the spoon gingerly.

'You saw the cook pour this?'

'I swear.'

He risked a spoonful, grimacing at the taste.

'It's barely edible. Still, I suppose if he wanted to poison me he'd serve something tasty.'

'There's no fear of that.' I watched him begin to rapidly spoon the stew inside him. 'The cook's stew never changes, though they say that on Good Friday he adds holy water instead of dishwater. If you die of anything from his food, it won't be of surprise.'

Looking up, he rewarded me with a laugh. 'It's warm and we survived on worse rations during the Tan War. What's it like compared to food in Dartmoor?'

'However the English built their empire,' I replied, 'it wasn't with their menus.'

He nodded. 'Spotted Dick wouldn't have got them too far in Calcutta. Instead they divided and conquered, using slaughter, starvation, torture, deceit, brute force and missionaries brandishing the bastardised King James Bible.' He inspected what remained in his bowl. 'This slop isn't far off the soup they tried to tempt starving Irish people with during the Famine – a bowl in exchange for your soul if you'd commit the mortal sin of attending a Protestant service.'

'My family starved but we never took soup in church,' I assured him. 'I'm sure your family were no soupers either.'

He nodded again. 'My grandfather escaped the Great Hunger on a coffin ship. He never spoke to my father about the sights he saw, skeletal figures dead in ditches, mouths green from chewing grass. He didn't have to say it: my father picked up those horrors from his silences. It made Pop determined to move to Ireland and fight to rectify those wrongs.'

'I remember your da,' I said. 'We didn't hear many Yankee accents in Drumcondra. I remember your mother too, her great style of dressing.'

A hint of caution crossed his face. 'You never said you were from Drumcondra.'

'Remember the small cottages near the Tolka?'

'I remember they used to flood.'

'If they didn't, my parents couldn't have afforded the rent,' I said. 'I played football once against your big brother – girls sitting pitch-side, hoping to catch his attention. He'd have given Rudolph Valentino a run for his money. It surely broke your father's heart when he enlisted in the British Army.'

'My brother liked to be in the thick of things,' the colonel replied, 'whether at the Somme or Béal na Bláth. He made me a pall-bearer at Collins's funeral, though some said this was only because I was his kid brother.'

'Still, you were centre stage at Collins's funeral. I was so jostled among the crowd that I barely glimpsed his coffin.'

'But if you were there that day,' he said, 'it means you were on our side.'

'Is that how you still see the world?' I asked. 'Divided in two?'

The colonel shook his head as if having to explain to a child. 'There were more than two sides. We hated the Irregulars, but hated the new officers the government appointed to ride roughshod over us even more. With Collins gone, who could you trust?' He inspected the stew. 'You're certain the cook put nothing in this?'

'He only adds meat during Board of Guardians visits,' I said. 'When I got released from Dartmoor I still thought we were all on the one side. The screws gave me my boat fare and not a penny more. I didn't mind going hungry because I remembered the jubilant scenes after the 1916 prisoners were released – men hoisted on shoulders. I didn't expect that big a welcome but I thought I'd get some welcome.'

'I'm sure Collins sent someone,' he said.

I nodded, remembering my walk down the quays before Collins's legman grabbed my shoulder and said, 'Jaysus, Jimmy, what the fuck did they do to you?' He took me into the Liffey Bar and left me in the snug while I heard him telephone Collins to say how fierce shook I looked, my hands shaking each time I tried to lift my pint. He'd had the decency not to mention how I'd soiled myself with fright when he put his hand on my shoulder.

'Collins's legmen brought me straight here and told the Super to sort me out.'

'You were admitted off the boat?' the colonel asked.

I nodded. 'Only for four weeks at first. I longed to get home, but when I got there, that cottage in Drumcondra didn't feel like home. I hated my family seeing me so broken, when the younger ones once looked up to me. They never turned me away but I destroyed their peace, shouting in my sleep. I left home, thinking I'd another family – my fellow volunteers. But every old comrade asked the question you asked – what side was I on now? I didn't want a side. I wanted the kinship we'd known when risking our lives together. I'd never given much thought to what a republic looked like. Why would I, when we had older leaders to do the thinking?'

The colonel nodded. 'The Squad didn't like the Treaty, but if Collins accepted it as the best on offer it was good enough for us.'

'That was easy for you,' I said. 'You knew Mick personally. The Squad were paid more than my father earned as a labourer. Ordinary volunteers never saw a penny but we were at his beck and call. I didn't even know what Collins looked like until a Dartmoor screw showed me a photo of him, leading the Irish delegation into Downing Street. Everything changed while I was getting kicked to a pulp in Dartmoor. Now half my friends were kitted out in National Army uniforms, with the rest slouching about in trench coats, muttering about having been sold a pup and bunking in with Rory O'Connor's breakaway Four Courts faction.'

'Friendships were shattered,' the colonel admitted, 'but we all had to decide.'

It was simple for him, I thought. He hadn't needed to flit around, trying to find food, too broken to follow Collins's argument about accepting an oath or the arguments of hard men talking about the need to establish a military dictatorship to force British troops back onto the streets. All I could do was bunk down anywhere I could, listening to some lads argue that the army was answerable to the government, and others that the government was answerable to the army, and we volunteers were not answerable to the living but to the dead.

'I couldn't decide,' I said. 'I walked the streets by day, hoping that a pal could sneak me into Beggars Bush barracks at night for food and shelter. But I never saw such drinking as went on there. I remembered you all being so disciplined once.'

'I never drank until we visited the Isle of Man,' the colonel said. 'Once you start it's hard to stop. Joe Dolan bought me my first whiskey, the others laughing as I spluttered when it burnt my throat.'

'How long did it take to get used to whiskey?' I asked.

'The murder of several friends. There's something trustworthy in a 70 per cent proof bottle. After Collins died, whiskey was often the only company I felt comfortable in.'

'Beggars Bush was full of men arguing all night, quaffing requisitioned whiskey,' I said. 'When it ran out, many wandered over to visit pals in the Four Courts, taking guns with them. At first nobody seemed sure where anyone else stood.'

'You never visited Oriel House so. Collins's intelligence staff stayed true to a man.'

'Nobody visited Oriel House voluntarily,' I replied. 'Black arts were rumoured to be practised there and in Wellington Barracks.'

'Black lies were told about us.'

'And printed on handbills pasted around Drumcondra.'

He glared at me, his voice suddenly defensive. 'Are you making an accusation?'

I shook my head. 'Stumbling across dead bodies during the Civil War taught me to keep my mouth shut.'

'Then keep it shut. The lies spread about me have me in here.'

'And not your conscience?'

'I sleep sound. Only my brain gets addled.'

'I wanted my brain to stop being addled back then,' I said. 'Especially when new sentries at Beggars Bush turned me away. I was neither fish nor fowl, scared to enter the Four Courts but more scared of being left on my own.'

'Why didn't you enlist in the National Army?' the colonel asked.

'I tried to,' I said. 'The recruiting room was as packed as a dockers' read. No idealism there, just unemployed young men with no notion of soldiering, attracted by the wages. It's no wonder so many of your casualties were self-inflicted, with fellows not knowing one end of a rifle from the other. When I reached the top of the queue, the recruiting sergeant stared through me, because I was shaking uncontrollably. He said that whatever class of work I was doing before, it certainly wasn't fighting and he needed lads who won't faint at the sight of blood. I wanted to say that I'd probably done more fighting than him and more killing too, but the whole queue of greenhorns sniggered and I just turned and walked away.'

'You should have asked for an officer who could vouch for you.'

I shook my head. 'He was right. I was a busted flush. I didn't belong in that new army with shining uniforms. My pal from Beggars Bush had defected to the Four Courts and so I crawled over a bridge under sniper fire, hoping he'd vouch for me.'

'You fought in the Four Courts?' the colonel asked accusingly.

I shook my head. 'Fighting was beyond me. I just wanted to feel like I belonged somewhere. I'd try to look tough in the doorway of local shops where lads requisitioned anything not nailed down, telling the shopkeepers to claim the cost back from Arthur Griffith in Dáil Éireann.'

I was cautious now, sensing him analysing my words for any hint of betrayal. I remembered how passionate the atmosphere was in the Four Courts, but also chaotic. Some volunteers diligently fortified the building with sandbags and leather-bound documents and others just did whatever they wished. One day I casually mentioned how I'd never set foot in the Wicklow Mountains. Seán MacBride and Ernie O'Malley beckoned me out onto Chancery Lane. They flagged down a motorist and requisitioned his car, saying they wanted to take me for a spin up to the Sally Gap, but really because they were too restless to stay still. Their jitteriness made me nervous. On our way back past St Stephen's Green I mentioned the pogroms up in the North. MacBride stood up in the open-topped car as if addressing the disinterested passers-by and said, 'Those Orange bastards are nothing compared to Griffith. The people will rise with us just like in the Easter Rising.'

When I said that in the Rising the people just looted shops and pelted his father with eggs, MacBride called me a Free State coward. He might have done worse but O'Malley's driving was so erratic that he crashed into a British Army truck bringing troops to the docks. MacBride brandished his Colt .45 before thinking better of it. He and O'Malley merged into the startled shoppers, anonymous young men again, leaving the car crushed like a concertina and me to make a run for it. Back at the Four Courts the trip was never mentioned again.

'What was it like in there?' the colonel asked with genuine curiosity.

I shrugged, unsure of what to say. 'They were earnest and passionate to a man and woman. But I sensed that nobody quite knew what to do next. Or maybe they knew with absolute fierce conviction but no two people could agree on it. There was camaraderie and arguments only halted by the nightly rosary. It felt like play-acting, but that stopped after one assassination too many. Suddenly your brother was raining down shells on us with artillery borrowed from the British.'

'He had no option,' the colonel said. 'The British didn't mind killings in Ireland, but got twitchy about one of their senior officers being shot outside his home in London. It was a deliberate provocation. If my brother didn't open fire, the Brits said that they would. We'd have been back to square one. It's what the Irregulars wanted.' He glared at me. 'It's what you wanted if you were among them.'

'I wasn't there for long. They told me to fuck off back home when I curled into a ball and screamed every time a shell landed. The Free State soldiers circling the building didn't even bother arresting me. They took one look and decided I couldn't have come from the Four Courts. I looked too much like a village idiot. I'd done my fighting for a glorious republic. This felt like rats cannibalising each other. That's what you all became, betraying the things you claimed to love. I didn't know which side scared me most.'

'We had the support of voters and of the government.'

'You fighting men despised politicians,' I said. 'No wonder the government cut you adrift after those three boys were murdered at the Red Cow.'

The colonel angrily pushed away his bowl. 'What interest have you in those boys? I should never have eaten your bloody stew. I'll not be poisoned for a crime I didn't commit.'

'There's nothing in the stew,' I said. 'I'll eat it myself to satisfy you.' I made a show of pretending to swallow a final spoonful. 'We were out of our depth, impossibly young. When they kicked me out of the Four Courts, I tried to hold up a National Army truck in the spot where I'd tried to hijack a British truck ten months before.'

'Why?' the colonel asked.

'I was so hungry and tired and befuddled that I wanted someone to put a bullet in me. With all that killing, it shouldn't have been hard. The recruits in the truck were about to open fire when an older lad shouted at them to stop. "That's poor Jimmy Nolan who went daft. I thought Collins had him locked up in Grangegorman." They drove me back here and I was never so glad to find asylum. My fellow lunatics were the sanest folk I'd met since leaving Dartmoor.'

'You're no lunatic,' the colonel said. 'Once a soldier, always a soldier.'

'Then treat me like one.'

'I will, Volunteer Nolan.' He paused. 'I didn't kill those three boys. They were my neighbours.'

'Then who killed them?'

'If I knew the answer my brain wouldn't feel tortured. I just know that I'm blamed by strangers on the street and by the gang who were watching my house at night.'

'There was no gang, Colonel.'

'That's what doctors keep saying.'

'Why won't you believe them?'

'Can I trust doctors?'

'Would you trust the word of a fellow soldier?'

'Yes.'

I stood to attention. 'I swear that no gang has been watching your house at night.'

'How do you know?'

'I accepted your word on Bloody Sunday. Will you not accept mine now?'

He pondered this, battling against his paranoia.

'Are you saying you have the inside track?'

I nodded. 'Trust a fellow volunteer.'

He nodded back, still a little uncertain. 'That will be all, soldier. Dismissed.'

I saluted and picked up his bowl. He rested his elbows on the table. It was the closest I'd come to seeing him relax his guard. I left the cell, glad that he had eaten everything in the stew, including the three large spits I had added when walking from the kitchen – one for each of the young neighbours I once knew.

Fourteen

Dillon

Asylum time

This time I would get the measure of this doctor. An intelligence officer knows how to spot undercover agents because they can never leave a mission half-finished if they feel there is more information to glean, stones to turn over. This was his nature. I couldn't tell if he was a real doctor or a spy. But if real then, just maybe, he might be my ticket out of purgatory – a point man able to guide me back to my wife and family – if I could trust myself enough to trust him with the truth.

Twenty years on, did I even know the truth anymore? I didn't even know how many days I'd sat in this cell, awaiting his arrival. But throughout this vigil I faced the door, ready to confront him, eyeball to eyeball, and prove that I was no longer the scared inmate he last encountered.

This time he came on his tod, not chaperoned by that lackey, Gus, whom I didn't trust. There was something too familiar about Gus's face. People like him know more than they let on. Grudges lurk inside them like cancer. But the doctor's Englishness meant that anything he knew about me must come from files, and files are too impersonal to hold vendettas. He stood on the threshold after unlocking my door, awaiting my permission to enter. A tactic to gain trust.

'How are you today, Colonel Dillon?' he asked.

I shrugged noncommittally. 'I'd tell you if I could keep track of the days.'

'But you remember who I am?'

I nodded. 'My interrogator.'

He took this nod as permission to enter. 'I wouldn't wish to call myself that. But the unfortunate truth is that by law I am tasked with being both physician and jailor. But just now I'm here on my own time, to listen if you'd like to talk.'

He sat on the other stool, awaiting my response.

'It wouldn't feel like a true conversation without a smoke,' I said.

He opened his cigarette case. 'These are Irish-made. I exhausted the supplies I brought with me rather quickly.'

'That's because you're a soft touch,' I scolded. 'That latchico Gus has you wrapped around his finger.' My first inhalation brought on a coughing fit. When it subsided I apologised. 'Sweet Afton Virginia. The first puff always makes me want to cough.'

'Does it also make you want to talk?'

'You're obsessed with talking,' I joked. 'Maybe you should see a psychiatrist.'

'I'd rather see a psychoanalyst.'

'And which class of headshrinker are you?'

'Both,' he replied. 'If I wasn't a psychiatrist by training I couldn't prescribe medication. But I'm a psychoanalyst by vocation.'

'You'll make money from neither with an address on the North Circular Road.' Mentally I felt enough strength to toy with him.

He smiled. 'You recall our conversation. That's a good sign.'

'I recall a freezing attic and feeling exhausted. I'm thinking more clearly today.'

'And would you consider talking to me?'

'To what purpose?' I asked.

'Psychoanalysts try not to just prescribe drugs. Psychoanalysis probes the conscious and subconscious mind, to see if subconscious memories can be unlocked to cure a malady. Sigmund Freud championed it. A Jew, so the comrade you smuggled off to America might not have liked him.'

'I spoke too loosely in that attic,' I said guardedly. 'Jimmy Conroy was so sloshed after the Civil War that I doubt if he remembers who he killed.'

'Amnesia is a handy weapon,' the doctor replied. 'Freud might say ...'

'I'm not talking to you.' The equilibrium I had built up while waiting for him was fracturing. 'I'll find a way to recover without bleating like a baby.'

The doctor rose. 'Do you wish me to leave?'

I beckoned him to stay. I had waited so long for this caller, or any caller to remember that I existed, that I didn't want to be left alone with just silence. Silence was a lonesome companion who rarely proffered cigarettes. 'I said I won't talk *to* you. I never said I won't talk *with* you.'

The doctor sat back down. 'What's the difference?'

'All doctors – no matter what titles they give themselves – take notes. But younger brothers like us ... we can simply chat with no notes taken to prove what was said. Some days I chat to people who aren't actually here. When my brain gets cloudy it's hard to tell who's real.'

'How do I prove I'm real?'

'No spectre ever offered me a second cigarette.'

Laughing companionably, the doctor reopened his cigarette case. 'Two is the limit of my generosity, alas. I hadn't realised how rationed cigarettes are over here when Gus was cadging Pall Mall from me. Lately I've become his best customer for wherever he lays his hands on Sweet Afton. He claims he owns a share of a greyhound with someone who works in the Carroll's cigarette factory in Dundalk, but I suspect that only a coalminer could dig deep enough to reach the bedrock of truth in anything Gus says.'

I inhaled deeply after lighting up. 'I'm not ungrateful. How is life on the North Circular?'

The doctor sighed. 'I'm marooned in a sea of faded lace curtains. Threadbare gentility. My landlady has a shrine on the landing to someone called Rory O'Connor and a map of Europe to let her keep track of Hitler's progress. She claims he has promised the IRA a 32-county republic, with all of Belfast forced to speak Gaelic.'

'And does she speak Irish herself?'

'She says Hitler won't expect patriots of her age to learn such a difficult language. But since discovering that I possess rudimentary German, she pesters me for simple phrases. She wants to be hospitable when stormtroopers march across the border with the keys to Armagh and Tyrone. For a woman not overly fond of anything except masses and money, she's remarkably fond of Germans.'

'We have a soft spot for Germans,' I said. 'One signatory of our proclamation wanted to install a German prince as our new king.'

The doctor furrowed his brow. 'Is having a king compatible with a republic?'

'We were too busy fighting for a republic to define what one was.'

'That rather sounds like a recipe for trouble.'

I was disinclined to explain that if we had started saying what we all wanted, we'd have been too busy fighting each other to fight the British. So I said, 'If your landlady has a shrine to Rory O'Connor, you'd best not tell her you are treating me.'

'Am I treating you?' he probed. 'Beyond dispensing whatever drugs the Superintendent prescribes.'

Taking another pull of my cigarette, I looked around at my cell. How dangerous could it be to just talk to someone, even if it went against every instinct drilled into me? 'How does psychoanalysis even work?'

'You lie on a sofa or, in this case, your bed,' the doctor explained. 'I sit behind you, as silent as possible, to not distract you from describing your dreams.'

'If we try any codology, you'll sit where I could see you. And what have my dreams got to do with anything?'

'You tell me. The treatment is dependent on the patient's willingness to talk.'

'Waiting might cost you a lot of cigarettes.' Another inhalation of smoke clogged up my lungs.

'Are you all right?' he asked, when I was breathing normally again.

'I'm fine. It's just the dampness here. If you want to hear a man really cough, listen to an asthmatic puff their way through a packet of Woodbines. In Ireland we swear by Woodbines to cure asthma. They clear out the lungs entirely.'

'That's not a treatment I've ever heard of.'

'How would you have?' I replied. 'No disrespect, but you're an outsider.'

'How often was your Yankee father called that?'

I fixed him with a stare. 'From the day my father moved to Ireland, he was respected as a good nationalist. We were a respectable family.'

'Is respectability important to you?'

Gazing at him, I could imagine this man's life, from being wheeled by a nanny to his days in prep school and boarding school that coated him in such an ingrained veneer of wealth that nothing could disguise his caste. 'You were born into money,' I replied. 'My family struggled. If you're rich from birth, respectability doesn't matter. People tug their forelock without you even noticing. It's easy to become the black sheep of the family, play-acting with psychoanalysis.'

'Maybe you're right and I'm a mere dilettante.' The doctor sounded unruffled. 'Perhaps I was wrong to ask the Superintendent to delay plans to give you the full electroconvulsive treatment. Does that prospect scare you?'

'I don't easily scare,' I said, although my stomach lurched at the thought.

'Your medical records say that you were seen crawling upstairs for fear of being shot through a window.'

'I wasn't thinking straight,' I said. 'But who wouldn't go daft if constantly harried for crimes he didn't commit?'

'Why would your enemies still want to strike all these years later?'

'To pin all blame on me and get away scot-free.' I felt unsettled by his questions. 'Ask your landlady how Liam Lynch thought he could win support by describing ordinary people as sheep to be driven in any direction?'

'I have no idea who this Mr Lynch even is,' he said calmly.

'Then ask her what the Irregulars thought to achieve by blowing up trains and robbing banks, trying to cripple the country and leave us incapable of governing ourselves? Those lads wanted the Tan War restarted, but making war is easy. It's peace that's hard work. Ask her what they hoped to gain by blowing up the railway viaduct into Foxford, with all the women losing their jobs in the woollen mills there? Anything I did it was done to restore law and order and decency.'

I was getting worked up when I desperately needed to stay calm. If cracks appeared in my mind, I could not control what phantom might slip in. The doctor seemed unmoved by my agitation.

'The Finns had a proper civil war,' he said. 'Thirty-six thousand dead – one third executed – in just four months. Who knows how many died in the war just ended in Spain? It makes me disinterested in exploring the rights or wrongs of your minor family squabble.'

'Then what are you interested in?'

'The damage you're doing to yourself by still fighting it. What if Collins had rejected the Treaty? Would you have not blown up bridges too, if he'd asked?'

I shifted uneasily. 'If Collins had asked his Squad to walk across broken glass we'd have done it without thinking,' I said. 'Mick did the thinking for us. We survived on idealism, knowing that when the time came, he would sort out the details. He was three steps ahead of everyone, never making a false move till he made the mistake of going home to Cork. War changes you. Your childhood home is no longer your home.'

I sighed, forced to remember events I had spent years trying to stop reliving. 'The one weakness in Collins's armour was nostalgia. That day he was shot, he kept standing rounds of drinks in village pubs, greeting old neighbours, turning a mission to secure the area into a homecoming. My brother tried to hurry him along, like he urged him to drive on through the ambush later that evening, when Collins's own neighbours blew his brains out. My brother held him in the armoured car as they drove away, fingers on Collins's skull, trying to press everything back together – all of the gaiety and strength, all the plans he never bothered to share with us. Jimmy Conroy beside them in shock, too numb to curse or pray for Mick's soul. That dumdum bullet to Collins's skull unhinged Conroy entirely.'

'You make it sound like losing a father,' the doctor said quietly.

I nodded. 'A father who never thought to tell us where he was keeping the deeds to the house. When news of his death reached Dublin, I'm told there was total silence among the Irregular prisoners in Kilmainham Jail before a rosary for his soul spread to every cell. No rosaries were said in Wellington Barracks. There was blue murder – hardened men out of their minds with grief.'

'What did you do?'

I paused, hating to even think back. 'I knelt by a dark window in a storeroom where nobody would find me. I didn't cry, though I was shaking. I just stared out, trying to spy who was hiding in the shadows, although I knew there was nobody. But it gave me something to do, so I didn't have to go down and start preparations for the lying in state when his body finally reached Dublin. My brother accompanied it on a boat that sailed past Cobh, where locals knelt on the streets and the British soldiers on Spike Island lined up to salute a gallant foe, while we were gathering, hours too early, on the Dublin quays to await his arrival.'

'You remember every minute of that night.'

'Who could forget?' I felt raw and vulnerable, overcome by memories.

The doctor nodded. Then, after a long companionable silence, he spoke. 'Then how come you remember nothing about the night those Drumcondra boys were shot dead at the Red Cow?'

I glared at him, feeling ambushed.

'What has the Red Cow got to do with me?' I said angrily.

'I don't know,' the doctor replied. 'But the Superintendent told me not to mention those murders in case I drove you over the edge.'

'Then why do so?'

'I've found that, if you wish to cure someone instead of just stupefying them with drugs, the only things worth mentioning are the unmentionables.'

I wanted this man to go. To be left with my thoughts or left alone to block them out. But it was too late, even if he left now. He seemed puzzled that I wasn't looking directly at him. But I was too distracted by the woman standing behind him. She hadn't changed in twenty years; she had that same bitter look I remembered from when she used to turn up at the Sweepstakes offices, as cunning as a shithouse rat, slipping past the near-blind front-desk porter. That wasn't hard, as Joe McGrath only employed this ex-volunteer from sympathy because he'd lost most of his sight when a half-cocked concoction exploded in his face during the Tan War. But surely she should not be allowed to dodge her way into a locked asylum. I glared at the doctor, annoyed at his casualness in leaving the cell door open. But he seemed too caught up in his hocus-pocus notions to have noticed her presence.

'We're not alone,' I said, sharply.

'Trust me, we are,' he replied. 'Anything you say is in confidence.'

His denial angered me. It had echoes of my rows with the Sweepstakes porter who used to cover up his ailment by indignantly protesting that nobody had got past him.

'Do you honestly think we're alone here?' I asked.

The doctor looked perturbed. 'What has you so suddenly agitated, Mr Dillon?'

'Are you so blinded by your psychoanalysis that you can't even see behind you?'

The doctor turned and stared towards the angry woman before turning back to me. 'I see a bare wall. You look anxious, Mr Dillon. Would another cigarette calm your nerves?'

I pushed back my stool and rose, unsure if the doctor was in on this trickery. 'You should have heeded the Superintendent's advice. Take your fags and go.'

'I'd never heard of the Red Cow until the Superintendent mentioned it,' the doctor said. 'I'm told it has a disused quarry.'

'I wouldn't know. I was never there.'

'Then why was I warned not to mention it? I specialise in trauma. I'm sure your paranoia stems from trauma. Initially you only piqued my interest for your involvement in Bloody Sunday.'

'I felt no trauma on Bloody Sunday,' I insisted. 'I did my duty and got away in time for Mass.'

'Then, does your trauma relate to the boys found dead at the Red Cow?'

'Their deaths had nothing to do with me.'

'Or with any officer serving with you?'

I tried to focus on him, but the woman encroached on my eye line. 'I'm not my fellow officers' keeper.'

The doctor mimed washing his hands. 'That sounds a bit like playing Pontius Pilate.'

'I don't care what it sounds like. We were trying to defend a freedom assailed on every side. When did law and order become dirty words?'

The woman spoke for the first time. 'When my son died in a disused quarry.'

'I refuse to be judged by the likes of you,' I told her sharply.

'I'm not judging you, Mr Dillon,' the doctor said. 'My only interest is in healing. I believe you are here because of your inability to talk about the past.'

'I'm here because of innuendos and slanders. I've spent two decades coping with stares of reproach from strangers.' Looking directly past him, I told the scowling woman: 'I was no more present at the Red Cow than you were.'

'Are you sure?' the doctor asked.

I glared at him. 'The gutter press needed to make someone the villain. Pantomime villains sell newspapers but newspapers are not courts of law. The coroner declared me innocent.'

'A country doctor bullied by big-shot government lawyers or so I'm told.'

'He was officially the coroner. I shouldn't need to answer those same accusations from other people.'

'I'm different from other people,' the doctor said.

'You're asking the same damn questions.'

He nodded. 'But I'm asking as a doctor.'

'I don't care if you're asking as a priest.'

'Would you tell a priest?'

I looked away. 'Certain sins are beyond absolution.'

'What does that mean?' he probed.

I stared towards the woman now pacing the room. Why couldn't the doctor see her?

'Priests can only forgive sins you actually commit.'

'If you didn't commit them, then why do they haunt you?' The doctor's eyes tried to follow mine as I studied the woman circling us.

'All my life I'm haunted by shadows,' I said. 'My childhood bedroom overlooked a railway embankment. At night, I couldn't quell a fear that someone was lurking there to rob us after my father put out the light. I remember being unable to stop myself peering out into the shadows. The fear of shadows never leaves you, the shadows just change. I can see things you can't.'

The woman stopped directly behind the doctor and leaned to whisper in his ear. 'Ask him why my son was left riddled with bullets.'

The doctor seemed unaware of her presence, yet her words must have permeated. He leaned forward and said, 'Mr Dillon, let's talk about the Red Cow murders.'

'Why are you so keen to do so?' I noted the woman's triumphant look as she stepped back.

'Because you're not.'

'Whoever killed those boys was a cur,' I said. 'But senseless things happen in civil wars: slaughter we must forget or we'll drown in a quagmire of bitterness and recrimination. What makes their killing any different from the others on both sides?'

'The fact that it seems to haunt you. And am I right that you did arrest those boys in Drumcondra?'

'Arrest is too strong a word,' I said. 'I took them off the street for their own safety. My neighbours were sick of war. I only spied the boys when myself and another officer were driving past, because they attracted such a hostile crowd. Originally a girl was sticking up those posters, but she got such abuse that our three young heroes took over to impress her. They weren't hoping to die for Ireland; they were hoping for a kiss and a squeeze down some alleyway later.'

'How do you know?' the doctor asked. 'Why do you feel it necessary to devalue their motives?'

I didn't reply. I was too distracted by the woman. I knew what she was going to produce before she reached into her coat. The scrunched-up poster was streaked with mud, just like I had left it, thrown into the gutter on Clonliffe Road. The crudely printed words were barely legible as she defiantly held it aloft. But I didn't need to decipher her tattered copy. I remembered every word and remembered my fury at reading them, on a street where I had often played, a few hundred yards from my parents' home.

> To all it concerns:
>
> Any person employed by the Free State Forces in uniform or in mufti found loitering in Drumcondra shall be shot on sight. This death threat applies to every member of the murder gang known as Military Intelligence. A new generation is taking up the fight. Any person found defacing this handbill should be drastically dealt with.
>
> Signed
> Irish Republican Defence Association – Drumcondra Branch.

'I asked a question,' the doctor said. 'Why devalue their motives?'

I tried to focus on him. 'Men like me who risked our lives were sick of the young fellows we nicknamed the Trucileers. Kids who belatedly joined the volunteers so they could act like big men despite having never fired a shot. The Truce was a great inducement for cowards to crawl from the woodwork, wanting a share of our reflected glory. Those posters called for officers who'd done the real fighting to be shot.'

'How did that make you feel?'

I raised my eyes, exasperated. 'How would you feel? I'd risked my life from the age of fourteen. I'd given up ...'

'What?'

I struggled for words to properly explain. 'The things they had. Youth, enthusiasm, a zest for life.'

'You were still only nineteen,' the doctor said. 'Just two years older than them.'

'How old did you feel after returning from France?' I asked. 'Compared to boys younger than you who didn't have to go?'

The doctor nodded. 'The younger lads with whom I'd once played cricket were still schoolboys, full of larks and high jinks. I had more in common with the men I served with, ten or twenty years older than me. Undoubtedly those veterans saw me only as a boy, but I was no longer one thing or the other.'

'Living on the run, forced to sleep with one eye open, not knowing where you will lay your head, ages your bones,' I said. 'I felt like an arthritic old sheep dog compared to those boys – too young and too old at the same time. That night on Clonliffe Road I was wearing a colonel's uniform, with leather boots up to my knees. But I was lost inside it. I felt like a cabin boy forced to take over steering the ship. I needed to save Ireland from crashing onto rocks, because our captain died at Béal na Bláth. Collins knew he had signed his own death warrant by being a signatory to the Treaty in London. But I wasn't going to let a snot-nosed kid, who'd only joined the IRA days before, claim they had a right to sign my death warrant.'

I gazed at the boy's mother, but either my eyes were failing or she was barely there now. She seemed made of gossamer because I could see straight through her.

'So you were angry that night?' the doctor asked quietly.

'Who wouldn't be? Now are you happy?'

'This isn't about me.'

The woman was almost gone, like a mist seeping into the wall. But her voice remained strong as she made every word sting. 'My child's flesh still warm when the priest anointed him.'

'Just go,' I told her angrily. 'Give my head peace!'

'Do you wish me to leave?' the doctor asked. 'Is that what you're saying?'

She was fully gone now, but the last thing I wanted was to be left alone. I reached across to grip his hand, struggling to regain composure. 'I'm saying that all I remember about that night was getting drunk, later on in the officers' mess, after I rounded up four other suspects. Those four men testified at the inquest that they were released unharmed after interrogation.'

'Did they testify willingly?'

'They testified anonymously in case the Irregulars burnt down their houses with their families still inside, like when Seán McGarry's seven-year-old son was burnt alive in Fairview. A fellow officer swore at the inquest that I was still interrogating those other suspects in the barracks at the time that locals heard shots at the Red Cow. If a car resembling my open-topped Lancia was seen out there, it was coincidence. Or if it was my car, then some officer must have borrowed it. I don't know. I was so drunk, between the whiskey and interrogations, that I blacked out. Drunk men have blackouts.'

The doctor was silent for a moment. 'Were you drunk on whiskey or on power?'

'I never wanted power,' I said. 'I wanted to be seen in my own right. Not as just my brother's kid brother or a baby-faced intelligence gatherer, with older volunteers thinking me too scared to pull a trigger. What I wanted, especially on the streets of Drumcondra, was the respect I'd earned as an officer.'

I paused, fearful of who might step through another crack in my imagination. I had known all three of those boys and their families. During the Tan War they would nod in awe when I risked visiting my parents, and take turns to stand guard on the corner during the few minutes I snatched at home. They were always thrilled skinny if I as much as deigned to nod at them when leaving my parents' home, thereby letting them share in the glory of seeming to be part of the struggle. But on that night on Clonliffe Road, their hatred stripped me of that sense of being respected by my own kind.

'I willingly accept hatred from any man who had once fought beside me before they joined the Irregulars,' I said. 'Even while I was torturing such men and they were cursing me, I still sensed a mutual respect. They hated me enough to want to kill me, but it was honest hatred between men who'd fought.'

'But the hatred shown by these boys was different?' the doctor asked.

I got up and paced around the cell, touching the wall to reassure myself that it was solid. 'Those boys hadn't earned the right to feel such hatred. They were puppets, doing the bidding of older men.'

'They sound like you at their age when Collins pulled your strings.'

'Collins possessed a plan,' I said. 'He could see within the Treaty the stepping stones to full freedom. The men manipulating those boys had no plan except anarchy. Ordinary people were sick of violence. None of us got what they wanted in the Treaty, but now people just wanted to get on with their lives. Whatever happened to those boys after I released them had nothing to do with me. If I gave them a slap around the ears, it was for their own sakes. If their puppet-masters didn't see a few bruises, they might be suspected of being informers when they got home.'

'But they didn't get home,' the doctor said.

I shrugged irritably. 'My fellow officers provided alibis clearing me of involvement.'

'So why does that night still plague you?'

Sitting down, I asked for another cigarette. For a doctor meant to calm my nerves, he was doing the opposite. My hand shook as I lit up. It took three puffs before I regained my composure.

'Any harmless clatter I gave those boys was no worse than the Christian Brothers in O'Connell's school gave us. That doesn't turn me into an Igoe.'

'You've mentioned this man before,' the doctor said. 'A sadistic detective.'

I nodded. 'Igoe could do what he liked with prisoners, knowing the British authorities would lie to cover up his actions.'

I had thought the blasted spectre of the woman was gone but she seemed to reappear behind me because I heard her whisper clearly in my ear.

'Like those Free State officers lied for you.'

'Get out of my head!' I stood up to confront her but when I turned nobody was there. I was aware of the doctor watching closely.

'Mr Dillon, I'm not in your head,' he said.

I took a deep breath, knowing I had to regain my senses and not let down my guard. But I felt a desperate need to talk.

'When we threw those three boys into a cell that night – just for a few minutes, to give them a fright – their terrified stares made me feel like Igoe. But they were crazy to be fearful. My mother knew their mothers. I'd have given them a lift home to Drumcondra if they'd still seen me as a neighbour. But there was a stink of piss in that cell and not stale piss from the last occupant who'd had good reason to piss himself. It was from one of these boys, shaking in fear. Do you know what the smell of fear does to a dog?'

'It excites him. He feels a compulsion to attack. Is that what you're saying?'

'I don't know what I'm saying.' I felt dizzy from talking about things I never discussed. I went on the offensive. 'Aren't you the brave man, sitting here,' I sneered. 'Why aren't you off fighting Hitler with your brother?'

'Because I'm fighting your war with you.'

'I'll fight it by myself.'

'Let's return to that smell of piss,' the doctor probed. 'What happened after you smelt their fear?'

'Nothing. I told you, I'm no Igoe. The duty log states how the boys were released after twenty minutes. The rest of the night involved drink and mania because everything felt super-real back then, yet totally unreal. I don't recall all the details of that time; I just remember being trapped in a new uniform that people feared. I sensed the fear of rank-and-file recruits and the mistrust of politicians unable to fill Collins's shoes. You are a queer class of doctor to torment me with questions when you could prescribe a horse tranquiliser to make me whole again.'

'If we patch Humpty-Dumpty back together with sticking plaster, do you think that makes him whole?' the doctor asked.

'It would make him appear whole. In Ireland it's appearances that matter. I'm not asking you to make me well. Just make me look well enough to return to my job and put a wage on the table again.'

'If you just want to bury your trauma, the Superintendent can apply electroconvulsive therapy. After enough volts jolt through your brain you won't remember what was bothering you because you'll barely remember your name.'

'But I'll be free of all this, won't I?'

'Will you?' The doctor gestured with outspread hands. 'How can you be free of something still bottled up inside you? When the numbness wears off your fried brain, all this will resurface in your subconscious and you'll start to imagine men lurking outside your house again.'

'There were men,' I insisted. 'Or at least one man. I couldn't see him but I sensed him. Not every night but some nights and he wished me ill.'

'What if he was inside your imagination?' the doctor asked.

'What if all your talk is a waste of time?'

The doctor shrugged. 'In here all you have is time.'

He had a point, I thought, scanning the cell in case any other phantoms appeared. 'Can you guarantee that this psychoanalysis we're doing will cure me?'

'We haven't been doing psychoanalysis,' the doctor said. 'You're too agitated. We have just been talking. But if you want, I can come back and try it. I will sit quietly and let you talk. If you're asking me to guarantee results, then I can't. I can try to open up your subconscious. But only you can make yourself well. It takes time and I don't know how long the Superintendent will allow us. He has you down for ECT on Friday. I can stall him for a bit longer if you want. But it's your decision.'

I smiled ruefully. 'For the past twenty years, faced with any decision, I ask myself: what would Collins do?'

'What would he do if he were here?' the Englishman asked.

I laughed. 'Mick would wrestle me into a headlock, because he liked horseplay. Then dole out a few slaps and tell me to cop myself on and not fall for foreign shite.'

'Your Mr Collins sounds like he wasn't slow in saying what he thought.'

'He told you straight.' Then I went silent, scanning my cell, realising I'd no idea of how long I had been in here. 'But I'm a grown man. Grown men must do their own thinking.'

'What do I tell the Superintendent about Friday?' the doctor asked.

'Tell him I'm thinking about it. It's funny, but I feel lighter after our talk.'

'Maybe that's psychoanalysis.' The doctor rose to his feet.

'Maybe it's just hunger,' I replied.

Opening his cigarette case, the doctor placed two more fags on the table. 'I hope we get to talk again, Mr Dillon.'

I nodded. 'We just might. But I'll consult my ghosts first. They all seem to be locked in here with me.'

'Then maybe it's time to release them,' he said, 'I'm leaving this door unlocked.'

'Do no such thing,' I protested. 'Your job is to keep me safe.'

He shrugged. 'You said it yourself, Mr Dillon; your ghosts are in here. This corridor just leads out to an exercise yard where broken men walk in circles. None of them will know you or accuse you of anything. They are too preoccupied by their own woes to worry about yours. It's time to learn to sit among them. They may not be much company, but they make better company than ghosts.'

He smiled and I managed to smile back until he was gone. Then I looked behind me to ensure that nobody was there, eavesdropping, waiting for me to let down my guard. When I was certain that I was alone, I tentatively opened the cell door. The corridor was empty. I could see a shaft of light come through the bars on the door at the end. Sunlight or the possibility of sunlight. All I had to do was step out into that corridor. I just didn't know if I could.

Fifteen

Gus

Asylum time

It was the time of evening I liked best, when there was a lull - or as much of a lull as ever occurred - before lights out, with patients letting themselves be shepherded back to their wards. Soon, outbreaks of crying or shouting would start again, with some patients ambushed by despair once they lay on their bunks and confronted the prospect of sleepless hours ahead. I pitied them in their loneliness but pity was rarely a useful poultice. I had already done my day's work, but the Super had asked me to stay on until dawn, just to keep an eye out, as he enigmatically said, knowing he didn't need to say more. In an hour's time I would make my unofficial rounds, telling the odd joke or slipping a half cigarette here or there, hoping to, however briefly, distract a few old lags from sinking too deeply into those malaises that felt bottomless to them. I knew what ward I would finish up at, the attendant bribed to turn a blind eye as I sat beside one particular bunk to share a cigarette and some disjointed chat with a patient starting his eighteenth year here.

For the past hour I had been happy to loiter, seemingly by chance, out here in the exercise yard, in the doorway that led to the private cells. I was so alert for any noise from Dillon's cell that I didn't hear the Super's footsteps until he was behind me.

'That's a cold night, Gus,' he said quietly, by way of greeting.

'Perishing.' I turned to face him. 'You're working late, Sir.'

He nodded. 'Trying to play catch up as usual. I could be here every hour of every day and I still wouldn't clear my desk. It's the Board of Governors tomorrow.'

I raised an eyebrow slightly, knowing the additional work this entailed. 'Who is doing the visitors' report this month?'

The Super took out a packet of cigarettes and offered me one, not replying until we both lit up. 'A jumped-up scut of a Fianna Fail TD who decided to inspect the Portrane asylum instead of here.'

'Funny how often that's the case,' I said. 'I'm sure it has nothing to do with the extra mileage allowance.'

The Super exhaled a lungful of smoke. 'You can say such things, Gus. But you know well that I can't.' He lowered his voice. 'I can only think them. The matron says he scuttled around the women's wards so quick you might mistake him for Jesse Owens. He claimed that, unfortunately with the train timetable, he hadn't time to inspect the male wards, but still found time to stuff his face with tea and apple tart.'

'Inspections are hungry work,' I said wryly.

'Not when old Jim Larkin or Alfie Byrne get their turn. They go through every ward with a fine toothcomb and that's no harm: we need honest voices to speak up for us at Corporation finance meetings. Reading the flowery language in other reports about how wonderful life is in here, I'm never sure if they are trying to butter me up or just trying to avoid putting down anything in writing that might make them feel duty-bound to find me extra funding. But I produce the daybook at every meeting and give it to them straight, every incident logged, so they can see how we're forced to constantly make do and mend. I've nothing to hide.'

I glanced down towards Dillon's cell. 'Almost nothing.'

The Super followed my gaze. 'Everything that has happened to the colonel since he was admitted is set down in black and white.'

He paused. 'Obviously anything prior to his arrival isn't, because it didn't happen here.'

'Obviously.' I remembered my nights spent watching that house in Donnybrook.

'And obviously nothing about any private conversations that Dr Fairfax is having with him. That's all psychoanalysis is really: well-meaning, long-winded conversations, going round in circles, and not any actual form of treatment.'

'I wouldn't know,' I replied, neutrally, aware of his deep suspicion of this practice. Some years ago, I had stumbled on a curt note in his filing cabinet, detailing his response to an approach from that Quaker woman, Rosamund Jacob, asking for a recommendation for a psychoanalyst. She had been plagued by nightmares since her imprisonment in the Civil War. He had been blunt in saying that no reputable Irish doctor would engage in any practice disapproved of by the Church and suggesting that she went to London instead.

The Super glanced down the corridor. 'Speaking of which, is the Sassenach still jaw-jawing in there?'

'No. I saw him leave a while back.'

'Did he see you?'

'I'm good at being unseen.'

He nodded. 'How long was he with Mr Dillon?'

'A fair while.'

I sensed his unease and how he now regretted agreeing to allow any conversations to happen that might veer beyond his control.

'I don't suppose you peeped in on them?' he asked.

I shook my head. 'That would be more than my job's worth.'

'That's true.' He nodded in a way that gave me permission to discreetly continue.

'However, if I had peeped in,' I added, 'I'd have found that they were not up to much, with Fairfax chasing shadows and poor Dillon imagining he was seeing shadows.'

'And nothing else?'

'Like the Yanks say in the motion pictures, Fairfax didn't get past first base.'

He nodded thoughtfully.

'If Mr Dillon has anything troubling him, I'm sure he has spoken about it to a priest in confession. If a priest can't solve it by granting absolution, I am not sure how talking to any doctor, no matter how well-meaning, will help. Brooding on the past helps nobody. It exposes wounds and lets them fester. Our English friend thinks that speaking about such things is cathartic but it's not. Some wounds aren't physical or psychological, they're spiritual. Fighting for Ireland was like a religious experience for lads like Dillon. They would have happily accepted martyrdom. It isn't just his mind that's wounded, it's his soul. While we can patch up his mind as best we can, I may have been unwise to let Dr Fairfax try to interfere with his soul.' He paused. 'Keep this to yourself, Gus.'

I stubbed out my cigarette butt. 'Who did I ever talk to? Dillon is not the first poor soul in here plagued by that Civil War and he won't be the last.'

He nodded. We were thinking about men like Seosamh Mac Grianna who was put in a padded cell when first admitted, but somehow managed to write himself well – or at least well enough to be released – by scribbling reams of Donegal Irish that even the Irish-speaking doctors on the staff couldn't make sense of.

The Super broke the silence. 'You never came across anyone who's heard of this Willoughby chap that Fairfax mentioned but was suddenly not keen to talk about?'

I weighed up my options. Cigarettes were one currency in here, but information was an even more precious commodity. 'I asked around the pubs but couldn't find anyone who ever heard of him,' I lied.

He nodded and glanced towards the corridor again. If I wasn't watching, he might have slipped down to peer in through the spyhole. 'Don't get me wrong. Dr Fairfax is a good man. He means well.'

'I don't doubt it.'

'But sometimes it's best to let sleeping dogs die.' He paused. 'You think he's getting nowhere?'

I made my shrug as non-committal as possible.

He nodded. 'If he's doing no harm, then well and good. But I've a duty of care and that includes letting no man torment another man's soul.'

He took out his cigarettes and offered me another one. 'Don't feel you need to stay all night, Gus. But you might just keep a watchful eye all the same.'

I put the cigarette behind my ear. 'Sure, I've nowhere else to be, Sir.'

He nodded again and then slipped away, burdened by a hundred responsibilities.

Sixteen

Dillon

Asylum time

What I experienced was no dream. That is all I can say for certain. It was definitely a real window I was kneeling at, peering out. I couldn't tell if it was the window of my childhood bedroom or the master bedroom in Morehampton Road. If I'd had more time I would have recognised my surroundings. But a voice disturbed my thoughts, the voice I longed to hear. When I turned, I did so joyously. Agnes stood in her white nightdress. I wanted to reach out my hand but an anxious expression on her face, lit by a solitary shaft of moonlight, stopped me.

'Agnes, love, what's wrong?' I asked. 'You look so worried.'

'I am worried, Francis,' she said. 'After all your promises, you're back peering out of windows again.'

'I'm not,' I lied. But maybe I wasn't lying because my thoughts were confused. When I turned back to the window, I felt relieved – like a schoolboy at not being caught – that it had shifted position. Its new location, high up on the wall, helped me recognise where I actually was – back in this blasted cell from which I needed to find my way home.

'Then what are you doing?' Agnes asked and I told her that I was trying to pray for guidance from God about what he wanted me to do.

'That's simple,' she replied. 'God wants what we all want – for you to be a good husband and father again.'

I nodded to show that I understood. Then I told her that what I just could not understand was why our Lord had put me in this Gethsemane, with she and our children forced to sleep each night in the next cell, surrounded by lunatics crying out at all hours. My family did not deserve this fate. Any retribution for my sins should be endured by me alone. If I wasn't so cowardly, I would have found the courage to face my executors like a man. Instead of hiding under my bed, I would have stood in our front garden to confront the gunmen coming for me, so that she and the children would not have been put at risk by those men needing to enter the house.

Agnes shook her head softly as she listened. 'Can you still not see?' she said. 'Nobody was coming back then, Francis, and nobody now.'

'There is,' I replied. 'That's why I'm praying for guidance. An English doctor is coming for me. Not with bullets but questions. He claims that my answers might unlock these doors so we can all go home. What do I do, Agnes? Maybe my secrets are safe with him because he's a Protestant and they go to hell, where nobody can hear what they repeat amid the flames.'

Agnes looked at me, serenely but sternly. 'But I would hear, Francis.'

'You wouldn't, Agnes. You're not in hell, even if Grangegorman feels like it.'

'If he spoke out, it would mean he had heard some secret worth repeating.' She stepped closer, yet withheld her touch. 'And how could there be when, before our marriage, we had such a long talk, walking in rain all the way from Arbour Hill to the Poolbeg lighthouse on the Great South Wall. You knelt on those stones and swore that you knew nothing about the deaths of those boys? So what can you possibly want to tell to some stranger?'

'All I want, Agnes, is to be back home with you.'

She stepped further back, her gaze resolute. 'Then don't let them break you. If you confess to one person, you will have confessed to everyone, when we both know you have nothing to confess to. If you had, you would have told me that day, where we stood in the rain at the Poolbeg lighthouse, not caring that we were soaked because all we cared about was our love for each other. We swore to have no secrets and let nothing ever come between us. If you weren't truthful with me that day, then our marriage has been a lie, after all my years of defending you against false allegations.'

I reached out my hand, hoping that she would take it in hers, but this only made her step even further back.

'Are you saying that if I talk to this doctor, you and the children won't be able to bear sleeping every night in the next cell, just to stay close to me?'

Agnes shook her head but the light was playing tricks. I could barely see her now. I just sensed her essence starting to seep away.

'Francis,' she said, 'I don't sleep here. Nor do the children. I'm not even allowed visit you. This is your madness talking. I sleep in Morehampton Road when I can sleep. Mostly I lie awake, fretting about how to feed our children and whether a spiteful neighbour might undo the lies I've told them about you having to be abroad on Sweepstakes business. Sleep is hard, but tonight I am sleeping soundly in our old bed because I know that I'm married to a good man, who is simply stressed by being overworked, and not to a man associated with murder.'

Then her aura was gone. What rushed in to replace her benediction of love was such an ache of loneliness that I cried out her name so agonisingly that I heard a key turn in the lock. I prayed that my cry had summoned her back as I watched the cell door open, longing to glimpse her white nightdress. Instead it was Gus, my jailor. There was something disconcerting about him, something discombobulating about this asylum where people seemed able to come and go.

'What the hell do you want?' I asked.

He shrugged. 'A bit of shuteye wouldn't go astray. You're doing some fierce shouting in your sleep. Can you keep it down?'

'I wasn't sleeping.'

'Than what were you at?'

I looked around the cell, trying to scramble together some shards of sanity. 'There was a woman here just now.'

My jailor raised his eyebrows. 'Well, I hope it was Greta Garbo in a negligée. If you're going to dream about women, you may as well go the whole hog.'

'I wasn't dreaming.'

Gus didn't say anything but he didn't need to. How could I have thought that my children were in the next cell? Hopefully they didn't even know that I was in this asylum. But I could have sworn I had heard their voices.

'Who's sleeping in the next cell?' I asked.

'That's top secret,' Gus said. 'In other words, it's a monsignor from Leitrim, but I'm not meant to know.'

'And there are definitely no children in there? I thought I heard children crying.'

Gus blessed himself, but not piously. It was like a blasphemous gesture, a word to the wise. 'God forbid. Any child left alone with the dirty fucker would soon be crying, from what I've heard, which is why they have him closeted away here until they can post him off to the foreign missions. But I'm saying nothing. Now, will you settle down, man.'

'I will if you lock that door and keep them all out.'

'Keep who out?'

I raised a finger to my lips. 'I'm saying nothing either.'

'Fair enough.' He gave me one last look, but it was an honest man-to-man look of concern, as if we were the last two souls awake at whatever strange hour this was. I was grateful because his look made me feel less alone.

I nodded and tried to calm my voice to reassure him. 'You were right, Gus. I was just dreaming. Good night.'

Seventeen

Nolan

Asylum time

I don't know what hour it was when I woke, but I was certain that a man's anguished shout woke me. Nothing strange there. Some man or other will cry out on most nights, but I was so used to such sounds that normally I sleep through them. Why was this one different? When I looked around, nobody else was stirring, so the amadán, whoever he was, had not even woken himself. But that was only true if the sound came from within this packed ward. Surely it had not only been in my head, because it sounded different from the usual cries locked in there. But, whether real or imagined, this was the cry of a man in pain and I felt convinced that he had been calling out for me.

So who could it be? I had few real friends in here, even though I knew everyone. I had gone to bed angry and scared, because that bastard English doctor was trying to come between me and the one person in here that I wanted to feel close to. I had not even been able to sleep at first, worrying about what confessions he might wheedle from the colonel. Those secrets were the glue that held the colonel and I together. Two fighting men who knew what it felt like to kill, in the moment of killing and in every moment that came after. This was an indelible burden and indelible bond that I had needed to wait almost two decades to find someone in here to share it with.

That which God hath joined together let no man put asunder. The colonel's presence here gave me back the kindred sense of companionship I had only truly known once, in a hideaway above a dispensary on Bloody Sunday night when, just for once, I was permitted to lay my head among the crème de la crème, the apostles anointed by Mick Collins. I could not recall how many nights I had awoken in a dozen other crowded wards like this, hoping that, even for just one second, I would be made feel whole again, by looking around to glimpse those young brave faces around me and not the broken and maimed, the fractured and destitute.

I turned and saw that old Tomas, who had slept in the next bunk to mine for the past three years, was also awake and watching me.

'Did you hear anything?' I whispered.

'Divil a thing.'

'There was a man shouting.'

'Not in here.'

I lay back, trying to make sense of it. My thoughts strayed back to Colonel Dillon's cell, big enough for two bunks. If we could lie side by side, like Tomas and I, then I might feel that sense of kinship again. But the Super would never allow me to sleep in his cell. Instead, the mountain would have to come to Muhammad. I turned again to Tomas.

'You'll not be sleeping in that bunk much longer,' I told him.

'What do you mean?'

'Another man will be needing it.'

'Well, he can go to fuck.'

'You can go. We'll find you somewhere.'

'I'm going nowhere.'

'I killed three men once,' I said. 'Do you know that?'

'I've heard other men say that this is why they steer clear of you, but I never believed them. I mean, look at you, Jimmy. You wouldn't hurt a fly.'

I fixed him with a stare. 'I've known my share of killers. They were all quiet men until roused. And so quiet again afterwards that nobody ever suspected them.'

He looked so petrified that I felt guilty at alarming him.

'Jimmy, don't kill me,' he pleaded. 'I don't want to die, honest.'

'Don't fret, Tomas,' I assured him. 'I won't kill you, I'll just find another bunk for you when the time comes. I've a friend who might be coming to stay.' I leaned back to look up at the flaking ceiling. 'No, not a friend,' I said quietly, almost to myself. 'A true comrade.'

Eighteen

Dillon

Asylum time

I had no objection to Nolan starting to see himself as my unofficial batman, a trusted obedient orderly. But if I were back in the army I would have been affronted by the manner in which he entered my cell to brusquely slam down my bowl of food. The tepid mush was as indistinguishable as ever, but previously he'd always scavenged a bowl for me not disfigured by cracks and a spoon less buckled by decades of use. This swill never filled your stomach, but just left you more acutely aware of your underlying hunger. But I was less perturbed by the meagre fare than by his abrupt manner as he made for the door, without responding to my expression of thanks.

'I said, thank you,' I said loudly. He stopped but declined to turn around.

'I heard. I'm not deaf or blind.'

'Then what ails you? Normally you're dying to chat.'

I thought he was about to walk out into the corridor, slam the door and leave me in this isolation. But eventually he turned, his tone wounded like I had betrayed him.

'Why talk to me now that you've found yourself someone more important to talk to?'

'What do you mean? I thought you enjoyed our talks.'

'The way I see it, there's too much talk going on in this cell.'

'What are you implying?' I asked.

'You and that English doctor had a grand conflab. What did you tell him about me?'

'Why would he ask me about you?'

'I'm a patient here too, even if few doctors condescend to address me. What makes you special?'

'I never invited the man into my cell,' I protested.

'He invited himself, you fucking eejit.'

'Mind your language. Remember whom you are addressing.'

'An intelligence officer gone as rusty as a nail left out in the rain,' he said scornfully. 'From years of soft living when I was kipping in here, sometimes with only a half-share of a bunk. You're as naive now as when you were a kid in an officer's uniform. It's no wonder that the only place you and your Squad co-conspirators could think of to stage your botched coup against the government in 1924 was a bloody pub. And no wonder that the officers sent to break it up didn't even bother arresting you for treason. You were so unimportant that they just let you all limp away home with your tails between your legs.'

'I'm warning you,' I said angrily. 'Mind your tongue!'

'And I'm warning you.' Nolan clenched his fists with tension. 'Mind yours, especially when talking to a British army officer.'

'For God's sake. The man only spent two months in the trenches. He's a doctor now.'

'Are you sure?' Nolan asked. 'What class of British doctor would willingly work in this madhouse? Have you asked yourself what he wants? Collins had men shot for only being half as suspicious.'

'I'm not sure what he wants.' I sat down wearily, too ill at ease to remain affronted by the man's tone. 'I've lain awake half the night asking myself that question. And when I finally slept, my wife kept asking me other questions in dreams.'

'What class of questions?'

Studying Nolan as he stood hunched there, I realised how lonely his life was in here. 'It's never wise to come between a man and his wife, even in their dreams.'

'I meant no offence, Colonel.' His tone was apologetic now. 'But the thought of you alone in here talking to him has me rattled.'

I gestured to the other stool. 'Please sit down. I know you're just trying to watch an old comrade's back.' I stirred the spoon with lacklustre around the cracked bowl. 'What culinary delights have we today?'

Nolan shrugged. 'The leftovers from yesterday, diluted with boiled cabbage water.'

'You'd make a great restaurant critic.'

My remark coaxed a smile from him. 'I'd terrorise the chef in the Russell Hotel for fear that he'd get a bad review.'

'Were you ever inside the Russell?' I asked.

He shook his head. 'No, but I lodged a few times in the Morning Star Hostel for Homeless Men. Rough and ready but run by good souls. That's been the height of my high living.' He nodded towards my bowl. 'Eat that when it's still hot. It mightn't taste of much but it will taste worse when it congeals with a scum on top.'

'I'm too stressed.'

'You need to eat.'

'I need to get out of here.' I lowered my voice into a confiding tone. 'Maybe something in this doctor's notions might help. I just don't know whether to trust him. He wants me to lie on my bunk and talk.'

Nolan nodded. 'That's the Brits all over, plaguing a man with questions. I had it with the Dartmoor screws who didn't ask too politely.'

'This is different. He calls it psychoanalysis.'

Nolan snorted dismissively. 'That's a posh word for informing. We know that anyone opening his mouth to the Brits risks meeting Vincent Fovargue's fate after Sam Maguire left his corpse on a golf course.'

'This doctor claims that talking might be good for me.'

Nolan leaned over the table until our heads almost touched.

'How can talking be good for anyone? Stirring up things best left unsaid? You and I can talk among ourselves about the terror of men being shot and the terror of doing the shooting because we know what not to say. But how could you trust an English doctor? Grangegorman is packed to the rafters with every class of headcase. Imbeciles and old men weaving baskets like their lives depended on it. How could a doctor who isn't a spy find time to chat to just one patient? The other staff here can be brusque but they keep me safe. I told the Super about how scared I am of the local latchicos who have started to throw stones over the wall, and he has gone and found the money to raise the wall. I'll still hear those corner boys playing pitch and toss against the wall but all they will be able to hurl in at us are insults. The Super is a good man who protects us from the world. But at night I still get scared.'

'Of what?' I asked.

'That a new Super will discharge me, when I can't cope in the outside world, although I've tried. Last year the asylum got so crammed that the Super ordered my release to free up space. But where could I go? My siblings are kind but I'm a stranger to them really. If I stay with them I feel like a scrounger. An old comrade lets me sleep on his floor but I scare his children by shouting in my sleep. He finds me work on building sites through the old comrades' network.' Nolan glanced at me. 'Not the ex-officers' network where men like you get prestigious jobs. A network of ordinary volunteers willing to turn a blind eye to an out-of-practice joiner who gets the shakes up a ladder. I knock out a week or two's work from any new job but even one bang of a roofer's hammer sets me off with the shakes. I'm such a danger to myself on any building site and so ashamed of losing yet another job that I disappear into myself. I end up walking the streets, sleeping anywhere I can kip down, until I return here and beg to be let back in. Last year when the Super saw the state of me, he promised I wouldn't be exiled again. In here, among men rocking back and forth and toothless lads talking to themselves, I feel I belong. Grangegorman is my only country left, Colonel. But it's not yours. I've seen where you belong.'

'What do you mean?' I asked.

'Every patient tries to recall the moment their lives went off-kilter. I tell folk that those Dartmoor beatings drove me mad because we love to blame the Brits and sympathy gets me an extra ladle of soup. But I can't lie to myself. On Bloody Sunday morning I pushed my way past a terrified eleven-year-old boy into a house on Morehampton Road and helped to shoot three men. When I ran back out, my mind was astray, though it took months to realise it. I was so young that I knew nothing about life, but suddenly I knew an awful lot about death.'

'Bloody Sunday had enough victims without you trying to sidle in amongst them,' I said curtly.

He nodded. 'I'll not deny that. I wasn't among the innocent match-goers butchered that afternoon, like Jenny Boyle due to be married or wee Jerome O'Leary, lifted up onto a wall when he got shot. Only ten years old. What happened to me was nothing in comparison. But part of me got knocked so badly off-kilter on Morehampton Road that I could never find my old self again. That didn't stop me looking on nights released from here when I'd nowhere else to go. I know every inch of Morehampton Road.'

'Not as well as me,' I said. 'I live there.'

Nolan went silent, as if summoning the courage to speak. 'I know,' he said at last. 'A hundred yards from where I committed murder.'

'How do you know that?' I was perturbed by how he was looking at me.

'It's funny,' he replied. 'After everything I've seen in here, you'd think there was nothing I wouldn't know about madness. But you were the first person I ever saw go mad before my very eyes, peering out from your bedroom window.'

'What are you saying?' I glanced around my cell to ensure we were alone. This felt stranger than any hallucination.

'Last year when I spent three months living on the streets I didn't haunt Morehampton Road every night. But on any night when my conscience led me back there, I always saw you. At first I thought you could see me watching. I got scared of being arrested for loitering, because what explanation could I give for being there? But you saw nothing. I started to think you were not staring out, but somehow staring in.'

My hands moved so fast they surprised both of us. Knocking over the stools, I gripped his flannel shirt so tight that I felt the worn material start to rip at the seams. His startled eyes, inches from mine, brought back flashbacks of midnight interrogations, nights when I had been so enraged that it felt like I had stepped outside my own body and was no longer in control.

'It was you all along,' I hissed, pinning him to the wall. 'You backstabbing Judas tout, hobo snake-in-the-grass tormentor. I was right about being spied on, despite the doctors saying I was hallucinating. If I'm insane, it's you who drove me mad.'

'Or your conscience.' Making no effort to loosen my grip, he stared with equal intensity back into my eyes.

'My conscience is between my confessor and me.'

'Then don't blab to an English doctor. His gobbledygook term is just another way to make you talk. For God's sake, Frankie, release me. I can barely breathe.'

I let go of his shirt. The bowl had been upturned, a gunge of lukewarm stew spreading across the floorboards, dripping through the cracks. We were both breathing heavily, trying to regain our composure. How long was it since anyone called me Frankie, the version of my name affectionately used by Squad members? Nolan was watching me carefully, afraid that my temper might erupt again.

'Can't you see, Frankie? Only we can discuss such things. People only want to hear about good wars with bold deeds to sing of. You and I had bad wars. Bad wars are best kept quiet. I serve my country by staying put behind these walls where no one need witness the aftershock. I live quietly with my ghosts. My presence didn't drive you insane when staring out your window. You never saw me. You say you were looking out for enemies coming to kill you, but I think you were looking out for ghosts.'

'You know nothing about me,' I replied. 'You were a lowly volunteer promoted for one day because we needed extra hands on Bloody Sunday.'

'I know the pain we both deal with and the pain we can't deal with,' Nolan replied.

'I built a respectable career. I toured America on Sweepstakes business and took my parents to dine in fine restaurants they couldn't have dreamt of eating out in when we lived in Drumcondra. I've made a success of my life. You and I have nothing in common, because I'm haunted by no ghosts.'

Nolan quizzically cocked his head. I wondered was he this small, back in 1920, or if the stale air and poor light here had hastened the shrinkage of his bones.

'Tell those fibs to the English doctor if you want,' he said. 'I'm a certified lunatic but even I see how Ireland is only barely held together by the invisible sticking plaster of everyone keeping their secrets. In here, I hear whispers you wouldn't believe, because the people who do the whispering are locked up for refusing to keep their traps shut. I hear things about priests and teachers and Christian Brothers. Bank managers sending servant girls to Nurse Caden for her little bag of tricks to make unborn babies disappear. We patients in here can talk about the sins of powerful men, because nobody outside cares to hear us. And I've learnt to spot those patients who can't talk about the things done to them, but starve or pray themselves to death instead. I know more about secrets than you ever will. I wasn't spying on you when I haunted Morehampton Road. I wouldn't have recognised you as the scared kid that Seán Lemass and I soothed on Bloody Sunday night. I only recognised you from that *Irish Times* photograph of the Sweepstakes Golf Society outing, you posing haughtily among the chaps who had good wars – young faces I once knew, now fattened up by twenty years of steak dinners.'

I rose and used my boot to gingerly touch the stew dripping between the floorboards. I wanted the sound to stop. It brought back memories of that night when I was convinced I could still hear the trickle of blood gurgling in a shot officer's mouth.

'It's a long time since I tasted steak,' I said. 'God knows if my children will even have a meal today as good as this slop.'

'At least you have children,' Nolan said. 'I've neither chick nor child. I'll die in here and nobody will notice because who would make a ballad about my life? The first night I saw you at your window I felt insane jealousy. You in such a fine house. Then your wife came into view, urging you back into bed. Imagine lying with such a fine-looking woman? Imagine lying with any woman?

That first night I hated you as much as the families of those three Drumcondra boys hate you.'

I kept my focus on the stew dripping between the floorboards. 'Those boys should not have been allowed to wander about in the middle of a savage Civil War.'

'So savage they ended up riddled with bullets.'

I turned to face him. 'The coroner found me innocent.'

Nolan nodded vigorously. 'That's what you must tell the English doctor, it's what you must keep telling yourself. We all need a sticking plaster. The more you can forget, the more you can stick yourself back together.'

'Why should I take advice from a certified lunatic?'

Nolan's penetrating gaze was deeply serious.

'If that's how I'm described in my file then nobody will ever listen to me. I'm safer to talk to than any doctor who might blab. When I was sleeping rough last year, I watched you every time I passed your house until I realised who you were waiting for. I'm so dim-witted that the truth only dawned slowly. But as you stared out, I realised you were waiting for those Drumcondra boys. You've had a long wait because they have a long walk from the Red Cow. Two seventeen-year-olds, shot once in the head. A sixteen-year-old sprayed with bullets after trying to run.'

'My accusers don't know the truth of what happened that night.'

'Do you?' Nolan asked.

I shrugged. 'I know I drank neat whiskey. A man can drink himself stotious and drink himself sober. Now what do you really want to know?'

Nolan went silent, then looked at me. 'What happened to you all when I was in Dartmoor? We slaughtered more of our own than the Tans managed when they ran loose like dogs. Do you even know how many died in that Civil War?'

I shook my head. 'It was felt wiser not to keep official tallies but to let sleeping dogs lie. However there isn't a plaque to a single one of the six hundred young National Army soldiers shot dead, sometimes while leaving Mass or just walking along the street.'

'With seventy-seven Irregulars dragged from cells and shot in retaliation.'

I picked a spot on the wall and stared at it, like Collins trained me to do if interrogated.

'No day has passed in the last twenty years without the number seventy-seven being thrown in my face. I've come home to find it daubed on my front door. Leaving Fairyhouse after a day at the races, I found it scratched into my car door. But no one cares how many ordinary civilians died because of Irregulars robbing shops and post offices.'

'Your side gave as good as you got. Especially when the remnants of the Squad were let loose in Kerry after Collin's death. Prisoners tied to landmines and blown up. Army bands playing jaunty tunes when relatives came to collect bodies. Even when the war ended, you couldn't stop. What purpose was served by murdering Seán Lemass's brother?'

I kept my gaze fixed on the wall. 'If I could have found out what officers kidnapped and tortured Noel Lemass, I'd have shot them myself.'

'How hard did you try?'

'It wasn't wise to probe. We needed to put an end to it.'

'An end to what?' Nolan asked. 'The hatred continues.'

I lowered my gaze to stare at him. 'An end to the killing. It's asking too much to end the hatred.'

'I didn't see hatred in your eyes at your window,' he said. 'I saw fear.'

'What makes you think it was those boys I was scared to see?' I asked. 'Maybe I was scared of an even younger boy. A fourteen-year-old who stole his big brother's revolver, brought home from France. A child only allowed to join the IRA because he possessed a gun, back when revolvers were rare as hen's teeth, though it was so heavy he needed both hands to lift it.'

'What makes you scared of him?' Nolan asked.

'I stole his childhood,' I replied. 'If I ever acted dishonourably – and I'm not saying I did – only he has any right to be my judge and jury.' I found myself shaking. 'But I never had any part in those boys' deaths. That is what I swore to my wife, when she asked one day before we got married, out on the South Bull Wall where nobody could eavesdrop. I vowed that I didn't. If that vow was false, what would it make my marriage?' I fixed him with a stare. 'Never breathe a word of this to anyone.'

He saluted, solemnly. 'I swear. Volunteer to volunteer. But don't go blabbing to an English doctor.'

'Do you think I want to talk to him?' I asked. 'But I can't stay in here forever.'

'That's true.' Nolan sat back on his stool. 'You should have followed Jimmy Conroy to America.'

I shook my head, thinking of my father's struggle to start a new life there in middle age. 'It's not as easy to become successful in America as people think. Owning a big car and refrigerator.'

'I don't mean that,' Nolan replied. 'I'm talking about the miracle cure that's all the rage there now, because the Yanks always have the best mod-cons. I heard doctors discuss it. A new treatment called a lobotomy. They drill into your brain like an electrician to cut away and repair any bits where the wiring has gone astray. Patients are walking around America as good as new, because they've had their upstairs rewired. But God knows when that cure will reach Ireland.'

I shook my head, disliking the sound of it. 'It's very different from the English doctor's notion of talking things out.'

'It's safer,' Nolan insisted. 'I mean, who ever heard of an inquisitive electrician? I worked on sites with those lads. They just want to get in and out, with the problem solved and no questions asked, no confidences revealed that might be betrayed. You don't need a doctor; you need a tradesman.'

'It doesn't matter what I need,' I said. 'There's no chance of lobotomies reaching Ireland until this blasted Hitler war is over.'

Nolan nodded vigorously as if waiting for this moment. 'But we have the electric shock treatment. I've seen Friday's list. Your name has a question mark beside it.'

I sat on my stool again. The cell had gone so silent that I could hear my own breathing. We sat for the longest time before I looked up.

'How painful is it, Jimmy?'

'I won't lie, Colonel,' he said. 'It's worse than any torture in Dartmoor. Because so few attendants work here, they need old lags like me to help out. I've helped do it to patients and had other patients help do it to me. While the last poor soul is still lying there, shaking with convulsions, the attendant is ordering you to remove your shoes. Meanwhile he's unbuckling the straps to cart off their last victim. You feel the pit fall out of your stomach, knowing your turn is next. I've endured it four times. Each time, waiting for the attendant to put the rubber gag in my mouth, I wonder if this is what it felt like for the men I lined up in a bedroom on Morehampton Road. The attendant gets his helpers to hold you down to tighten the straps. Sometimes, if they are fellow patients who've endured this themselves, there's a moment before the horror starts when I see such compassion in their eyes. It reminds me of the sense of solidarity I felt as a volunteer, back when we knew what we were fighting for.'

'I remember that sense of belonging,' I said.

'Hold onto that feeling because when they prise the electric contraption off your scalp you'll have no feelings left.'

'I'll never forget the feeling of pride in fighting for freedom,' I said, 'even if this is the price we're paying now.'

'We'd have faced a hangman's noose,' Nolan replied. 'But electric shock treatment wasn't a price any of us ever imagined. You and I would have been better off getting ourselves hanged when we were young. We'd be immortalised as martyrs like Kevin Barry, who never had to answer awkward questions about what side to choose. But the people who see me now only want to look away.'

'Don't say that,' I said, seeing how upset he looked.

'It's the truth,' he replied. 'I went before the Military Service Pensions Board last time I was out, with old comrades providing statements that my torture in Dartmoor has me in here. The committee looked straight through me, as a man of no property or consequence, then begrudgingly awarded me the minimum pension to appease their conscience. It gets paid to Grangegorman. I'll never see a penny, but as I now bring in a few bob to the asylum there's less chance of me being chucked out. As I was leaving the Pensions Board meeting, one member said to me, 'It shouldn't all be about money. I notice you never claimed your active service medal.' I knew that I'd end up back here, in a ward of beds packed together. I wanted to ask him where I would keep it? But I said nothing. I wanted no fuss.' He looked at me. 'Have you medals?'

I nodded. 'I rarely wear them but my children like being allowed touch them.'

'You need to get back to your children, Colonel.'

'I know. But I'm scared of the electrics.'

'Would you have been scared to face a firing squad if the Brits had caught you?'

'Yes. But I would have faced one.'

He stretched out his hands across the small table. 'The Super has his monthly inspection of patients seeking release tomorrow. We'll go and see him. If you put your name down for the electrics on Friday, I swear that I'll be there to tie the straps around you myself. I'll hold your gaze. My salute will be the last thing you see before blacking out.'

I extended my fingers until they entwined with his. 'What if I make a holy show of myself?'

Nolan gripped my hands tight. 'I'll teach you the trick to survive it. Shut your eyes. Shut out everything from your mind. Go back to your happiest memory. Relive that memory over and over. Use it to block out the agony to come.'

My eyes were already closed. I felt his fingers grip mine and I knew that this volunteer would watch over me on Friday when I let myself be tied down. Already I had a terrible foreboding of how it would feel when the apparatus was placed like a crown of thorns on my head. But I pushed past that fear and sought out the bedrock of my happiest memory. The landlady in our Isle of Man digs is warning us that boarders are under curfew in her lodging house. Unless we're back when she locks up at eleven o'clock there will be war. We hope she is not watching as the five of us spill out onto the pavement outside her house in Douglas, bent with laughter like schoolboys, so carefree that any small thing sets us off into fits of giggles.

'There will be war!' Joe Dolan impersonates her snobbish accent. 'That biddy wouldn't know war if it bit her on the arse.' We saunter off in newly purchased holiday flannel trousers, waving walking sticks as we swagger down to the nearby amusement park to clamber onto helter-skelters and the switchback railway rides. Our shouts are joyous when we glance down at a bewildered man in British Army uniform gazing up at us, with no clue as to who we are or why we are savouring this freedom so much, after Collins gave us the nod to take our first ever holiday.

Last night we had sat up late, laughing and reminiscing, until the landlady banged on our bedroom door to demand that we keep our voices down, already regretting having taken us in. But we refused to spend that night like we had spent our previous four hundred nights, afraid to make a sound. We not only left on the light, but opened the curtains and took turns standing at the window, waving out at the empty street as if defying snipers to shoot us.

And today nobody in this fairground in Douglas can understand why we're so raucous. They can't grasp the strain of living in constant fear, never knowing what torture might be inflicted if lifted by the Tans. This constant stress has shifted since the Truce was declared five days ago, amid such public euphoria that we have barely slept. We are leaving it to Collins and Dev and Griffith to sort out the incidentals, the loose ends best left to politicians. None of this concerns the Squad because we have fulfilled our task. We've won our war because while the British needed to beat us into submission to win, all we needed to do was not to lose and we would be declared the victors. This truce means that we have forced them to see us as equals at last.

And now we can relax. We fall about laughing at the carnival booth where Joe Dolan can't hit a single thing at the coconut shy, despite his reputation as a crack shot. Joe soon gets annoyed with us ragging him. He claims that all carnival booths are rigged and we are too naive and trusting. Why waste our money on shysters when it could be spent on them finally achieving their ambition to get me drunk.

We enter a nearby bar so loudly that the barman has doubts about serving us, not least because I barely look old enough. But Jimmy Conroy has a quiet word, half-cajoling and half-menacing.

The drinks are served on a tray and the lads crack up, watching me splutter as raw whiskeys hit my throat. Joe Dolan says, 'Whoa there, sonny boy, take it one gallon at a time.' I try another sip. This one goes down easier, although it is already making me feel light-headed. I may still be with Jimmy Nolan in that cell but the memories are overwhelmingly vivid as in my mind's eye I see us once again raise glasses in the triumphant toast of men who have accomplished our task. As I drain my first ever glass of whiskey, already I am imagining myself arriving back in Dublin. I can envisage tricolours hung in every window and crowds pouring out from houses around East Wall and Ringsend to line the quays and cheer as the mail boat carries us home like heroes. Every man jack of us with tales of unsullied deeds of valour to tell our grandchildren, about how we brought joy to a people united in their bliss and dying to embrace freedom.

Nineteen

Fairfax

10 April 1941

While crossing the yard to finish my evening rounds I became aware of a presence at my back. When I turned, a patient was standing very close behind me. I had glimpsed him before, helping Gus with odd tasks. I waited for him to speak but he took his time, staring in a belligerent manner. Finally, he spoke.

'So you're the English officer who shot an Irish lad in France?'

His remark took me aback. 'That wasn't quite how it happened.'

'Either you shot him or you didn't.'

'How do you know about this?'

He glanced around at a work party of patients drawing turf from the coal yard in the dusk. 'You've as much chance of keeping secrets in here as you have of keeping your own shoes if you don't sleep with them under your pillow.'

'What's your name?'

'Nolan. Jimmy. Volunteer. Second Dublin Brigade. I've a message.'

'What do you want to tell me?'

'I want to tell you nothing.' His voice took on a protective edge. 'And I'll make sure that no other comrade falls for your tricks either.'

I was tired after my shift and not looking forward to the diminishing novelty of another night amid the *médiocrité* of my lodgings. 'Have you a message or not?'

'The old gotcha on duty at the gateman's lodge says there's a young woman asking for you. He says she might be in some class of trouble. Jesus, it didn't take you long.'

'If that's an insinuation, I resent it.'

'I've insinuated nothing.' He turned to walk away. 'I'm not even talking to you. And, God willing, nobody else will.'

Perplexed, I walked down the avenue to the gate lodge with its heavy wooden door that so many patients saw close behind them, never to open again. A young woman sat on the wooden bench, a cardboard suitcase beside her. The gateman gave me a sharp look, as if annoyed to be disturbed at this hour. I placed a cigarette on his desk. He nodded and stepped outside for a smoke, affording us some privacy. Jem Bourke's widow glanced up.

'You're looking well,' I said, confused by her presence.

'Maybe it's the bloom of pregnancy. I'm sick as a dog half the time.'

'Is that the half of your time spent smuggling sacks of flour over the border or the half spent cycling home?'

Her look was withering. 'Haven't you become the right comedian? Barely a wet week in Dublin and you've mastered the Jackeen cynicism.'

I sat beside her, realising how lonely I was here. Despite us having only shared one fraught conversation on the mailboat crossing, she was the only person in this country to whom I felt any connection.

'I'm sorry. I didn't mean to sound cynical. I'm just surprised to see you.'

'I had to stop pretending to be pregnant. It turns out that I am. Soon I'd be so big that the customs men would think I'm carrying twins.' She paused. 'Mother of God, I hope I'm not.'

Her palms were pressed flat on the bench in a sign of tension. I risked patting her fingers. 'What are you telling me?'

'Me and Jem had been trying but there seemed to be nothing doing. I thought he was firing blanks or something was wrong with me. It turns out there was nothing wrong with either of us. We just didn't know it. Now Jem never will. My time of month was due a few weeks before that bomb, but I was never that regular. Blundering around dark streets in London to find bomb shelters, it's hard to keep track like normal, because nothing is normal. When my time didn't come after Jem's death, I thought nothing of it because shock can send everything haywire. You'd know this if you're not just a quack but a real doctor too.'

'The shock endured could disrupt any woman's cycle,' I said.

She nodded. 'That black marketeer in Cullaville isn't the worst, though he's always eyeing me up. I said I wasn't feeling well but hadn't the money to see a doctor. He told me to stay in the back of his shop. A retired doctor owed him a favour. I felt scared, not knowing who he might bring back. But it was a real doctor, old as the hills, but kind. After I answered a few questions, he told the black marketeer to go out to the front of his shop until called. Then he examined me and said he reckoned I was ten weeks gone. Who'd have thought it, with Jem sharing a pauper's plot in Camberwell cemetery?'

'What did your family say when you told them?' I asked.

'I didn't. I'd a few bob saved up. Enough to get me here.'

'I'm sorry,' I explained, 'but we don't take in women in your condition. I've heard mention of a home on the Navan Road, run by nuns. I don't know much about it, but I can go there with you if you want.'

The woman flinched angrily. 'I'm no fallen woman or unmarried mother-to-be. I'm Jem Bourke's widow. Why would I go into a convent to scrub clothes?'

'Where will you go?'

'I know where I'm going but I need to ask a favour first.'

'Is it money? I have some savings if I can help.'

'I don't want your money.' She was affronted. 'When men aren't thinking of sex why do you always think of money?'

I shook my head in apology. 'Sorry. I just want to make sure that you are alright.'

'Why? We're hardly family.'

'To be honest,' I said, 'I don't have any family.'

She nodded, mollified. 'I know the feeling.'

'You have a whole family in Monaghan.'

'I don't know why, when I first went to England, I was homesick for Monaghan. I was barely home before I realised that I'm more homesick for London. Isn't that funny? Bombing raids and fires blazing at night. Who in their right mind would want to risk going back, especially with a child who, please God, will be born safe there?'

'Are you saying you're taking the boat?'

'I still have my travel permit.'

'What about the danger?'

She shook her head. 'I never felt more scared or alone as on my first night in London, hearing an air-raid siren. Not knowing where to go, but following other folk down stairs that seemed to go on forever. I was lost, not knowing a soul but then I realised, with a flood of release, that not a soul knew me. But they made room for me to sit among them on that packed platform, with one man offering me a fag and wanting nothing in return. An old woman put a hand on my shoulder because she saw me shaking and said we'd all be snug as bugs down there. She asked my name and said it was pretty when I surprised myself by claiming that my name was Meredith. My family would think Meredith a pretentious name. But in that tube station I could be Meredith or Mabel or Margarita with no snide busybody neighbour to contradict me. I felt suddenly free in the middle of a war. Isn't that funny?'

'Do you not feel free here?' I asked.

She shook her head. 'It's only after tasting freedom that I realised how unfree life is here. Traipsing to Mass and confession where a priest can ask any personal question he wants; standing in shop queues and accepting how the woman behind you will be served first, over your head like you don't exist, because her husband owns a big farm. I was nobody in London, yet I was never happier, even before I met Jem. I was barely home before I felt the parish closing in on me, all arriving to express sympathy, *moryah*, but really just to gawk at the emigrant returning empty-handed. I'm taking tonight's sailing because London at war beats Monaghan in stagnation.' She looked up. 'You and I have no family. But we can pretend to be in-laws. In-laws rarely see or even like each other. But they can call in favours.'

'What can I do? Just ask.'

'Only two men know I'm pregnant. You and that doctor in Cullaville. No woman knows yet, but I know who I want to tell first.' She hesitated for the first time. 'You said you might look out for my aunt.'

I nodded. 'They have her working in the therapy room, knitting and darning. She rarely leaves her ward except to go there. I stop by occasionally. She's partial to the few sweets I bring her.'

'That sounds like her.' The young woman paused. 'The boat doesn't leave for a few hours. Is there any chance of seeing her?'

'Visiting hours are over,' I said. 'Even if I could bend the rules and bring you up to her ward, you don't want to see her there and I think she'd prefer you not to see her in that ward with no space for privacy and dignity.' I paused. 'It's a long shot, but there is a quiet pub just down the road. Can you wait there?'

She shook her head. 'I can't go into a pub alone. They'll think me a prostitute.'

'It has a snug. I've seen women enter it to get jugs of porter filled.'

'And covered over with a cloth to be taken away. Do you ever see a woman stay there on her own?'

I rose. 'Would the free young woman you described, sitting in that crowded tube station during an air raid, care what some Dublin barman thought of her?'

The woman smiled ruefully. 'She wouldn't care a toss.'

'Then why do you care?'

'Because I'm still in Ireland. I won't feel free until I see the lights of Howth disappear.' She paused. 'Are you saying you have the power to bring her out to meet me?'

The Superintendent had left for the evening. But the gateman had a spiteful streak and would be sure to inform him of any breach of rules. Still, the man could only tell of something if he witnessed it. This would cost me more than a few packets of cigarettes, but if anyone could smuggle people in or out of this asylum it was Gus.

'I don't. There are strict procedures. But the worst they can do is send me packing on that boat. Maybe that's where I belong for all the good I'm doing here. But give me half an hour and I'll meet you at that pub, either alone or with someone. If you feel unable to go inside, just wait on the corner.'

We heard the gateman's footsteps return down the gravelled driveway. The woman picked up her suitcase.

'I'll be sipping a sweet sherry in the snug,' she said. 'I'll pay with English coins. That always impresses folk. And I'll have a glass of lemonade ordered, just in case.'

I opened the door for her and locked it again. The gateman came back in, unable to hide his curiosity. 'What did she want, calling at this hour?'

'Her freedom.'

He laughed. 'She picked a queer place to look for it.'

'Are you not cold out here?'

'Perishing, but what can you do?'

'It's warmer up in the kitchens,' I said, 'if you can cope with the clouds of steam. You've a long night ahead. Maybe I can get someone to relieve you for a spell.'

'I doubt it.'

I walked back up the unlit driveway to the main courtyard. One patient – a tall, thin old man who seemed unable to stay still – was pacing around the mucky football pitch, locked in a ceaseless agitated conversation with an imaginary companion. The usual jeers and catcalls came from the direction of Kirwan Street Cottages on the far side of the boundary wall – local urchins trying to outdo each other in thinking up new insults to shout at the patients they couldn't see. Last week a group of them scaled the wall to trespass on this strip of recreation ground, scattering patients and taunting the attendants who confronted them.

The Superintendent was attempting to raise the height of this perimeter wall and top it with glass embedded in cement to stop the nightly avalanche of stones thrown in to frighten the patients. But each day's work was being maliciously destroyed during the night before the cement could properly set. A night watchman was coming on duty now to patrol the wall until dawn to allow the cement to dry. He shouted an oath at the urchins to make them aware of his presence, but this only encouraged them to try to impress some girls, whose laughter I could hear, by trying to hurl more rocks over the wall. Few succeeded in landing in the muddy recreation area and the inmates still allowed to exercise so late in the evening seemed impervious to this nightly name-calling.

I needed to find Gus. He seemed impossible to locate in the main hospital, but when passing the back stairs that led to the attics I saw a glimmer of light up there. I called his name, though I could think of no reason for him to be up there. After a few moments he appeared. It was the first time that I sensed him looking ruffled.

'What's the story?' he shouted down.

'I need a favour.'

'Can't it wait?'

'No. And I will be hugely in your debt.'

He disappeared again. I saw the dim light being switched off. He had always seemed a decent if unfathomable man, but his surreptitious manner caused me to wonder if he had been pilfering from personal possessions of deceased patients up there. He descended the steep stairs, a little too briskly. But this was no time to question him. When I mentioned Bridie Kerr, he nodded so immediately that I wondered if he might be the only person in this asylum to know every patient by name.

'As harmless as a lamb and as easily startled,' he said. 'Her brother pulled a fast one by claiming that she lived in Dublin and therefore fell under our care. The Super has been trying to get the Monaghan County Manager to fork out the hundred and fifty smackers needed for her upkeep, but you'd squeeze a kiss out of a Mercy nun quicker than you'd squeeze money from some Monaghan men. It's no wonder she's never had a single visitor in all her time here.'

'She has one now.'

I didn't explain how I knew Bridie's niece and why she was calling so late in the evening. I admired Gus's deliberate avoidance of curiosity. He simply nodded when I asked if there was any possible way to do what I wanted.

'It's possible,' he replied. 'It's also possible that you and I will get the sack and the nurse in change of Bridie's ward will be given a choice of being dismissed or going to work in the piggery – although you earn more here caring for the pigs than caring for the patients.'

'So are you saying it's not possible?'

Gus shook his head. 'I haven't said anything because we are not even having this conversation. Though I might mention in passing that there's a secluded bench outside the mortuary building near the gate lodge. If you just happen to be sitting there in fifteen minutes' time, it's always possible that the impossible might happen.'

Gus strode out the main door in the direction of the female hospital where staff would be already steering the dayroom patients towards their wards to commence the nightly count and lock in. I walked back outside. The jeering from Kirwan Street Cottages had stopped. The elderly patient continued to walk in such a rapid, jerky motion that, if he stopped suddenly, I suspected that he would topple over. An attendant started to call in the last few stragglers. This was the most likely time of night for escape attempts, although most patients were easily recaptured. They almost invariably made for the home of their nearest relative, except for those who were mad for the motion pictures. Gus was generally dispatched in search of these and had told me how his first port of call was the Bohemian picture palace in Phibsborough. He always had the decency to wait until the main feature was over before quietly apprehending them and walking them back here with no need to file a report with the Garda Síochána.

I found the bench that Gus had mentioned. Ten minutes later he appeared with Bridie. She looked confused and uneasy but seemed to have sufficient trust in Gus to allow herself be swept along, accompanied by a nervous but defiant young nurse who was quietly reassuring her. I had previously only seen Bridie wearing a tattered cardigan over a flannel nightshirt but it looked like the nurse had rifled through the clothes allotted to every patient in her ward to fit together a mismatching outfit for her. Gus told us to wait on this bench, shaded from view, while he walked towards the gate lodge.

'Leave this Holy Joe to me,' he said. 'I've a patient in the kitchens primed to ask him about his work with An Ríoghacht and the Irish Vigilance Association. The old codger loves to boast about helping to keep Ireland safe from indecent literature.'

'I take it you didn't get your copy of Joyce from him.'

'That gobshite can barely read *Ireland's Own*, though deep down I suspect that he'd secretly enjoy being given a good working over by Joyce's Bella Cohen.'

I was trying to focus on reassuring Bridie who kept glancing fretfully around, but Gus's remark caused an unexpected ambush of grief. It brought back memories of lying in bed with Charles who had been gifted a copy of *Ulysses* that a friend procured in Paris. Charles had flicked through it in exasperation until he stumbled upon the scene where Bloom fantasised about being unmanned by this fearsome brothel keeper. I could hear Charles's booming laugh as he read it aloud, savouring the outrageous dialogue while I spooned into his naked body. How could this man have betrayed me and what right had I to still feel such anger after the fate that befell him?

The nurse kept trying to arrange Bridie's lank hair in some tidy fashion.

'Thank you for taking this risk,' I whispered.

'Gus says that Bridie has a niece taking the boat. I'll be for the chop if the Super hears of this, but that might be the best thing to happen. My mother loves boasting to neighbours in the Oliver Bond flats of being me a nurse here, like it's a step up in the world, like a mental nurse is treated the same as a hospital one. But the only qualifications that I needed was to be over five foot four, unmarried and have no ailments that might stop me dealing with the violence that can happen here at any moment.' She brushed back Bridie's hair again. 'Most patients are dotes like Bridie who wouldn't harm a fly, but some of the paranoid schizophrenics with delusions can turn on a sixpence: calm one minute, tearing at your hair the next. Half the time it's not even their illness, it's frustration boiling over at being so hemmed in. There's fifty trying to sleep in Bridie's ward alone. At half-six we lock them in, their faces in summer staring out the barred window at all the daylight left. Then at eleven sharp, we're locked in too, at the nurses' home, except for once a week being allowed go wild entirely and stay out until half-eleven.

'When Gus asked me to help you I was scared. Then I thought of Bridie's niece taking the boat, despite the air raids and ructions over there, and I said to myself, it will take me twenty years to get any promotion in this place, but if I'm sacked I'll walk into a better job in London, with better pay and more respect than I get here where I'm only treated as a handmaiden for doctors to wipe their hands on.' She paused. 'All the doctors except you. You treat us with courtesy. All the nurses regard you as a man of mystery. We spend our breaks speculating on why you're here.'

'What's your theory?'

She hesitated, shy suddenly. 'When I see you on a corridor, lost in thought, something about your eyes makes me think you're suffering from a broken heart.' She blushed and added quickly. 'I'm speaking out of turn, I'm sorry.'

'You might just be right. I hope you're not sacked for this; we're all not sacked.'

'You're safe enough, they're short of doctors. Gus will be all right too.'

'Why is that?'

'The Super relies on him for things that never make it into the Board of Governors reports. Gus knows where all the bodies are buried, in every sense of the word. I'll be the only one sacked. But if I am dismissed and have to take the boat, just promise me one favour. Will you write me a reference?'

'I'll do better than that,' I said. 'I'll give you the name of a doctor I know in London who will ensure that you get proper training and real qualifications.'

We both went quiet, hearing the door of the gate lodge open. I squeezed Bridie's hand to caution her to stay silent, although she had yet to utter a word. The gateman walked up the unlit avenue without seeing us. The nurse waited a moment and then slipped away. I realised that talking to her had been the first open conversation I'd had with anyone here. Bridie finally spoke.

'Will there be sweets?'

'It will be better than sweets.'

Gus appeared in the lit doorway. 'I told the gotcha there was hot cocoa going in the kitchens and I'd fill in here for quarter of an hour. He'll be sure to drag it out for another ten minutes for spite. Now out you go and neither of you are to come back fluttered.'

He opened the door that led onto the deserted street. Bridie peered out, scared to cross the threshold.

'You'll be grand, Bridie,' Gus assured her. 'It's only for a few minutes. We'll save you your slice of black bread for supper.'

She allowed me to take her arm and lead her onto the street. I needed to coax her to enter the pub. A row of solitary men sat nursing pints. The barman went to speak. I ignored him and opened the door into the snug. Bridie peered in at the young woman waiting there.

'I know your face,' she said at last. 'Or I think I do.'

'Of course you do. Didn't we often share a bed, driving your mother daft by giggling at night?'

'Is it Margaret? Mags?'

The woman nodded. 'I brought you sweets, Aunt Bridie. And I've news too.'

She glanced at me. I held up both sets of fingers twice to indicate that she had twenty minutes, at most. Then I closed over the snug door, aware of every eye in the pub watching me, every ear straining to hear what was being said in there. I ordered a brandy and tried to engage the sullen barman in loud conversation to give the women some privacy. The barman was disinclined to talk, suspicious of what was happening in his premises. I heard Gus's voice behind me.

'Seeing as you're buying, I'll have a Bushmills and a glass of stout as a chaser. I left little Jimmy Nolan holding the fort in the gate lodge. He loves any bit of status.'

'Are you not afraid of him absconding?' I asked, after ordering his drinks.

'Jimmy?' Gus watched the barman measure out his whiskey. 'We've patients like Bridie who shouldn't be here and then others like Jimmy who can't cope anywhere else. This asylum gives him asylum, if you get my drift.'

'He spoke to me most aggressively, earlier, like he harboured an animosity towards me.'

'That's not animosity,' Gus said. 'It's a pathological jealousy.'

'Of me? I don't even know the man.'

'But you are trying to get to know the man he's desperate to feel close to. I'm working here so long, overhearing doctors talk to each other, that I've learnt every class of odd medical term. Are you familiar with morbid jealousy disorder?'

I nodded, surprised that he knew the name for this psychological obsession. 'Some doctors call it Othello syndrome or delusional jealousy. It's where a man becomes convinced, with no logical foundation, that his wife is unfaithful. But I'm damned if I know what that has got to do with me.'

Gus savoured his first sip of whiskey. 'I'm no doctor, so maybe I'm wrong, but you acquire a gut instinct for things in here, even obsessions without rhyme or reason. Jimmy never had a wife. He's always been popular, but a loner. The Old IRA man that even the

Old IRA forgot about. He's obsessed with Dillon because it's the first time in here that he hasn't felt totally alone. All old gunmen share more secrets than any married couple. He sees your attempts to get Dillon to talk as a threat to that bond between them.'

'That's illogical,' I said.

The attendant raised his glass again. 'What has logic got to do with this place?' He took a sip. '*Uisce Beatha*, we call whiskey: The Water of Life. You should buy a full bottle and save yourself the trip tomorrow.'

'What do you mean?'

'You've lost your bet. The Super was doing his monthly inspection today, seeing the patients who hoped their families had sent in letters, promising to take responsibility for their release. Francis Dillon marched in his office, with a military swagger and with Jimmy Nolan trailing behind like his bugle boy. Dillon demanded to be put first on the list for the old electric shocks tomorrow.'

'But the Superintendent promised me more time with him. I'm getting somewhere.'

Gus shrugged. 'Maybe you were getting somewhere where nobody else wants you to go. All superintendents rule their asylums like feudal lords. They eventually stamp on anything that might challenge their authority. Your novelty has worn off. Have you experience of administering electroconvulsive therapy?'

'Yes,' I said. 'Why?'

'The Super has you listed to do it. The doctor who dished out the volts last week was a tad overenthusiastic with his bag of tricks. A patient was left in agony with her left shoulder. The X-ray shows that fragments of bone became detached during her spasms. I could see that the doctor was going too heavy, with one eye fixed on his tee-time. But it's more than my job's worth to say boo to a Blackrock College boy.'

'And did the anaesthesiologist not notice?'

Gus stared at me with incredulity. 'What anaesthesiologist? You're not working in the Ritz. In Ireland all we can do is to tell the patients to offer it up for the holy souls in purgatory.' Gus looked towards the snug. 'This is a good thing you're doing here.'

'Maybe it's the only good thing I'll ever do here.'

'Then it's one more good thing than some of your colleagues will ever do. Still, you're against the clock in case that gotcha returns early. I'd better get back.' He downed his glass of Guinness. 'What did you hope to get Dillon to confess to you during psychoanalysis anyway?'

'How would you even know how psychoanalysis works?' I hadn't intended my tone to convey anger, but it arose from pure frustration.

Gus set down his empty glass, his voice icy. 'Don't get shirty. How would you know what things I know, about psychoanalysis or about you?'

'I didn't want Dillon to admit anything to me,' I said. 'I wanted him to admit things to himself.' I put down my own glass, adopting a more conciliatory tone. 'You've taken a big risk this evening. How many packets of cigarettes do I owe you?'

The snug door opened. Bridie emerged slowly, clutching a paper bag of boiled sweets. Gus glanced to me. 'Do you think I'd risk my job for you?' he said quietly. 'I did this for Bridie.'

Bridie looked around, scared by all the staring men, then her gaze settled on Gus. He held out his arm to link hers.

'Will we be going, Bridie?'

She took his arm, allowing him to lead her out. She never looked back. I entered the snug. Margaret, Mags – I finally had not one but two names for her – had been crying. I went to speak but saw that she didn't want to talk to me or anyone. She brushed away any remaining tears, then picked up her suitcase and ran the gauntlet of staring male eyes until she reached the pub door. She stared back, before disappearing into the night.

'This whole country needs locking up, not my aunt.'

Twenty

Nolan

Asylum time

In all my years as a patient, I never saw a sight to match the first time they strapped the colonel down to riddle him with the electrics. I'd had to wheedle my way into the low-ceilinged outhouse converted into a ward for this purpose. The operating theatre, or abattoir as we called it, was tiny, but I wouldn't be budged. Despite the colonel's demand – or maybe because of it – the Super put his name halfway down the list. I pretended to make myself useful by helping to hold down each patient, lest they did themselves damage during their involuntary spasms. These mini-executions – this is how they seemed like – happened in one corner under a single electric bulb. The rest of the outhouse was cordoned off into a holding pen where other patients on the list moaned aloud in fear as their turn drew closer.

A set of screens blocked their view of the beds on which this procedure was done. Two tables, covered in lacquered cloth that could be easily wiped down, were positioned behind it. The first one held the forceps and sterile drums; the bowls of swabs and saline solution to be smeared on the temples of each patient before the electrical apparatus was attached to their skulls. The second table held the doctor's magical black electric box with its knobs that he fiddled with each time before unleashing the torment.

Even hardened patients who had endured numerous sessions lost their nerve when their turn drew close. In addition to the three people needed to hold them down on the table, extra staff – or liberty patients like me if no staff were available – were needed to cajole and half drag each new patient from the pen. Some ran for the door, even though they knew it was locked, or lay rigid on the floor, trying to make their bodies as heavy as possible while being lifted and carried to their fate. The colonel was the first patient I ever saw voluntarily step forward. Perhaps I hadn't fully drilled home what would happen or maybe he didn't want to lose face in front of a mere rank-and-file ex-Volunteer like myself.

But what was so extraordinary that even the nurses paused and looked perplexed was that, when Dillon gingerly stepped forward, suddenly there wasn't a sound to be heard in the pen. Every patient seemed to hold his breath, waiting to see if fear would make the colonel lose his resolve and beg the English doctor to halt the procedure. I let other people hold him down. Instead I took his hand and gazed into his eyes to show that I had kept my word and was offering my support again, just like when we broke curfew on Bloody Sunday night. Back then we were mere boys. Now we were broken men, but we could win this last battle against a British officer wanting to interrogate one of us.

I had only told a few inmates about the doctor's ploys to trick the colonel into turning informer. But walls have ears. Every patient here seemed to realise that a duel was being fought between a doctor and a patient and, just for once, the patient would win.

Part of me knew there were no winners in that torture chamber. The look of trust that the colonel gave me only lasted as long as it took a nurse to use pliers to force open his mouth wide enough to insert a padded rubber strip to bite down on, in case he lost every tooth or bit his tongue in half. But even the initial noise of this involuntary struggle provoked no sound from the patients in the pen. Normally the nurse gave the word, but I beat her to it.

Staring up belligerently into the face of the English doctor, I gave the nod to start.

I never saw a doctor move with greater reluctance than Fairfax when he attached the electric terminal to each side of Dillon's skull and pulled the switch to apply the first electric stimulus. Only then, when the air filled with the usual screams and sparks and stink of scorched flesh, did a great shout of triumph erupt from the men waiting their turn in the pen. Their shout perturbed Fairfax, who could not explain it. It was just as well that he wouldn't ask for an explanation, because I wasn't really sure that I – or the men doing the shouting – fully understood it. For some men it was a shout of revenge. The Super had tried to keep Dillon's presence a secret. But everyone knew from the moment he came in. Dillon was always a marked man. Perhaps no patient here had suffered torture under the hands of his tight-knit crew in Wellington Barracks, but many knew friends who had emerged from that barracks as jabbering wrecks. And even patients who knew nobody who personally suffered there, understood the sense of terror that any mention of Wellington Barracks or Oriel House could still evoke.

For others, the shout was one of triumph at an Irishman outwitting an Englishman by refusing to break the code of silence that bound us together. Some others, so bewildered that they barely knew where they were, probably shouted because the men around them did so and they needed to join in. The few who didn't shout were already unconscious – drugged patients wheeled up from the locked ward where anyone who attempted suicide was kept sedated.

Electroconvulsive therapy puts the heart crossways in me, no matter how often I have witnessed it. But this time felt different. Previously I'd only seen it administered by imperious doctors, unquestioningly self-confident in thinking they were doing good. But looking at Fairfax, I knew how repulsed he was by this torture.

Still, he had no time to think. The queue of patients waiting to be done began to moan and quake again, with the sideshow of Francis Dillon now over. Fairfax removed the terminals from Dillon's skull as his body still jerked with spasms. The next patient was already waiting on the second bed as Dillon was wheeled off to be placed on a stretcher to let the first bed be reused. I moved away, preparing to help bring him back to his cell. Dillon wouldn't be there for long. It was rumoured that his cell was needed for the next important patient whose presence they wanted hushed up. I felt relieved of any need to call him Colonel now. His air of superiority and higher military rank had been dissipated by his screams. We were equals at last. He was one of us now. Soon he would become just another patient in these crowded wards and would truly need me, clinging to me, grateful that I was minding him.

I looked back at Fairfax adjusting the knobs on his electric apparatus. He was shaking. I knew he hated every moment of this. Even I could sense the Super's message in allotting him this task. The novelty of having a posh English doctor around was gone. Soon Fairfax would be another lowly house physician, summoned at all hours for dogsbody tasks, like force-feeding elderly patients who longed for the respite of death. Gus would summon me, if short-staffed, and we would look away as Fairfax struggled to ram a tube down the patient's throat and funnel gruel into his stomach, while we held down the man's shoulders. Finally, Gus would take pity on Fairfax by silently removing the rigid rubber tube from his shaking hands, because Gus was an expert at bringing ordeals to an end.

Fairfax glanced across at me as the door was unlocked for us to leave with Dillon's unconscious body. I nodded back, as if at an old acquaintance, feeling no sense of triumph. This ward held no victors, but only the vanquished.

Twenty-One

Gus

11 April 1941

Fairfax was in a sullen mood during his shift on that day when the Super first ordered him to apply the jump leads to Dillon's brain. Even the patients who were sufficiently compos mentis could sense his disconsolateness during his curt dealings with them. It seemed more than just frustration at having been denied a chance to try out tête-à-tête psychoanalysis with Dillon or his realisation that slow-motion cures held no place in this meat factory. Grangegorman was so overcrowded that its raison d'être was not so much to cure people as to care for the unwanted while corralling them in.

Maybe the fact that he spotted me moving about in the attics on the previous evening provoked his suspicion. But for whatever reason, having lost face before those patients in the electrics ward, he seemed to need to reassert his authority. That evening, when his shift ended and he should have already left the asylum, I became his target.

Perhaps Fairfax thought that he was bringing psychoanalysis to Dublin, where most people presumed it was sacrilegious to tell your secrets to anyone other than a priest. But I knew that the practice already existed here, in its own hidden world, in a house in Belgrave Terrace in Monkstown, which wisely displayed no medical brass plate.

I knew about furtive worlds, from spending much of my life flittering between them. In Grangegorman I had made my own hideaway in a corner of those attics that no one frequented. For years I conducted a weekly rendezvous up there, with blankets and a horsehair mattress hidden among the shelves of unclaimed handbags. Nobody had ever followed me up there, because curiosity wasn't a big commodity in this asylum, with folk too wrapped up in their own despair. But Fairfax took it on himself to investigate my suspicious movements, out of a sense of moral duty or the conceit inbred into his class or perhaps because I pushed him too far in that pub on the previous evening.

He crept up the stairs so quietly that, despite my usual antenna for danger, I had no idea how long he stood watching the pair of us silently lie on that mattress. It was my companion who noticed him first, his head resting on my chest as he luxuriated in inhaling the Pall Mall cigarette I had kept for him to savour. An agitation in his eyes made me look up. Fairfax was standing over us, clenching his fists, torn between his own nature and his role as jailor and custodian of the souls incarcerated here.

'Thank God you are both still clothed,' he said. 'It makes what I must report to the Superintendent less onerous, if I am correct in assuming that this man is a patient?'

'Who else would he be?' I tried to gather my wits. 'Outsiders don't queue up to get in here like it was the Crystal Ballroom.'

'Did you coerce this patient to come up here with you?'

'Does he look coerced?'

'He looks scared. You did me a great favour with Bridie Kerr. I'm not unappreciative. You know enough about my actions last night to get me sacked. But I have a duty of care to every patient and I must report even the slightest hint of exploitation.'

'Report what you want,' I said. 'There's no exploitation here, but yes, he is scared. Scared of doctors and authority figures, scared by his nightmares and often scared of his own shadow.'

'Let him speak for himself.' Fairfax studied the man beside me who crouched into a ball, his discarded cigarette in danger of setting fire to the mattress until I stubbed it out.

'He doesn't speak much. The habit got beaten out of him years ago.'

Fairfax knelt to touch his shoulder and he flinched. 'This man is petrified. What have you been doing to him?'

'What I do once a week when his ward attendant turns a blind eye. I feed him cigarettes and morsels of food I've squirrelled away. I spoon into him for a short time, the way we used to lie, spooned into each other at night. He's so lost inside his own purgatory that I don't always know if he understands. But I try to make him aware that, even in this place, he is still loved.'

My companion put his hands over his ears to block out our voices, muttering to himself while rocking back and forth.

'Why have I never seen him before?' Fairfax asked, genuinely concerned.

'Who says you haven't? Every doctor has the memory of his first day here etched in his mind. After that – though you try your best – it becomes a blur of faces or sedated figures placed on the line for attempting suicide, like this man tried more than once. You try to remember faces, but there are too many. Don't feel bad about it.' I placed a protective arm around my companion to try and stop him shaking. 'You're a reasonably honest man doing your best, but in here nobody's best is good enough.'

Fairfax rocked back, affronted, repeating my phrase as if it was intended disparagingly. '"A *reasonably honest man?*" When I want an attendant's opinion of my character I will solicit it.'

'Be careful what you try to solicit in Dublin,' I said. 'Back alleys have no street lights, but that doesn't mean they don't have prying eyes.'

'I've had enough impudence,' he replied angrily. 'You wouldn't last a day in an English asylum.'

'Lower your voice.' I nodded towards my companion. 'You're scaring him. I wouldn't stay another day in this asylum if it wasn't for him.'

Fairfax took a deep breath. 'I'm not in the business of judging your feelings towards this or any man. Nor do I want to know details of your life outside these walls. I came to Dublin to try and make a difference. Maybe I can't. But I can still ensure that no harm comes to any patient under my care.'

I disentangled my arm from around my companion and arranged a coat under his head to make him comfortable, before I rose to confront Fairfax.

'Any harm done to him was done before he came in here,' I said. 'And no harm will come to him in these attics.'

'Let's see what the Superintendent says about that.'

'The Super is too busy pondering the gaps in your curriculum vitae.'

'What would you know about my curriculum vitae?'

'Only what I've read in the growing pile of correspondence the Super keeps in the same filing cabinet where he stashes his whiskey. You claimed to have worked at the Tavistock Clinic for five years, treating damaged soldiers who couldn't afford private psychotherapy. But the doctor in charge there says you were persuaded to resign after just two years, in circumstances that he declines to go into.'

'You know nothing about my life.'

'I don't know why you left the Tavistock. But I know that you're a liar. It takes one to know one.'

He bristled with defensive nervousness. 'What exactly are you implying?'

'That you and I have been telling different lies, but about the same thing.'

Fairfax drew himself up to his full height. 'I may be attacked or imprisoned. But I won't be blackmailed.'

'Neither of us can be imprisoned for the lie I'm referring to,' I said. 'We've each lied about our big brothers. Whatever type of freedom Dillon lost his sanity fighting for never included freedom for men like me. I just keep my head down and savour any brief liberty worth the risk.' I glanced back at the figure lying in a world of his own on the mattress. 'But the only liberty I ever took with this man here was to erase all trace of his name and the shell of an existence that his torturers left him with. He's my lie. Your lie is about your brother still being off fighting Hitler. I've read the letters the Super has. Your big brother was killed in the Battle of Mons, hours before the Armistice. There was a huge rumpus in the hospital you worked in after the Tavistock where you tried to introduce a man with whom you shared a flat as being your older brother. Perhaps that's why you have airbrushed that hospital from your CV and claim you were still working in the Tavistock at that time.'

'I told a white lie at that hospital,' Fairfax replied. 'I'd no idea that a doctor there knew my father. Occasionally, in certain social situations my flatmate and I would claim to be brothers. It was just easier. My flatmate would have made a better brother than my actual one, who won medals for gallantry but was decidedly ungallant towards me.'

'There's nothing wrong with white lies. For twenty years I've been telling the opposite one. The lie that keeps me here so I can watch over my big brother.' I addressed the figure on the mattress. 'Eamonn, you're safe, my old segotia.'

My brother raised himself up onto his knees to glance fearfully at the doctor, then curled back down into a foetal position.

'When Eamonn and I first curled into each other, we were chislers,' I said. 'I hero-worshipped him. No braver boy in James's Street. Eamonn was set up for life. As the eldest son, he was guaranteed a cooper's job in Guinness's.'

'You said your brother was killed in your Civil War,' Fairfax said.

I nodded. 'It's what I told our da after a neighbour tipped me the wink about where to find Eamonn when thugs left him for dead. Their rifle jammed and they tried to batter his head in with the butt. I don't know how long he lay in that ditch, with passers-by hearing his cries but hurrying on, not knowing what side they might be accused of supporting by helping him or what retaliation they'd receive for an act of Christian charity. I got Eamonn admitted here under a false name, thanks to a doctor who owed me big time. When I realised he'd never recover, I told Da how I'd got word that Eamonn was shot and secretly buried. That wasn't uncommon back then. I suppose that Eamonn got lucky compared to Lemass's brother or Archbishop McQuaid's brother who were both killed on opposite sides, but on some days when I look at him, I wonder. I tried to fill Eamonn's shoes in Guinness's for a while but then I came to work here. It keeps me close to the only person I've ever felt close to.'

'Were you lying when you said you took no part in the fighting?' Fairfax asked.

I nodded. 'I had my skull cracked open by a Dublin Metropolitan Police baton when Jim Larkin called the workers onto the streets in 1913. That was a fight I understood: workers against toffs, no misty-eyed mysticism. We knew exactly what we were fighting for, with even Joe McGrath making fiery speeches about workers' rights. I respected Eamonn's idealism in his fight, but no matter what the outcome, I knew I'd remain an outcast, one careless action away from jail. You feel that way about your country too, I suspect.'

Fairfax said nothing but in our coded world, silence was often an affirmative reply.

'Before working here,' I continued, 'I laboured on building the Ardnacrusha hydroelectric power station, for slave wages in County Clare. We were trying to organise ourselves to demand better wages when Joe McGrath turned up. Only this time with Dillon and a posse of other former National Army officers whom he used as strike-breakers. McGrath knew what way the wind was blowing. His strike-breaking helped get him the Sweepstakes license. However, Eamonn was a genuine idealist, obeying every order to attack the Tans. He and his pals were the cream of the crop. But cream turns sour.'

Fairfax knelt again to touch Eamonn's shoulder. This time my brother didn't flinch, but I sensed he was still cowed. The doctor looked at me.

'Which side in the Civil War left your brother in this state?'

I shrugged cautiously. 'Does it matter? Not that I didn't ask around, hungry for revenge. I stopped asking after I learnt that – amid the recriminations and land grabbing and personal jealousies being settled – Eamonn did equally terrible things to his former comrades. I decided I didn't want to know what atrocities he committed. Nor did I want to know the names of those who left him for dead. Killing them won't bring back the son I told Da he had lost. It was better for Da to think of Eamonn dying a martyr's death instead of being left a crippled half-wit. It's been an easy lie to keep up. Nobody wants to ask about Eamonn, no more than they want to know about some of the women in here, unable to go home because folk want no reminding of the outrages committed against them during that Civil War by men drunk on the power of simply having power.' I gazed at him honestly. 'That's my excuse for lying. What's yours?'

Dr Fairfax considered his words before replying.

'It was unprofessional to tell Dillon my brother was alive. I did it on impulse, hoping to establish a connection, make him feel we had something in common.'

'You're a convincing liar, but something about you being in Dublin doesn't add up. I've spied you slinking into the Bohemian pubs and the United Arts Club where I thought you'd surface, but you rarely stayed long.'

He nodded cautiously. 'I never saw you.'

'I'm good at being unseen. But if you'd come to spread the gospel of psychoanalysis, then I'd be hard to miss. You see, I'm an occasional attendee at the Sunday evening gatherings of the Group, as they call themselves, in Jonty Hanaghan's house in Belgrave Terrace.'

He looked puzzled. 'I've never heard of him.'

I nodded. 'That's interesting. Surely the first thing you'd do in a new city would be to seek out other pioneers. Jonty is the first person to offer psychoanalysis here. He works ten hours a day, six days a week, to support a family on the pittance he charges patients who find their way to him by word of mouth. He won't risk a rosary crusade outside his door by advertising. Sunday is his day of rest, when his friends gather, those he's training to follow him and others who think it's all tosh but are equally welcome. It's a hidden world, but easily found by anyone interested in psychoanalysis.'

'I wouldn't have taken you for a disciple of Freud,' Fairfax said.

'I'm nobody's disciple. I'm a slave to no faith or ideology. When I die, nobody will notice. I just hope to outlive Eamonn, so he is not left alone. But I like Jonty and like to know that there's one place where, even for just two hours, I'm welcomed as who I am, with no need for disguises. We're a motley crew – writers,

Jews, dissenters, Marxists, open-minded doctors hoping that news of their attendance won't filter back to the Catholic hospitals where they work.'

'What first brought you there?' Fairfax asked.

'I accompanied a young man, too scared to go alone, who hoped that Jonty might be able to cure him of a particular affliction.'

Fairfax nodded, digesting my meaning. 'And did this Jonty succeed?'

'The young man was too scared to ask. On our way home I took him into a field to prove it was no affliction and give him the sort of cure he needed.'

Fairfax glanced uneasily behind his shoulder, even though we were alone, apart from Eamonn, who was making no attempt to follow our talk.

'You may be free with your favours,' he said. 'I'd caution you to be less free with your talk.'

'There's nothing free in this Free State,' I replied, 'beyond the tea and homemade cake that Jonty's Quaker wife serves after we've dutifully listened to another talk on delusions or dreams or hysteria. I can't follow the half of it but I like it there. I'm a people-watcher. I look around the room and wonder about the lives led by the well-heeled strays who find their way there. Lately I've asked myself why you, as a passionate advocate, have never shown up. If you want victims of traumas, you'll find enough of them there, brushing cake crumbs off their knees. A Lieutenant-Colonel Duckworth attends Jonty's gatherings. His family had land in what was called King's County. IRA men arrived and gave them ten minutes to leave, taking whatever they could carry. He took a copper-plated daguerreotype of his mother as a girl. Jonty goes on about the significance of him choosing this over his Great War medals. Duckworth claims the IRA delayed torching the house to let everyone within miles scavenge chairs and tables and even chamber pots before the flame was lit.'

'Why burn Duckworth's family out?' Fairfax asked.

'If they'd nothing to return to, they wouldn't return,' I replied. 'That means more land to be divided into smallholdings. I don't know how many people willingly died for Ireland, but I've rarely met a small farmer who wouldn't kill for an extra half acre of land.' I paused. 'It's an unusual name, Duckworth.'

Fairfax shrugged. 'It's not uncommon in England.'

'It stands out here. A bit like Willoughby. Duckworth loves his Sundays in Jonty's, although he'd kill for a sherry or something stronger. I suspect he spends most nights alone, drinking cheap whiskey from an expensive decanter. In Jonty's he can talk about the burning of his family home without having to look over his shoulder. He likes talking. Last Sunday I asked if he'd ever heard of any army officer named Willoughby being in Ireland.'

Fairfax was suddenly deeply cautious. 'What's that to do with me?'

'You asked the Super if he remembered an army officer by that name. He offered to ask me and, because you became flustered, he did naturally ask me.'

'I was making conversation. I knew someone of that name stationed here.'

'During the Tan War?' I asked.

'And the Great War. He got invalided out of front line action in Egypt and stationed here to recuperate. I really didn't know him well.'

Once he said this I sensed him regretting it, as if it contained an element of betrayal. But I needed to keep him on the back foot. The Super knew nothing about Eamonn. Nor did anyone else beyond the attendant on his ward. I intended to keep it that way. My brother wasn't dead to me but I was determined to retain his right to be dead to the rest of the world. So I pushed Fairfax further, hoping to use anything I could gauge from his replies as a means to barter for his silence.

'You knew him well enough to ask if anyone remembered him.'

'He was the man who told me about this asylum. He'd visit shell-shocked soldiers here when part of it operated as a war hospital.'

'What did he tell you about Grangegorman?'

'That I would never be tough enough to work here.'

'Is that why you came? To prove him wrong?'

Fairfax took a moment to reply. 'It's too late to prove anything to him. He died in the Blitz.'

'When?' I recognised the raw grief he struggled to conceal.

'A few weeks ago.'

'Not long before you applied to work here?'

Fairfax nodded. 'A coincidence. Like I say, I didn't know him well.'

Peter betrayed Jesus thrice on the night of his arrest. The strain in Fairfax's voice suggested how it hurt him to do the same to someone special.

'You know a lot about him.'

'His death was reported in the *Times*.' Fairfax went on the offensive. 'I'm not here to be interrogated. I only have your word that this patient is your brother.'

'Is my word not good enough?'

'I want him returned to his ward. This is inappropriate.'

'That's the exact word Duckworth used about Herbert Willoughby's behaviour during the Great War.'

'His name wasn't Herbert,' Fairfax replied, more softly. 'Well actually, Herbert was his middle name. But I ... we ... his friends knew him as Charles.'

'His fellow officers knew him as Herbert and as a bit of a cad. He had a high-pitched laugh like a hyena, Duckworth said, totally out of character with how he spoke. Duckworth claimed that his superiors grew uneasy about his penchant for taking young recovering soldiers for spins in Wicklow. He did it a bit too often, and some soldiers who were taken for spins weren't keen to be taken a second time.'

'I don't like what you're implying,' Fairfax said.

'What do you care? You say you barely knew him.'

'I still won't have his reputation impugned. Charles was a good man. He ...'

Fairfax stopped. I felt sorry for him now. This had gone far enough. I would have loved if, just once, somebody felt this strongly about me.

'If you ever want to talk,' I said in a quieter voice, 'I'm a good listener.'

'I don't care what you think you are.' He seemed to need to reassert his authority.

'I'll shut up so,' I said. 'I'm just saying that when I took that young man into a field coming home from Jonty's, he came willingly. I'm no saint, but no bully either.'

Fairfax's frustration got the better of him. 'You are impugning a man you never met, relying on an old duffer who sounds close to being an alcoholic.'

'I'm relying on more than Duckworth,' I said.

'What do you mean?'

'Duckworth says he was moved from the Royal Barracks to Tipperary to make it harder for him to conduct Florence Nightingale visits here. When the Tan War started, he was caught up in an ambush and moved back to Dublin because he knew his way around, although any British officer who ventured out alone surely had a death wish. Indeed, Michael Collins once considered having Willoughby shot.'

'How would you know such a thing?'

'I made enquiries.'

'From Dillon?'

I shook my head. 'No disrespect to Dillon, but he's a delusional headcase.'

My brother's disappearance still gave me some leverage over his former comrades. Half of them treated me with sympathy, imagining that Eamonn was in an unmarked grave. The other half treated me with caution because they had left Eamonn for dead but his body was never found. I rarely asked questions, but when I did, I got answers because they were relieved I wasn't asking about my brother.

'An IRA man told me that Willoughby liked to talk a bit too freely, especially if keen to impress seemingly naive young men. When he went on the hunt, I think he liked the smell of cordite and liked risk. The IRA men tasked with tailing him were baffled when he'd leave the barracks in mufti. At first they presumed he was trying to spy. British officers who pretended to be Republican sympathisers tended to end up shot in country lanes where they thought they were being taken to meet Collins. But your friend never wanted to pump any young man he met for information. He was more interested in paying them a half crown to pump him.'

'I won't have that talk about him,' Fairfax said.

'Why not?' I asked. 'Being queer saved his life. Collins had no time for such shenanigans. Mick was a bog-standard conservative Catholic. But in an intelligence war, you use any source available and your friend had no real loyalty to anything except his cock. It seems that his fellow British officers ostracised him, not just because of suspicions about his behaviour but because he had no stomach for the butchery they wallowed in. He told the rent boys he was so fond of that it disgusted him and they told Collins that if you opened his trousers he sang like a canary. Thanks to his careless talk, the Tans raided a lot of makeshift offices to find every scrap of paper gone because the IRA were tipped off. It didn't stop the occupants of each house being beaten to a pulp, but it prevented the capture of men on the run.'

'A shambles of brutality and brandy, best forgotten,' Fairfax said. I looked at him quizzically and he added: 'The only thing he ever said about his time in Ireland. Even then, he only ever said it once, when drunk.'

'I reckon he knew exactly what he was doing by talking. He savoured his acts of betrayal. Maybe betrayal was in his nature.'

'He served his king and country well, in Egypt and France and the Dardanelles,' Fairfax replied, a little too sharply. 'He saw things that gave him nightmares. You know nothing about his nature.'

'I know that rent boys said he liked an occasional hint of violence just to add spice. Collins told them to put up with it or they'd get worse. They reported back every word he said. They're probably unique in being the only people never to apply for active service pensions. Many ordinary British Tommies disliked what they saw in Dublin.' I stared down at my brother as he now slept.

'Eamonn used to meet other Republicans in a room above Phil Shanahan's pub in Mabbot Street, while, in the bar below, Tommies left their revolvers on the counter in exchange for a pound note to spend in the Monto brothels. Decent lads willing to risk a week in the glasshouse and maybe a dose of the clap, because this wasn't their war. Maybe your friend felt the same. He sounds an intelligent man, unsullied by jingoism. Maybe snitching didn't feel like betrayal to him because you can only betray something you love or still believe in.'

I realised I had pushed Fairfax beyond his limits. I doubt if this man had punched anyone but this was probably the closest he ever came to it.

'You are an uneducated attendant,' he said, 'trading in cigarettes, secrets and lies. Pilfer whiskey but stay away from my file. If the Superintendent has questions about my previous employment, I'll answer to him. I never heard of this Jonty chap. I checked with the British Psychoanalytical Society before I left London and they have no Dublin members listed. I'd have no interest in tracking down an unregistered quack.'

'That's what other doctors here see you as,' I said. 'They think it's time you cracked on with doling out pills and injections like them. They look at you a bit like how your friend's fellow officers probably looked at him; an outsider who is too much of a loose cannon.'

'I don't give a damn how you, or anyone in this asylum, sees me.'

'I never said that's how I see you,' I replied. 'I see someone grieving. Did you love him?'

I was trying to make a genuine connection, but his defences were up. 'Your opinion of me is irrelevant.'

'Did this man hurt you?'

'Don't push your luck.'

'Men sometimes do. But there are different shades of violence. It sounds like your friend liked it as a foretaste of pleasure. He understood his kink. But if you think that questioning Dillon will help you to solve any contradictions within your friend, then you're wrong. Dillon's violence was a thousand times worse and came from a different place. The rage of a young man out of his depth. You could spend years talking to Dillon, but you'll never get him to admit to murder. To do so, he would need to admit those murders to himself.'

'Don't presume to diagnose someone as if you were a doctor,' Fairfax said coldly.

'Doctors only see each patient for a few seconds once a week,' I replied, 'I'm with them every day. You know the Latin names for what ails them, but I know their pain.'

Fairfax took a deep breath. I sensed how he wanted to be gone, from this asylum and this city. 'I will say nothing to the Superintendent about you being up here. But I want this patient back in his ward and these attics considered out of bounds.'

I nodded. 'I'd have had my brother in bed long ago if you hadn't butted in.' I roused Eamonn gently. He opened his eyes, uncertain of where he was. 'You're grand, bro,' I reassured him. 'In safe hands. Not a sound now. We don't want to wake any craw-thumping caterwaulers.'

Eamonn rose or tried to, but even after all these years his injuries made it hard for him to stand unaided. He glanced at the doctor but I was not sure if he truly saw him or what he saw in this state, where I was the only person whom he recognised. He flinched whenever anyone else touched him. He had gained weight over the years – a rare achievement on the rations here – and it took me a moment to steady myself and steady him before I made my way towards the stairs. Fairfax saw the effort involved and stepped forward, anxious to help, but I knew that a stranger's hand on Eamonn's shoulder would induce flashbacks and fear.

'My brother and I are grand,' I said, perhaps too abruptly. 'We don't need anyone's help. I've always managed on my own.'

I left him standing on those stairs, watching us make our slow descent.

Twenty-Two

Fairfax

11 April 1941

I couldn't face going home after the gateman signed me out. I couldn't face the frayed lace curtains, the gunman's shrine on the stairs, the table on the landing with its array of Catholic icons and dusty bottles of discoloured holy water. I needed release; to lose myself for a few hours in the louche disreputability of Le Boeuf sur le Toit in Soho. Such clubs were hard to find on Dublin's North Circular Road. Here the sole vice seemed to be a competition among rose-growers to scoop up the most cow dung soiling the road after each batch was herded from the cattle market down to the docks. Like Gus had said, I had visited the few Dublin pubs brave enough to place coded advertisements in *The Bell* magazine about being 'continental' in atmosphere as a rendezvous for artists, aristocrats and fashionable ladies. But I had felt lost in them, unsure of the local handkerchief codes and nuances. Now, after my attic encounter with Gus, I was too rattled to try and decipher furtive conversations with strangers.

I owed the Superintendent a bottle of whiskey and was determined to present him with it before he mentioned our wager. I felt uncomfortable about returning to that small local pub so I walked on towards Phibsborough. The stained-glass windows were lit up in the triumphalist Catholic church that dominated the skyline there, with its soaring Gothic tower. Its doors were open, an obedient flock pouring in for what looked like a men's confraternity. I'd never held strong views about Popery, but their sense of belonging reinforced my loneliness.

I purchased the Bushmills in a pub and walked on until I reached a stretch of filled in canal. One side was occupied by a small public library, framed against the backdrop of Mountjoy Prison. How many men were in there, jailed for possessing the same feelings that plagued me and being caught acting on them? I was tired of wrestling with these desires that had seen me, as a young man, seek help by consulting an older doctor in the Tavistock Clinic, long before I ever worked there. I still remembered my shock at grasping the implications behind his suggestion that perhaps I needed an experienced man, like himself, to counsel me on such matters.

When studying psychotherapy, I had attended lectures about aversion therapies to suppress homosexual feelings; about using electric shocks or drugs to induce nausea at any thought of sex; about whether freezing ice baths or scalding the skin with hot metal were the most effective methods to plant a mental association between homoerotic thoughts and memories of pain, so that even thinking about another man sexually would induce vomiting.

Working in asylums, I'd heard American colleagues praise the use of ice-pick lobotomies to treat homosexuality, with more traditional European doctors arguing that chemical or surgical castration were the only effective cure. Often during such discussions, I would excuse myself to be sick in the toilets. Once or twice I had been trapped into being the consultant psychotherapist on duty, with some anxious, shame-faced young man on the far side of my desk, describing his struggle with the feelings I spent years learning to live with. No doctor ever brought me to an acceptance of my nature. It was Charles who finally gave me that equilibrium. If that hard-nosed stockbroker felt no shame, but accepted our shared condition with the right modicum of necessary discretion but without guilt, then I knew there was nothing unnatural in my orientation.

But Charles was gone, dead in the arms of a Dominick Street labourer. I couldn't rid myself of Gus's description of him twenty years earlier with Dublin rent boys. This was long before I knew him, yet a sour sense of betrayal overwhelmed me, bringing back the emotions I had felt on the night his body was found. I sat on a park bench opposite the library and, opening the whiskey, took a slug by the neck. I welcomed the burning sensation on my throat that almost made me gag. This was surely what Dillon felt as a boy, on the Isle of Man when his companions urged him to prove his manhood by downing whiskey neat.

A tramp on the next bench was eyeing me with great curiosity, hoping against hope that I might bestow generosity. I reached out to hand him the bottle. He held it to his lips for a long time as if terrified that I would snatch it away. Finally, he gasped and handed me back the bottle with a nod of thanks.

'Christ, that's the real McCoy,' he said. 'It would put hair on a nun's chest. Are you drinking for a reason?'

Charles always said that a real man needed no excuse to drink. He had often mocked my caution and fear of losing control.

'I'm drinking because I want to,' I replied.

The tramp nodded sagely. 'That's the best reason. Your good health. If this doesn't kill us, it will definitely cure us.'

I drank again, a long gulp, feeling its effects on my empty stomach. 'Some things are beyond curing,' I said. 'And I should know. I'm a doctor.'

He nodded, but would have agreed with anything to ensure that I handed him back the bottle. 'The only thing worth truly curing is a side of bacon,' he said. 'And I should know because I once worked in a slaughterhouse.'

'I feel I work in one now,' I replied. 'Only we do our slaughtering slowly, over decades.'

'Jaysus, what class of kip is that?'

'A zoo for the unwanted.'

He handed me the bottle. 'If I get your drift, I may have experienced its hospitality myself. Old men with long faces and long black coats walking around a shed with stinking floorboards warped from decades of patients no longer even aware of pissing their pants. You're bringing back memories I could do without.'

I raised the bottle and swallowed. 'I had a row with a man there this evening. I got angry with him but really I was angry with myself.'

The tramp accepted the bottle back. 'You were probably right to be angry with the bastard. If he has done nothing wrong today, he'll probably do something wrong tomorrow. There's a reason they count each blunt knife and fork before letting the patients out of the dining hall. Half the fuckers in there would stab you and the other half wouldn't even notice if they were stabbed.' He took a long drink, then looked at me in an almost fatherly way. 'Do you know what I'm thinking?'

'What?'

'That you seem a thoroughly decent man. I'm enjoying your company and your whiskey, so it pains me to say this, but you don't belong in this park. I'm thinking you might be wise to fuck off home with yourself. No offence, like.'

'None taken,' I replied. 'Do you smoke?'

'Only when I'm offered.'

Reaching for my case, I emptied the four remaining cigarettes into his lap. 'You're offering wise and sensible advice,' I said. 'But I spent my life being wise and sensible and it maybe cost me the only person I ever loved. I can never win them back but maybe I can find a way to stop their ghost from mocking me.'

The tramp looked genuinely concerned. 'Jaysus, man, getting pissed is one thing, but it sounds like you're torturing yourself. Would you not fuck off home?'

'I tortured patients today,' I said. 'I watched them being carried, screaming and struggling, to be strapped down to let me play God with their sizzled brains. One patient had his brain fried just to spite me and avoid having to talk.' The effects of the whiskey hit me as I swayed while trying to stand up. 'Can you point me in the direction of Dominick Street?'

The tramp rose and used a hand to steady me, worried that I – or the bottle – might fall.

'All you'll find in Dominick Street is scurvy and lice. Terraces of coffin boxes reeking of TB. Who would you be looking for there?'

'The ghost of a stranger I only ever saw on one occasion and on that occasion he was dead.' I held out the Bushmills. 'I have no further need for libation. Accept this gift.'

He took the bottle but looked deeply perturbed. 'Promise me one thing,' he said. 'I don't want it on my conscience. Promise you're not going to top yourself.'

*

Dominick Street was easy to find. Bookended by a huge church, those four-storey red-brick houses must have been grand residences in Georgian times, before being subdivided into ever smaller tenement rooms. It was impossible to tell how many families lived on this street where gangs of youngsters roamed. I had never seen children so thin, with some bow-legged from rickets. They looked hungry and frozen, yet possessed by a manic energy like whirling dervishes. Two boys mimicked my walk, while others pestered me for what they called 'any odds'. But most were so caught up in street games that I might have been invisible. These were the cobblestones on which Charles's last lover once played – a boy growing aware of his difference from friends who eyed up girls in short skirts waiting their turn to jump in skipping games. Or perhaps he was unaware of his nature until he reached London, because how could you articulate emotions, even to yourself, if lacking the vocabulary to comprehend them?

A woman opened a top-storey window and called down to her children. It seemed impossible for her to be heard above the hubbub of noise. But maybe it was like with the flocks of puffins that Charles and I once saw on clifftops in the Hebrides; every chick instinctively recognising their mother's call. Three girls stopped playing and waved to her before running in through an ornate doorway, bereft of any actual door. Curiosity made me peer into the unlit hallway. A door opened on the top floor. I spied the woman's face, lit by a flaming sheet of rolled newspaper which she dropped over the bannisters, a beacon of twirling light to guide her daughters as they raced up those bare flights of stairs.

More children swarmed in past me, like a signal had been given that meagre suppers of bread and margarine were ready. I cursed the effects of alcohol as I steadied myself by holding onto steel railings that led to a dank basement. Over the course of a few moments this bustling street had virtually emptied, except for three boys taking turns to push each other in a boxcar made out of a butter box tied onto the wheels of an old pram. I had the pavement to myself as I walked on, unsure of why I was even there. If I found the tenement room where Jem Bourke's parents lived and tried to express my condolences, how could I explain the circumstances in which I came across their son's body?

Perhaps I was seeking a sign from beyond the grave about how to resume my life and for a moment it seemed that I was being given one in the strangest way. Just before I reached the end of the last terrace, a window opened in a third-floor flat. A handsome youth gazed out, scanning the street to check that the boxcar was out of sight in the dark. I stopped, unsure if he could see me watching. If he could, he did the oddest thing. He disappeared for a moment, during which he turned around and undid his trousers. What reappeared over the rim of the windowsill was a dangled pair of naked buttocks, displayed like a grotesque yet erotic invite to me to enjoy his proffered body, if I found the courage to climb the dark stairs and knock on the right door. For a few seconds I watched, repulsed and entranced. Then, as he defecated down onto the basement, I realised that he was simply too lazy to queue for the communal toilet. Once he finished, he slammed the window shut. He had not even noticed my presence or, if he did, his act was not one of enticement but defiance. How drunk was I to have imagined that he was offering illicit solace, when he – like everyone else in this city – was indifferent as to whether I existed?

The sensible thing was to turn for home, but I preferred to be lonely out on these streets. O'Connell Street would be filled with window-shoppers and happy couples having their photos taken by street photographers when heading into the Metropole cinema and ballroom. On another night I might have enjoyed promenading along that wide boulevard where unofficial minders cadged a few coins by standing guard of rows of parked bicycles and anxious girls awaited their beaus under Clery's clock. I might have savoured that heady air of excitement and gaiety, heavy with hints of unspoken sexual rewards to come for couples whose desires were legally acceptable. But I was in a darker mood tonight as I slipped down the lanes by the closed-down fruit and vegetable markets that led to the quays. I kept remembering Dillon's face when I applied the voltage; kept hearing Gus's voice in the attics; kept trying to forget the surge of lust I had felt at seeing that youth in Dominick Street shamelessly display himself.

I reached the river. Quaysides are always dark and lonely, with troubled souls drawn to such darkness. I walked away from the city, counting each quay as I approached Kingsbridge Station. Inns Quay, Arran Quay, Ellis Quay, then Sarsfield and Wolfe Tone. Before me the darkness of the Phoenix Park with its dangerous possibilities. I didn't want to go there, but didn't want to go home. Charles must have known these quays well, from his time stationed in the Royal Barracks, slipping out at night to find rent boys, if Gus was to be believed. What grim sights had Charles witnessed during his time here? After hearing my accent, few people spoke about those times, but I sensed the memories that still rankled. Elderly men dragged from their beds and beaten half-senseless before being tied to the front of Crossley Tenders by Black and Tans, as a warning that any shot fired at the vehicle would result in their immediate execution. Rooms ransacked. Houses torched. Workers who could not reach home before the curfew, battered with rifle butts and left for dead.

Charles was not like that. In comparison, his kink almost had a refined delicacy, a sliver of pain to heighten pleasure to come. But maybe such distinctions counted for nothing when you were swept up in a situation where all notions of normal decency were suspended. Who would have the courage to stand up against such galvanised hatred? In France I'd seen horror, but horrors inflicted with a mundane set of rules. You in one trench and the enemy in another. Warfare on these streets must have been different. No whistles blown to commence attack, no rule books, often no uniforms or sense of where the next shot would come from. If you declined to fall into line with an unspoken consensus, then the next bullet could come from behind you, fired by sullen comrades who saw you as a renegade. The Superintendent had told me that the other National Army officer with Dillon on the night when they picked up those boys in Drumcondra was himself shot in the back by his own men during a raid, a week later. Seemingly by accident, but who could tell amid such chaos?

Maybe my need to probe Dillon about his acts of violence was because I had never possessed the courage to probe Charles about what things he might have done during his time here, back when normal military rules ceased to apply. But if faced with confessing his indiscretions or being tortured by volts of electricity, I knew what Charles's choice would have been. He kept his friends close but his secrets closer.

I crossed the river before Kingsbridge and walked slowly up the unlit narrow pavement bordering the river wall. Victoria Quay, Usher's Island, Merchant's and Wood Quay. People passed on the wider pavement on the far side, but I was alone on this side, although increasingly I had a sense that someone was following, always just out of sight. I'd stop and their slow and measured footsteps would stop also. Bicycles passed by, with girls balanced on crossbars, hair blown back, their faces animated. Town was starting to empty. Essex Quay, Wellington Quay. How long since I had eaten? I had no idea. The whiskey had robbed me of all sense of time. Aston Quay and then a strangely quiet O'Connell Bridge. The cinemas had emptied. Dancers in ballrooms were still engrossed in holding each other as tight as public decency allowed.

There was a dimly lit public convenience still unlocked just down from O'Connell Bridge on Burgh Quay. A youth leaned against the quayside wall outside it. He stopped gazing at the river for one split second to glance at me as I approached. A mercenary speculative glance I knew well. I pretended to be oblivious to his presence, but he knew that I was drawn to the bait. To hold my attention, he leaned over the wall as if intently gazing at something in the water below. His jumper was ragged and too short. His trousers were so ill-fitting that a triangle of bare flesh was on display, revealing a glimpse of the curve of his buttocks. It was impossible for my eyes not to be drawn to that exposed realm of skin. I was almost past when he turned his head.

'Fag?'

I paused, reluctantly. Every instinct cautioned me to walk on. 'I beg your pardon?'

'Have you a smoke?'

'I gave my last cigarettes away to a tramp.'

'More fool you,' he snorted. 'Handouts should come at a price.'

I walked on a few paces, determined to ignore his innuendo. In London I would not have stopped but that was because I used to have someone to go home to. However, I wasn't in London. My friend Christopher had sublet my Putney flat and put my possessions in storage, but it felt like they belonged to a different life I would never fit back into. I had come to Dublin on a wild goose chase, hoping to find a trace of Charles's ghost or maybe to forget him, because there was nothing to link him with this city. Except for one thing. I turned back. 'Do you know Dominick Street?'

'Of course I know Dominick Street.' The youth's pride sounded hurt. 'Wasn't I born, bred and buttered around the corner from it? Who do you know in Dominick Street?'

'Nobody.' He looked at me with such intensity that I felt I had to say something. 'I came across a young man's body in a ruined building in London after a German bombing raid. The air-raid warden said he was from Dominick Street in Dublin.'

'Poor bastard.' The youth shook his head. 'Still, at least he got out of Dominick Street. I'd risk getting killed in London to get away from here.'

'Why don't you?'

'I just don't. I make my living how and when I can. I can turn my hands to most things. I'm particularly good with using my hands.'

Maybe this was how Charles had met Jem Bourke, I tried to lie to myself. A meaningless cash transaction that accidentally got suspended in time, like the sleeping bodies preserved by lava in

Pompeii. It had meant nothing and I was making too much of it. Charles's pick-up had not looked much older than this youth, but his torso was toughened by years of manual labour. This youth possessed a different type of street toughness, like a stray dog having to forage wherever he could, desperate for scraps, yet ready to bite any hand that fed it. I was on dangerous turf. Two Gardaí appeared, walking up the far quay. They didn't look across, yet the youth was acutely aware of them.

'Fuck away off with yourself if you've no fags,' he said.

I had gone a few yards when he called after me, in a voice both low and lewd. 'I'm from Bolton Street. I bet you never came across a lad from Bolton Street but you wish you had the courage to, you penny-pinching coward.'

I walked on towards the Loopline railway bridge across the Liffey. A barman emerged from a pub called the Scotch House on the junction with Hawkins Street. He locked the door, donned bicycle clips and cycled away. No one else was around. If I crossed Butt Bridge, I could commence the long walk up Gardiner Street back to my digs. Every instinct urged me to do so, but I couldn't face the stairs up to my room and the loneliness after I closed my door. I knew I'd lie awake, thinking about this youth by the quay wall. Not because I was attracted to him: in truth I wasn't. But because thinking of him impersonally using his hands on me, imagining every outcome and scenario, would stop me from having to think about Charles's time here. It would stop me thinking about my failure to help Dillon in any way except by strapping an apparatus to his skull while other patients yelled as if mocking my failure. I looked behind me. The youth was still there. He knew full well I hadn't gone away. The old cat and mouse game. Risk and reward. Or no reward except a severe beating. But the last word the youth had said stung. *Coward.* If Charles hadn't known that I was a coward he would never have risked stubbing out a cigarette on my skin, defying me to be man enough to lash out. God knows how many casual handjobs Charles had enjoyed, knowing that I was too trusting to suspect, or if I suspected, I was too cowardly to interrogate my suspicions. Perhaps the closest I might ever come to truly understanding Charles was by walking back to do what Charles had done in this city, enjoying anything on offer without fear of risk. I was so drunk that I wasn't sure if my body would be able to let anything happen. Even if no pleasure occurred I could prove Charles's ghost wrong by showing that I was no coward. Besides, it wasn't pleasure I was after, but release of any kind.

I walked slowly back. The youth still kept his back to me.

'You were careless,' he said without turning. 'You dropped a ten bob note in the first cubicle inside there. I might have to kneel down to pick it up.'

Charles would barter to show who was in control.

'I heard no banknote fall,' I said. 'I only heard the tinkle of two half crowns.'

'A five bob a job?' He shrugged. 'It's all the one to me.'

The casual callousness of his shrug told me I could have suggested any sum. It made no difference. Once he got me in there, he intended to rob me. I'd fight back but I wouldn't be strong enough. There was still time to walk away, but instead I entered those foul-smelling toilets. His footsteps followed, light and alert, ready to flee once he landed a few kicks and grabbed my wallet. He nodded in the dim light towards the cubicle.

'What are you waiting for, bud?'

'Have you a name?'

'No. And no time for fucking around either.' He deftly undid my belt and yanked at my trousers, but I knew this was just to make it harder for me to run after him. 'You know what you want and I'm going to give it to you.'

A voice from the doorway startled us both. 'What do you intend giving him, you wee gurrier? We've been watching. This queer must be desperate. There's more meat on a butcher's pencil than on your scrawny rump.'

One of the two Gardaí I'd seen earlier entered the toilets. He blocked the doorway as the youth tried to flee. Pushing the youth back so that he slipped on the wet floor, he called to his unseen companion. 'Jerome, the sergeant is in the *Irish Times* night office, warming his arse chatting to the duty clerk. Give him a shout. This will enliven his night.'

Footsteps hurried away. The Garda leaned against the doorway, pleased with himself.

'Well, this beats Banagher and Banagher beats the Devil,' he said. 'I'll get mentioned in the papers when it goes to court. Gross indecency. Papers love this class of thing.' He nodded to me. 'For the love of Jesus, fix your clothes, man.'

I said nothing as I re-buckled my belt. Any sway that my accent held in London did not extend to here. I was out of my depth.

The youth addressed the Garda. 'Have you any butts? Go on, don't be a stingy bastard.'

'You mind your tongue,' the Garda warned him, 'especially in front of the judge when he's sticking you away in Kavanagh's Hotel.'

'Why would he put me in Mountjoy?' There were generations of practised indignation in his voice. 'You'd be amazed at the size of the half-smoked butts that rich fuckers toss away when having a piss. I was having an honest scavenge for butts when this toff came in and propositioned me. Cash in hand. That was the only thing that was going to be in hand. I'd no plans to give the fucker a hand shandy. I was going to take any money on offer and kick the shit out of him. So if you charge me, make it attempted robbery. My da will go ape shit, and he's in the Animal Gang, if anyone in

Bolton Street sees my name in the newspaper for anything except robbery. Do you hear?'

The Garda nodded. 'That doesn't mean I'm listening. The sergeant will decide on charges.' He produced a cigarette. 'Here, smoke this if it shuts you up.'

The youth took it and looked at the Garda belligerently for a match. 'What's the story? Is it a magic fag that lights itself?'

The Garda lit a match. 'For the last time, shut your gob.' He turned to me. 'I don't understand your sort but, even if I did, I couldn't see what drew your fancy to this sewer rat. Still, at least he's grown up. Last month we caught a fucker after luring an eleven-year-old up to the Phoenix Park. He had a jar of Vaseline and a candle. He said he was going to use the candle to break the boy in gently. Said it like he expected brownie points. We told the child to scarper. Then we broke the fucker in while arresting him. Jesus only fell three times during the Stations of the Cross. This geezer must be highly religious because by the time he reached the station he'd outdone Jesus twice over. I suppose you want a fag too?'

I shook my head. What I wanted was to be anywhere but here. Ever since I was fourteen years old and infatuated with an older boy who played cricket for the First Eleven, I had been awaiting this moment of disgrace. The end of my career, even if the judge spared me a prison sentence. I had not gone cottaging for years. Walking in here had not been an act of lust, but of public suicide. Even if the Gardaí hadn't caught us, this youth was always going to turn on me, maybe with a sharpened steel comb raked down my cheek. I had been asking for it, in every sense of the word. That unsought glimpse of a youth in Dominick Street had unhinged me. That and the whiskey and memories of Dillon buckling in torment. It was dim in those toilets but I could still see how this youth was nothing like Charles's last lover. Nothing that could have occurred in here would have yielded any clue as to what Charles felt in his final moments. If Charles's encounter with Jem Bourke had been a fleeting financial transaction, their bodies would have separated the moment they climaxed. Instead they were found in a post-coital loving embrace.

There were heavy footsteps outside. The young Garda stopped leaning against the wall and stood to attention. The sergeant who entered was heavy-jowled and near retirement age. He surveyed the squalid scene with a caustic air.

'Caught in the act, Sir,' the Garda said. 'Guilty as charged.'

'If I had my way they wouldn't be charged,' the sergeant replied. 'They'd be fucked into the Liffey with stones in their pockets.' He eyed the youth. 'I know you. Is your money-lending granny still defrauding widows and orphans?'

'She helps out neighbours when she can.'

'At five shillings in the pound and a hammering off your uncles if anyone is slow in paying. I thought you were locked up in Daingean Industrial School?'

'They let me out,' the youth said.

'You didn't learn this class of jiggery-pokery in Daingean.'

'I wouldn't tell you what I learnt from the Christian Brothers there. You wouldn't want to believe me anyway.'

'At least you won't have to go back. It's big prison for you now.' He looked to me. 'And as for you ...' He turned to the Garda. 'Have you taken down his particulars?'

'I was waiting for you, Sergeant. I ...' He stopped. Another set of footsteps were entering the public convenience. Footsteps that were not stealthy but slow and measured. Was it someone needing to relieve themselves or a lonely man walking unbeknownst into misadventure? The person I least expected to see in the doorway was Gus. His slow gaze took us all in.

'There you all are now,' he observed to nobody in particular, then addressed the sergeant. 'Is it yourself, Sean?'

'It's hardly the Count of Monte Cristo.'

Gus chuckled. 'No, but it could be MO-RI-AR-I-TY.' He glanced at the Garda. 'This gossoon is too young to know the song, but I remember it being your party piece.' Leaning his head back, he sang in a relaxed baritone voice:

> 'I'm a well-known bobby of the stalwart squad,
> I belong to the D.M.P.
> And the girls all cry as I pass by:
> Are you there, MO-RI-AR-I-TY?'

He looked at the sergeant. 'I suppose this isn't the time for you to give us a verse?'

The sergeant shook his head. 'You'd be well minded to move along out of here, Gus. This is police business. I've less pleasant things to do than singing.'

Gus had not yet looked in my direction. The situation was humiliating enough without him coming to gloat, although in truth I wasn't sure why he was here.

'But have you really, Sean? This isn't exactly leading a baton charge against the Animal Gang waiting to rob unsuspecting folk down the docks.'

'My father is in the Animal Gang,' the youth injected, as if this bestowed status on him.

Gus gave him a sardonic glance. 'I know your father. If the Animal Gang let that runt tag along it must be as a ragtag mascot. The best part of him ran down your grandmother's leg.' He glanced at the sergeant. 'This scut is beneath you, Sean. Why not send him up to Lugs Branigan in Kevin Street Station?' He addressed the youth. 'Will you take a beating from Lugs? Lugs has his own form of policing, no court appearances involved. His leather gloves barely leave a mark. You'll be as ugly coming out of the cell as going in.' He turned to the sergeant. 'He's not worth wasting time on. Being shown some ring craft by Lugs might be the making of him.'

'What has you so interested?' the sergeant asked. 'Who is this gurrier to you?'

'This sparrowfart?' Gus shrugged in disbelief. 'Nothing.'

'Then what are you doing here, Gus?'

'My job, like you're doing yours. But to be honest, I'm a bit tawdry tonight. My grip must be slipping.' Gus finally glanced at me. 'This English toff is one of my patients.'

I was about to protest but a shameful instinct made me stay quiet. The sergeant stared at me, like an exhibit in a zoo.

'Are you saying he's a nutcase?'

Gus nodded. 'Incurable. But we'll cure the fucker. I was minding him but I turned my back and he was gone. Still, patients like him never get far. He knows nobody in Dublin and nobody knows he's here. The Super took him in as a personal favour to a government minister who is doing a favour to Sir John Maffey, the British Diplomatic Representative. I won't say who he's related to across the water, but let's just say that the British government wanted him out of London to avoid public embarrassment. If this reaches our courts, they wouldn't be the only important politicians keen to avoid public embarrassment, if you get my drift.'

I could see the sergeant considering this but anxious not to lose face.

'Still and all, Gus, I can't just do nothing. It's gross public indecency.'

'Is it?' Gus glanced dismissively at me. 'I can't tell you how to do your job, Sean. You're a good man as everyone knows. But I'll tell you one thing: this patient can't do anything down below, if you get my drift. The Superintendent has him on a course of chemical castration. You'd raise the *Lusitania* quicker than you'd raise him. If he has forked out any cash here, it's a case of deposit and no return. You'd need to arrest this scut for embezzlement and not solicitation. I'm just saying that a bit of discretion mightn't go astray, for the sake of both our pensions. It might be wise not to rattle too many cages over an unfortunate incident where nothing actually happened. Maybe you should get Bolton Street's answer to Baby Face Nelson out of here, in case he has big ears. He'll have cauliflower ears when Lugs is finished with him.' He addressed the youth. 'Will you go into the ring with Lugs?'

The youth nodded nervously, desperate for a way out.

'That copper isn't as tough as people make out. If he wants to box, I'll go a few rounds or as long as it takes to floor him.'

The sergeant laughed. 'Lugs is a former Leinster heavyweight champion. There's a black market in Dublin for everything but I can't see too many touts flogging tickets for that boxing match.' He addressed the Garda. 'Take this gurrier up to Kevin Street Station. Tell them he's thrown down the gauntlet to fight Sergeant Branigan.'

The Garda seemed uncertain. 'Do you still want me to take down the other man's particulars?'

The sergeant fixed him with a stare. 'I want you to do as instructed. Why are you still here?'

He remained silent as the Garda led the youth away. When there was just us three left, he turned to Gus as if he found it too disdainful to look at me. 'I know it's a mental illness, but it's unnatural. It doesn't sit right with me, helping out his sort.'

'You're helping me out,' Gus replied. 'A favour you can call in anytime. My goose is cooked if the Super discovers he's been gallivanting. We have him as a day case, because Sir John didn't want him actually locked up. So he's out on *gur*, on parole as you might say, in digs he's not meant to leave except to attend treatments. Maybe you think this poor bastard deserves to suffer, but, trust me, he is. We have him lodging on the North Circular with the Widow Mhic Rághnaill.'

The sergeant laughed companionably, but I knew that I was excluded from his sense of bestowed camaraderie.

'That harridan windbag? We used to raid her house when she harboured every desperado willing to die for Ireland. She packed that in after discovering that they weren't willing to pay rent for Ireland.' He paused. 'Get him out of here, Gus. Once I don't find him in similar circumstances we'll say no more this one time.'

Gus nodded. 'You're a decent man, Sean. We're all entitled to an odd secret, as I said to you on the morning your sister-in-law was admitted.'

The sergeant's mood soured. 'Just get this fucker out of here. There was no call to go mentioning that.'

Gus seemed unperturbed. 'I look into Molly's ward when I can, Sean. She's doing well. Keeps hoping she'll be let out if your brother sends in a letter. I jolly her along as best I can. Good night to you.' Gripping my arm firmly, he steered me out the door, raising his voice in song a last time: *'Are you there, MO-RI-AR-I-TY?'*

We had gone a hundred yards before he slackened his grip. I glanced at him.

'Am I meant to be grateful?'

'You're meant to keep walking in case that two-faced bastard changes his mind. His sister-in-law is as sane and normal as you or I. She threw a mug of scalding tea over Sean's brother after discovering he was keeping a fancy woman on the side. The brother had to choose between giving up his wife or his floozie. Sean doesn't like being reminded, but you should never let a peeler have the last word.'

'Are you saying I'm sane and normal?'

He shrugged. 'Look at where we work, then ask yourself if any of us know what's sane and normal? But I do know you're drunk.'

'Mr Dillon would tell me that every man needs to go on an occasional spree. Or he would have told me that yesterday. This evening he looked placid but perplexed because I saw him trying to eat his stew while holding his spoon by the wrong end.'

'One session down,' Gus said. 'He has seventeen to go over three weeks. He gets Sundays off. The Bible must say thou shalt not electrocute people on the Sabbath.'

'I hope he'll be able to get through them,' I said.

'As three people will be holding him down, he won't have much say in the matter,' Gus replied. 'It's you getting through them that I worry about if the Super insists on you acting as ringmaster.'

I stopped, having reached the side wall of Trinity College. I remembered the awkwardness of our last conversation. 'Were you following me?'

He shrugged. 'Well, I hardly found you by accident. We had a bit of a barney in the attics. You caught me on the hop. I get a tad defensive about anything involving my brother. I picked up your trail after I got him to bed. I could see you weren't in a good state after the day you've had. I've been behind you since Sarsfield quay, although before that you made one tramp in Phibsborough a happy man. He told me you were a patient pretending to be a doctor.'

'Maybe he's half right.'

'You're a good doctor. You care. Maybe too much for your own good.'

'Are you here because the Superintendent told you to keep track of me?' I asked.

'He knows nothing about this. I'm my own man. I do my own thinking.'

'And what do you think?'

'I think it's ironic that you put all that effort in trying to get Dillon to speak. The minute I clapped eyes on you I knew it was you who desperately needs to talk.'

'I don't need your help,' I said. 'And I didn't appreciate your lies to that policeman.'

'My lies prevented you from appearing in court. Lies are useful. You know this. You need to live by them every day, walking a tightrope.'

'How would you know who I am?'

'Because I must live by those same lies. I know what we could both use, but it won't happen tonight because I'm not your type. I'm not saying that on certain nights I wouldn't be tempted. But after our little charade, the only thing I truly need is a strong drink and you need the exact opposite. Thankfully I keep a supply of black-market genuine coffee.'

I looked around at the deserted street. I didn't want to go with this man, yet I didn't want to be alone. I didn't want to be in Dublin, yet nowhere else felt like home. My head hurt. It would hurt more tomorrow. I was lucky that this was the only part of me which hurt. If my encounter with that youth had not been interrupted, he would have been anxious to prove his masculinity by beating me to a pulp. I might have fooled myself in thinking I was seeking sexual release, but really I had been seeking physical retribution – the more violent the better. If I had turned up at the asylum tomorrow with eyes so bruised I could barely see through them, I would be exposed and ruined, but maybe I would no longer have to live this lie, which was so hard to keep up. Or maybe I had needed to experience a physical assault in the hope that, just for a while, it might block out the mental pain of grief. I did need to talk but not to an attendant in the institution where I worked. I envied Catholics for being able to enter a confession box and speak openly to the stranger, although any priest who heard what was inside my heart would condemn me to hell.

Gus was watching me quietly. I wondered how often had he stood on such corners, waiting while men pondered which way to go.

'I took a ridiculous risk, didn't I?' I said at last.

He nodded. 'Desperate men do desperate things.'

'I'm not desperate, I'm a doctor. That's what I'll be tomorrow when we pass each other in work. But I'm not ungrateful. I'll leave two hundred cigarettes in that attic.'

'For what?'

'Payment.'

Gus shrugged in an annoyed manner. 'Fuck you,' he said. 'Do you ever get down off your high moral horse? I've never asked any man for payment for anything. Tomorrow you'll be a doctor and I'll be an attendant. But tonight we're just two men with no labels. I don't want two hundred cigarettes or anything else. I enjoyed scavenging the odd fag off you, one by one, just to see how far I could push it for my own amusement. But that was a game, almost a flirtation. I'm not playing games now. I need a whiskey and you need a coffee. I've a basement flat in Longwood Avenue in Little Jerusalem, not far from where Dillon's pal fired on those Jewish men. You've a long walk to your digs, but come back to my gaff first and let's just talk.'

'You once asked did my special friend, Charles Willoughby, hurt me.'

'Did he?'

'Physically at times, yes. But that isn't what really hurt. Betrayal hurts. I've changed jobs and countries, but can't change the questions and doubts tormenting me. Can someone have truly loved me and yet still betrayed me?'

'And what do you think?'

'If I knew the answer I wouldn't be tormented.'

'Maybe you know the answer, but just haven't talked it through. Talking to a stranger is good. Come and inspect my library. Every time I go back to a man's house I steal one book as a keepsake. My bookshelves are a secret diary that only I can decode. It's how I've read Shaw and Dickens and *Ulysses*, with a few Zane Greys thrown in. Tonight we can be like Bloom and Dedalus, except that I won't have lost my key and we won't companionably piss together in the garden while surveying the stars. My landlady gives me the run of the basement but would take a dim view of that.'

Gus walked on a few paces and paused to look back at me, still standing at the wall of Trinity, undecided. Then he walked slowly on, waiting for my footsteps to catch up. I hesitated and then, as I walked forward to join him, I knew that I would tell him everything about Charles. Once I started to talk I wouldn't be able to stop. I would talk my way through my grief, my fears, my worry that I would never again find companionship or be able to open myself up to the risk of love. Even if it took until dawn, I would talk myself through pain and finally discover if it was possible to heal myself with words.

Twenty-Three

Dillon

Asylum time

My name is Francis Dillon. For some time now – I'm not sure how long – I have needed to shelter in this hideaway because men were coming to kill me. I no longer need to worry about that. I have a protector, the truest of true friends, Jimmy, who has promised to keep me safe. I can't fully recall why they were coming to kill me, but Jimmy says not to worry; he will do all the worrying for us both from now on.

I remember that when I first sought sanctuary here, I was hiding alone in a cell. But Jimmy has arranged for me to share his hideaway. He is not short of friends because so many others choose to also sleep in here with us. I like the company, even if on most nights some guttersnipe will start raising Cain, hullabalooing about things that aren't even there.

But no matter what rumpus breaks out, Jimmy keeps me safe, wading in with shouts of *ciúnas*. He even fixed me up with a job, peeling spuds in the steaming hot kitchens. It's a doddle on freezing days when other poor buckos are working in the coal yard or thinning turnips in an east wind or making plant pots from old milk tins in that shed with a leaking roof. When they all troop into the huge dining room with their fingers blue from the cold, Jimmy and I are already chatting away at the best table, well away from the damp stains on the wall caused by the broken drainpipe and leaking gutters. Some days I can follow what Jimmy's talking about. On other days it's just words. But I like the sound of companionship in whatever he's saying, just like on some nights, when I wake in the big room and for once no one is shouting, I like to gaze around. It reminds me of sleeping in another hideaway, above a dispensary somewhere in town, the floorboards lined with young lads like me, sleeping peaceful with one soul always awake, standing guard near the window.

On such nights I can remember that hideaway so well, the sense of companionship and shared purpose, of belonging to a band of brothers. There was fear back then as well, constant danger that men might come to kill us. But the fear was different in those days because I never felt alone. We were part of something mighty and standing together we felt invincible. Some nights Jimmy wakes and sees me staring around.

'What are you at?' he whispers.

'Remembering being young. Back then was a good feeling, wasn't it?'

'It was.'

'Now there's just us two left, isn't there?'

'Two's company,' he always says. 'One is a lonely desolate place. Now back asleep with you, Colonel.'

I like it when he calls me that, which is rare enough. With undercover intelligence work you can't be too careful. Sometimes in the dining hall a smart alec will stand to attention and give me a mock salute. Jimmy loses the head altogether, with Gus, the good attendant, needing to intervene and haul Jimmy away, saying, 'For the love of Jaysus, Jimmy, you're a bantamweight. If you're going to throw an uppercut, pick on someone whose chin you can reach.' We both laugh then and, as likely as not, Gus will wink and dole out a fag to share, saying not to thank him but the English doctor.

On some days I actually remember being a colonel and having a swanky job and a house and a wife whom I love dearly. I know I must get well to get back to her and my children. I never mention Agnes to Jimmy. It seems to make him go quiet and sad, like he's lonely, which is confusing because I'm still here beside him.

Other times it's me who gets sad and quiet because all my memories are wiped clean. This happens after doctors sizzle my brain with sparks to make me well. I don't like that when it's happening and not even Jimmy can stop me shaking with fear. The doctors always say I will feel better after, but I don't know if I do, because I can't remember much after. But I remember that I have a home I must get back to in Drumcondra and when recalling that house I remember the smell of the perfume my wife wears: La Rose Jacqueminot – a scent distilled in Paris from Provence rose and jasmine that I buy every year on her birthday. I try to think about this when the smell of shit or piss gets too strong in this hideaway or men start to shout for no reason or scare me by glaring like they know something I don't. The doctors say that one day I will be well. Until then I have Jimmy to mind me as we shuffle around like an old married couple, with all our secrets safe because Jimmy remembers them for us both.

Last night was the first night I woke and Jimmy didn't stir. There wasn't a sound as I made my way to the barred window. Those small streets of Drumcondra were exactly as I remembered them. Behind me I could hear my little sister's cross voice scolding me because I wouldn't go out and play with her on the road. But I was scared to go out because I knew that the neighbours would just stare at me or call their children in and slam shut their front doors. Bad things can happen out on those small streets, although something stops me from remembering what they were. My sister scolded me again and I had reminded her that we could not go out anyway. We had made a promise to stay awake all night. I knew that we would never feel this close again as I turned and entwined her nine-year-old fingers in mine. We stood in silence at the window, keeping vigil over the three coffins lined up on the table in our father's front parlour.

Twenty-Four

Gus

23 May 1973

Some patients leave this asylum, but others never do. Harmless old codgers, which is probably the description that passers-by on the street use for me these days. I came to love every patient here in their madness and misery and euphoria. I did think about leaving Grangegorman when Eamonn died in 1968, but where would I go at this stage? It took a certain degree of skulduggery and subterfuge to get his body released so that he could be interred in our parents' grave in Goldenbridge. But the new Superintendent raised no objection to my seeming act of kindness towards a patient who had no family and no visitors during half a century here. The management are humane but practical folk and Eamonn's burial was one less expense for them. Other attendants offered to attend the burial but I said that this particular patient was always scared of crowds and I would sooner just be there alone with the priest and grave diggers.

I needed to insert into the official cemetery records the name I invented for Eamonn when I got him admitted in 1923. But I knew a guy who knew a stone mason who discreetly chiselled Eamonn's real name under the names of our parents. He charged two bob a letter, saying that he wasn't trying to fleece me, but a man needed to make a living and he'd knock me up a receipt if I could claim the cost back. '*Ná bac leis,*' I said. 'Sure, isn't this the best pound note

I ever spent?' Then I winked to discombobulate the greedy pious git and added enigmatically, 'The second most enjoyable pound note I ever spent, actually.' That grave is in the shallow part of the cemetery, where plots are only deep enough to hold three coffins. I don't know where I'll go when my turn comes, but I did right by Eamonn and beyond that I don't much care.

I knew a French bloke a few years back – knew him in the biblical sense, although, at our age, it was among the shorter sentences in the Bible. But as I looked out his window next morning, at the squat dome of Rathmines church, he taught me the only French sentence I've ever managed to memorise: *Plus ça change, plus c'est la même chose* – the more things change, the more they stay the same. That sums up Grangegorman in the years since Dr Fairfax hightailed it back to England in 1949.

During that solitary night in my Longwood Avenue basement, he talked openly until dawn light filtered onto the streets of Little Jerusalem; and we walked to get fresh rolls at Bretzel's Jewish bakery on Lennox Street, where German diplomats sent their children to queue, shame-faced, for the best bread in Dublin. After that, we rarely said much to each other. There was no need. We knew one another's secrets and knew they were safe. We were never anything less than polite when our duties in the asylum threw us together, but we were never anything more than polite either. Curiosity drew him to Jonty's once but I stayed in my corner, listening to old Duckworth lament the absence of sherry, and gave Fairfax his own space to talk to our host. I'm not sure where he worked when he returned to England but he must have become famous because, years later, I saw him being interviewed by Malcolm Muggeridge on a television above the counter of a pub that erected an aerial to poach the BBC signal. But with the sound turned low and the clamour of drinkers around me, I had no idea what he was talking about.

When Dillon first got released from Grangegorman, the Sweepstakes created a class of sinecure for him. This wouldn't have been too costly for them, with the amount of fiddling that goes on in that bleeding hearts racket. I'm told that for years at a time he was perfectly sane – if such a state exists – but then, at decreasing intervals, rats would get inside his mind and gnaw at the memories there, with Dillon enduring more spells in psychiatric hospitals, convinced that enemies were coming to seek revenge by killing him.

Whatever class of job his old IRA comrades invented for him in the Sweepstakes left him with enough free time to become a great man for the golf. This was how I learnt about his death last year. Few newspapers bothered carrying a complete obituary, despite him having participated in Bloody Sunday and being at one time the youngest colonel in the Irish army. But when glancing at a copy of *The Irish Times* that a drinker left behind on a pub counter, I saw that Woodbrook Golf Club had placed a small notice in the social and personal column. It announced, with regret, the death of a former club captain. There was his name, along with the military title he lost fifty years ago.

I hope that Dillon's funeral had a bigger turnout than Jimmy Nolan's burial last week. Even if their Ireland had little room for men like me, they both risked their lives to bring about Irish freedom, when barely more than boys. Both suffered for it too, in ways that nobody wanted to know, behind the high walls of asylums.

Jimmy Nolan wept as if he had suffered a bereavement in the weeks after Dillon was first released. But during his long years in here after that, he gained no shortage of friends who would have gladly stood at his graveside. However, we attendants would have had the Devil's own job, rounding them all up to bring them safely back in here. There were some family members at his burial, nephews and great-nieces who tried their best for this relation whom they barely knew. Two elderly men with old IRA medals turned up to salute his coffin, and a civil servant was in attendance, possibly just to confirm his death so the government could finally stop paying his IRA pension to the asylum. I was there with two other attendants to represent Grangegorman and because we were deeply fond of him. His relations didn't know to collect his personal effects – not that he had many, after his decades in here, shouting so often in his sleep that other patients grew accustomed to it and stopped being woken by the sound. But under his mattress I found an envelope with an official harp on it, which contained a medal so shiny that I doubt if Jimmy ever held it in his hands.

The new Superintendent wondered if a museum might want it but I told him that this seemed unlikely, what with nobody caring anything about Jimmy and his struggles, and with the present Troubles having kicked off again in the North. So the Superintendent nodded and I found myself climbing up these flights of stairs again. I stood in the vast attics where Fairfax once surprised me during my stolen hours with Eamonn. The shelves of unclaimed personal possessions have grown even more packed in the decades since then. But I found a prominent spot, amid the purses crammed with rosary beads and photographs of children, to place Jimmy's medal on display, so that if anyone ever comes looking for it, it will be easily found, though I'm not sure if anyone is interested in the folk who live and die behind these walls.

I could hear the television blaring in the common room downstairs. The patients love Hughie Green presenting *Opportunity Knocks*. Green is a right buck eejit but I enjoy his programme myself, so I didn't dally. I just patted Jimmy's medal lightly in memory of him and Eamonn and every young person who endured bad wars that nobody wants to remember. Then I closed over the attic door and left his medal there, amid the unclaimed handbags, gathering dust in the dark.

Author's Note

Grangegorman's old buildings have been transformed from wards crammed with troubled souls into a university campus, buzzing with the laughter of animated students, many of them with little awareness of what occurred here. But perhaps it is only now, with its high walls demolished, that Dubliners can truly visualise the physical scale of this former psychiatric hospital. Established in 1814 as the Richmond Lunatic Asylum, it became Grangegorman Mental Hospital in 1925 and was renamed St Brendan's Hospital in 1958.

Although primarily a place of respite, under the care of staff doing their best to provide succour, in my childhood it was whispered about in ways that made it feel like a distant location, despite being less than two kilometres from the city centre. Perhaps we didn't know how vast it was because we wanted to know little about this institution where wounded souls passed their days, hidden away in plain sight behind walls that people hurriedly passed.

Grangegorman became a prototype for a chain of asylums across Ireland. Admission was easily secured. In the mid-nineteenth century the most common cause listed for insanity in women was 'fright', but other reasons for admission included 'domestic disagreements and bad treatment by relatives', 'jealousy', 'pride' or 'love and disappointed affections'. By 1900 one in every two hundred people in Ireland were incarcerated in an asylum.

If being admitted was easy, being released was less so, with families often happy to be rid of bothersome relatives. At times asylums betrayed their patients' interests by continuing unnecessary incarcerations that drove them deeper into mental malaise. The constant demand for places meant that, no matter how laudable the intentions of staff, these asylums were ultimately dysfunctional. Their focus needed to shift from the needs of individual patients to simply keeping such overcrowded institutions running.

Hide Away tries to explore the trauma that had to be hidden away and remain unspoken in an Ireland suffering from such psychological wounds that society was often only held together by collective, and selective, amnesia. In a country where families hid secrets amid the iron grip of respectability, no event required more collective amnesia than Ireland's short-lived Civil War. Its worst large-scale atrocity was the Ballyseedy massacre. Major General Paddy Daly – a 1916 Rising veteran who took part in the armoured car hijack mentioned in this novel – had nine anti-Treaty prisoners chained to a land mine in revenge for the murder of five Free State soldiers, lured to their deaths by a booby trap bomb at nearby Knocknagoshel. Despite the ferocity of the Ballyseedy explosion, which left limbs scattered along the road, one of the nine, Stephen Fuller, miraculously survived after being blown into a field where he lay unnoticed while soldiers machine-gunned the other bodies to ensure no witnesses. When a relation of Fuller's was once asked if he spoke much about this massacre, the reply was short and simple: 'It hurt too much to talk.'

While the Civil War and War of Independence form a backdrop to the buried trauma in the book, the novel does not attempt to interrogate the rights and wrongs of a civil war from which neither side emerged with clean hands or any credit. Instead, it seeks to explore the aftershock of such events and what can happen internally to people when it hurts too much to talk, in a society where secrets – whether about a person's sexuality, or mental health, or violence they participated in when young – must be kept hidden away.

Numerous excellent non-fiction studies explore the complexities of both of these conflicts, while many veterans also published memoirs, like Dan Breen's ghost-written *My Fight for Irish Freedom* in 1924.

But while such memoirs provide vivid first-hand accounts of raids and ambushes, the novelist John McGahern (whose father was a Tan War veteran) noted in an early letter to his sister that, 'I have always found IRA narratives boring in the extreme. But then I never found these external dramas interesting. What curiosity I have is what impact they made on the individuals concerned. I've found they made none or only accentuated some stupid hatreds.'

McGahern would exclude Ernie O'Malley's great memoir *On Another Man's Wound* from such criticism, calling it 'the one classic work to have emerged directly from the violence that led to independence'. But while many memoirs glossed over trauma, the personal trauma of participants was intense, with some ex-volunteers ending up behind asylum walls while others like Tom Cullen (one of Collins's Squad) met tragic endings.

As a participant on one side, Dillon's character clings to his own entrenched perspective on the Civil War. Men and women who fought on the other side held divergent positions with equally heartfelt conviction. Indeed, it is simplistic to suggest that two clearly defined factions were involved. As with many liberation struggles, the republican movement was riven by jealousies and ideological contradictions, temporarily set aside to focus on a common purpose.

Todd Andrews took part in the Bloody Sunday raids. In his memoirs he noted how his early revolutionary fervour was 'based mainly on emotionalism and enthusiasm. I rarely thought; I felt.' During the War of Independence, a diverse coalition of idealists could be held together by such emotionalism and enthusiasm. The Treaty exacerbated divisions, leaving former comrades to grapple with the realpolitik of what happens when a ballad is no longer a sufficient blueprint for a future. It led to 'the Unspeakable War', as Eoin Neeson christened it in 1958.

People on both sides suffered from post-traumatic stress, although this term didn't enter common currency until the Vietnam War. In her detailed study, *Killing and Bloody Sunday, November 1920*, Professor Anne Dolan, Associate Professor in Modern Irish History at Trinity College Dublin, quotes a report to IRA headquarters by Michael Lynch of the Fingal Brigade. He witnessed the disturbances at a dance in Portrane Asylum where Squad member Joe Dolan and other volunteers needed to be bundled into a padded cell which they wrecked with knives. Lynch stated:

> if the newspapers got hold of it a grave scandal [would ensue] ... I make this report not to bring trouble on the heads of the men concerned ... but because I believe they were more than drunk. They were stark mad for at least ½ hour. I candidly believe that the present strains on their nerves is too much for them and has left them in such a condition that the taste of whiskey leaves them violent lunatics, and would strongly urge – after watching them for about three hours – that they be given a rest from all arduous duty.

At an army inquiry in May 1924 Major General Russell drew a similar conclusion about the mental stress endured by young members of Collins's Squad, stating how, 'the very nature of their work ... left [these men] anything but normal ... if such a disease as shell-shock existed in the IRA ... the first place to look for it would be amongst these men'.

Collins saw the mental toll their work was taking on certain Squad members, like Frank Teeling who committed a random murder in a theatre or James Conroy who opened fire on a group of Jewish men, with the artist Harry Kernoff lucky to survive.

Before his death, Collins was already attempting to send some men abroad to recuperate or start new lives.

Of course not every Squad member was traumatised. Most enjoyed successful later careers. Bill Stapleton became a director of Bord na Móna. Like Joe Dolan and Charles Dalton, Frank Saurin held a senior position in the Irish Hospitals' Sweepstake. James Conroy returned from America to openly play a role in the short-lived quasi-fascist Blueshirts. The pragmatic Seán Lemass – whose role in the Squad was more tangential – became a progressive, modernising Taoiseach.

I have used real names for such veterans when describing verifiable events. But I have created fictitious names for two Squad members who became patients in Grangegorman. My fictitious Francis Dillon shares many background details with and participated in similar military actions as the real life Charles (Charlie) Dalton, younger brother of Emmet Dalton.

Both Dalton and Dillon are raised on the same Drumcondra street. On 7 October 1922 both participated in the arrest of three young anti-Treaty activists in Drumcondra – Edwin (or Eamon) Hughes and Brendan Holohan, aged seventeen, and Joe Rogers, aged sixteen – who were pasting up posters advocating the murder of Free State army officers. All three boys were found dead at the Red Cow next morning. Following a contentious, vexatious inquest, to which the government dispatched senior legal figures to defend him, Dalton was cleared of involvement by a local coroner. However, this verdict was less clear-cut in the court of public opinion.

Most historians I have spoken to feel that the nineteen-year-old Dalton was implicated in the deaths of the three neighbours whom he picked up that evening. But no historian can categorically and unconditionally prove it. All I know for certain is that, even if not complicit in these deaths, he was burdened by the implication of being involved throughout his troubled life, probably sensing an unspoken judgement among many people with whom he interacted.

If you wish to read the actual words of the real Charlie Dalton, then seek out his memoir, *With the Dublin Brigade*, subtitled *Espionage and Assassination with Michael Collins' Intelligence Unit*, published in 1929 when he was twenty-six. Or his more sombre statement made to the Military History Bureau two decades later. Both accounts end with the Truce. 'The Unspeakable War' is not discussed. But in between writing these two testaments, he suffered periods of serious mental ill-health. This saw him admitted to Grangegorman, convinced that voices were accusing him of murder and suffering from paranoid delusions that men intended to kill him.

I don't claim to know the real Dalton's actual thoughts. But I live near his small childhood street and the adjoining streets that were home to the three youths murdered at the Red Cow. Perhaps if I lived in Fairview, my nightly walks might instead have brought me past 37 Philipsburgh Avenue, the house of Seán McGarry, the last volunteer to leave the GPO in 1916 as the blazing roof tumbled down. McGarry's seven-year-old son was less lucky in escaping a burning building six years later. If pondering that tragedy then maybe I would have written a very different novel, exploring the feelings in later years of the anti-Treaty volunteers who torched McGarry's house where his terrified child was trapped inside, with the boy's death from burns being dismissed by Liam Lynch as simply the fortunes of war.

But my nightly walks in Drumcondra brought home to me the truly claustrophobic nature of that Civil War. By pacing out the distance, I discovered that one of the Red Cow victims lived two hundred metres from Dalton's parents' house. Another lived a hundred yards further away. The origins of this novel began with me pondering imaginary conversations as I walked those small streets; posing the questions that I wanted to ask a man who either bore the guilt of these crimes or else had his life blighted by the burden of implied guilt in other people's eyes.

However, because Dalton died fifty years ago, I needed to create a doppelganger for him and a set of fictitious characters that would allow me to tease out one such version of such a conversation about trauma and its corrosive effects on the mental health of people who participate in violence when young.

And because I could only speculate on his actual feelings, once I tried to imaginatively immerse myself in the aftershock of those events, he became somebody different on the page, this fictional creation named Francis Dillon – an everyman figure whom I invented to represent not so much Dalton as all young participants in conflicts – be it in Dublin in 1922 or Derry in 1972 or Bosnia in 1995 – who have to carry, throughout their adult lives, the trauma of violence in which they were caught up.

Hide Away is set in Dublin, but Dillon and Nolan could as easily be members of the Algerian National Liberation Front during the revolution there in 1960 or French conscripts ordered to commit atrocities in that conflict. As Dillon joins the IRA at fourteen, he could even be regarded as in the same category as the thousands of child soldiers estimated by the UN to be currently fighting in wars.

Jimmy Nolan is very loosely based on a more forgotten figure, James Paul Norton, one of six volunteers involved in shooting three men in a house in Morehampton Road on Bloody Sunday. In a statement to the Military Service Pensions Board – who deemed his recurrent mania and cyclic insanity as attributable to his military service – Norton described how 'the strain of that operation played on my mind and nerves'.

His subsequent beatings in Dartmoor (that led to him being described as 'a complete mental wreck' on his release) contributed to his deteriorating mental health. This saw him committed for increasingly long periods to Grangegorman, diagnosed with manic depressive psychosis. He died there in 1974 – fifty years after first being admitted.

While wishing to acknowledge Norton's forgotten decades of mental anguish, once again I don't claim that any of Jimmy Nolan's thoughts echo those of the real-life Norton. Indeed, with two thousand patients packed into Grangegorman, I don't even know if these two Bloody Sunday participants even met while both were in there. But I have taken the liberty of using aspects of Norton's back story to forge a character to represent all the forgotten victims of such wars who find themselves left alone to deal with trauma.

Taking such liberties poses a moral quandary for any writer. These two men probably did not regard themselves as public figures in the way that Seán Lemass undoubtedly was. My sole defence is a belief that when anyone makes the moral choice to participate in a politically motivated murder, no matter how honourable their motives seem to them, they lose their anonymity by inserting themselves into the discourse of their nation's history.

Perhaps the root of my curiosity about such damaged figures stems from a story my father told me, from his wartime seafaring days on tiny Irish ships sailing to Lisbon. In between voyages he lodged in a Baggot Street boarding house, where the landlady told him not to mind the man who shook with nerves at the breakfast table and perpetually glanced around in an agitated distracted way. 'He was with Collins's Squad,' she whispered, as if no other explanation should be needed.

Dermot Bolger
May 2024